THE MEDUSA MURDERS

THE MEDUSA MURDERS

Joy Ann Ribar

A Bay Browning Mystery

BOOK 1

Wine Glass Press
U.S.A.

Wine Glass Press, U.S.A.
© 2023 by Joy Ann Ribar.

First Edition: 2023

Published in 2023
Printed in the United States of America

ISBN: 978-1959078-20-3 (paperback)

ISBN: 978-1959078-21-0 (ebook)

GENRES: Mystery, Amateur Sleuth, Women's Fiction

EDITOR: Kay Rettenmund
COVER | INTERIOR DESIGNER: Terry Rydberg, Fine Print Design

With gratitude to my Pardeeville High School

English students (2001–2017).

You made me fall in love with literature

over and over again.

I send you my best wishes

wherever life finds you.

Many of you hold little pieces of my heart forever.

CHAPTER 1
RIVALS

January sleet pelted the windshield as Bay Browning scurried to her car from Giorgio's and stuffed her dry cleaning into an untidy bundle in the back seat. Now that she had a free hand, she pulled her wool scarf over her head and clambered into the driver's seat, buckled up and headed down Grand Avenue toward home.

Giorgio had been on the phone when Bay handed him her dry-cleaning ticket, speed talking loudly, half in Greek half in English, likely to someone he knew. She waved her hand and tapped one booted foot loudly to indicate she was in a hurry.

The blue and white building, though clean, always smelled of chemicals and spicy Greek foods. Bay was sure one day she'd see a lamb or goat roasting on a spit out front when she pulled up to collect her clothes.

She'd been a customer at Giorgio's for a year and a half now, ever since she accepted a full professorship at Flourish College in the bustling community of Prairie Ridge, Wisconsin, the youngest person to achieve department chair in English literature since the college opened fifteen years ago.

Working in the Literature and Arts department came with a price, however. Stasia Andino was the associate dean and Giorgio's sister. She made it clear on day one she expected everyone on the staff to patronize her brother's business.

Wet and cold, Bay huddled inside her apartment elevator and pressed the tenth floor button. Disgusted that she couldn't carry the contents from her car in one trip, she left the dry cleaning in a heap in the back seat along with her tote bag. Dinner was more important. She hadn't eaten anything all day beyond coffee, a mini orange, and protein bar; and she was ready to dive into the Tuscan wedding soup and garlic bread she'd picked up at Piccolo's Italian Kitchen next door to Giorgio's. Hot soup would bring warmth and comfort before she would head back to the college for an evening meeting, a meeting she didn't want to attend now that circumstances had changed.

That ratty knave, McNelly. If not for his interference, the Lit/Arts office would be offering an assistant runner position to Bay's pick of the applicants. But McNelly recommended a new candidate based on hardship and twisted the arms of one or both head deans. Tonight, his candidate was up for approval beside Bay's recommended applicant.

"Come on L.L, get on board with this hire, would you? The girl needs the money for her own personal safety." Gabriel McNelly, Religious Studies and Ethics professor, stood over Bay's desk that morning. "She's a refugee for God's sake."

Bay was known as "L.L." by her colleagues and students at the university. The initials saved her from explaining the syrupy way she'd been named by her family and allotted her more authority in the professional world where gender bias lived on. Only her family and friends were invited to call her Bay. Only her closest family would dare to call her LuLu.

Bay raised her eyes from the college application essay she was reading and offered the professor a non-committal shrug. She didn't know much about McNelly. He'd joined the department before the fall semester after cajoling his way in, claiming religious studies included examining literature that incorporated the Bible, Torah, and Qur'an. Bay didn't debate the claim but argued McNelly belonged in social sciences since he primarily taught ethics and sociology. Bottom line, something about him bugged her, and she couldn't put a finger on it. Now his piercing green eyes bore into her accusingly.

"Explain to me how this girl is a refugee. She's from Canada, right?" Bay remained unconvinced.

McNelly hesitated, gazed up at the ceiling and proceeded. "She confided in me. The girl's gone through plenty in her life. She just needs a little help, like a job."

"If you want my support, you're going to have to tell me more." Bay could be just as relentless.

Again, the hesitation. Then McNelly folded his hands in prayer and lifted them above his head. "Forgive me, Father."

Bay snorted. "Don't tell me. This girl made a confession to you, didn't she? And just what made her do that, I wonder."

McNelly dropped his hands and scowled. "I knew she had a heavy heart, something weighing on her mind. I told her I used to be a priest and she could trust me."

Bay snorted again. "*Used to be* is the key term here, Professor. You need to tread lightly. You could get in trouble for hearing unauthorized confessions in your office, especially since you're no longer a priest." Bay's words were authoritative but calm. "Now, what's her story?"

The elevator door dinged loudly, announcing the tenth floor and shaking Bay back to awareness of the present. Dinner awaited. Takeout in hand, she fumbled through her handbag for keys.

She had snagged the corner apartment with a view on one side of Elfenham Park from the balcony outside her living room and bedroom. She spied on the variety of songbirds that made the park home, often able to look at them head-on in the tallest pines and oaks from the vantage point of her balcony breakfast table.

Mechanically, she unlocked the deadbolt and reached around the corner for the wall switch to illuminate the entry hall. Soft light spilled forward revealing the kitchen and dining area on the right and spacious living room dead ahead. *What was that lump of something on her couch?* She didn't remember leaving folded laundry out. Bay nearly always finished what she started, no matter the task.

Then the lump moved. Bay stifled a shriek and held her phone aloft to shine on the moving lump while she leaned forward to find more lights. The lump bounded off the couch onto the floor and let out a whiny meow. A black cat stood right in her path, glaring at the interruption of its nap.

Bay set down her precious takeout, placed both hands on her hips, and glared back. "And who do you think you are, kitty, and how did you get into my home, anyway?"

The cat answered by way of a languid arch followed by a luxurious stretch, claws extended. The feline yawned and pranced toward the counter where Bay's dinner emitted an enticing aroma.

Bay frowned. Had the cat been an unwanted gift from her father? Barrett Browning constantly encouraged his daughter to take in some sort of companion, despite her protest.

One surprise led to another. A shadow emerged from the guest bedroom, prompting Bay to turn on the overhead light and grab a large vase from the sofa table. The blue-green vase, a favorite of Bay's, was made from excavated Roman glass. As she grasped its lovely, curved ribbon-like handle, she wondered if she could come to break it over the intruder's head.

"Are you going to clock me with a vase—how cliché is that?" A blond woman called out of the shadows. "You live in the city, LuLu, and you still don't own a gun?" The blonde tossed her head back and snorted. "Oh, I see you've met Minerva."

Bay glared at the woman and held the vase up a little higher in striking pose. Several responses fought to be unleashed at the intruder, but anger and disgust were exactly what Cassandra expected from her sister, so Bay inhaled sharply before proceeding.

"What are you doing here, Cassandra?" Bay kept her tone cool and even.

Cassandra hesitated and drew a little farther into the living room. Bay could see Cass had helped herself to her sweatpants and T-shirt, but she couldn't see her sister's face.

"I'm out," she said simply, shrugging.

Anger rose upward from Bay's stomach and burned her chest scarlet. "Out as in on probation, parole, or did you break out?' The words came out at a higher-than-normal pitch. Best to keep her sentences short, Bay decided, or her anger would boil over.

Cass smiled, aware of the effect she produced in her younger sister. "I served my time with early release for good behavior." Cass's smile was too big, like a fat cat beside an empty aquarium.

Bay's reaction was impulsive. She scoffed and snorted. "Good behavior. You? Never." She barely managed to spit out those few words.

Now Cass walked into the light where Bay could assess the toll prison had or had not taken on her sister. Her blond hair had never been shorter. Bay imagined a pixie cut eliminated the possibility of hiding objects in one's hair for escape or violence. Cass still had a pretty face, but it bore a few creases, and the freckles that once danced across her nose as pretty specks of light, had darkened into a muddy stain.

She tilted her chin regally at Bay's words. "I can be quite convincing, Sister." She bent over to pick up Minerva and cradled the purring cat.

Bay knew her grifter sister could be convincing for certain. She'd made her living by swindling, but it caught up with her, and she'd spent the past three years in a women's prison in Florida where she'd been prosecuted for larceny and fraud. Bay shut her out completely, refused to communicate with her, and told her she never wanted to see her again. Bay felt guilty about those decisions, but Cass had caused so much hurt. Bay didn't know how to begin to forgive her.

"What's your plan with that vase? Are you going to break it over my head?" Cass regarded Bay with merriment mixed with caution. It was a feeble attempt at improving the mood.

Bay looked at the Roman treasure and calmly replaced it on the cherry table. "I'm going to eat my dinner before it gets any colder, and then I'm leaving." She turned her back on Cassandra and walked into the kitchen to retrieve the takeout from the counter that separated the two rooms. She pulled the shutters down over the counter to close off the space, shutting out Cass, willing her to disappear. Bay pulled a spoon from a drawer and set about slurping the soup as loudly as possible. Anger was gaining sway.

Bay heard the soft clicks of Minerva landing on the ceramic tile floor, but no sound came from Cassandra, who was more catlike than the black feline. Bay kept slurping soup, dipped the buttery garlic bread into the broth, and noisily sucked the doused bread. She hoped her sister felt as annoyed as Bay felt. Bay's phone jingled, interrupting her smacking serenade.

"Hello, Dad." Of course, Barrett Browning must know that Cass was out of prison and squatting at Bay's apartment.

"Oh-oh. You sound upset, LuLu. I take it you've discovered your sister then."

"Yep." Bay's response clipped like scissors. She inhaled deeply. "Did you tell Cassandra to come here? Did you let her into my home?"

Barrett lived in the same building, but on the second floor. After securing a professorship at Flourish, Bay chose Windflower Gardens for its proximity to campus, only a few minutes away. Father and daughter moved in the same day.

The elder Browning sighed, speaking like the brokenhearted man he was. "Lu, where is Cass supposed to go? She needs a second chance in life…and in this family." Barrett's voice was gentle and quiet as always. Bay could not recall many times when her father showed anger, so she wondered if her own fiery emotions came from her mother.

"Dad," Bay tamped down the urge to suggest a hot location where Cass could go. "I can't let her stay here. I don't trust her."

A quick glance at the time indicated she needed to delay the conversation and head to her meeting.

"I can't talk about this right now. I'm going back to campus for a meeting. Can you do me a favor, please?" Impatience took over. "Come up here and stay with Cass until I get home?" She considered asking her dad to take Cass to his apartment, but the fear that her ex-con sister would somehow swindle their father averted that idea.

"Of course." Barrett added, "Thank you, honey."

Bay bit back her response. *Don't thank me, Dad. I don't plan to help her.* She disconnected and resumed eating, but with less vigor. The garlic bread tasted bitter now and the soup was lukewarm. Bay dumped the rest of the container down the disposal, tossed it in the trash, and rinsed the spoon.

She hadn't removed her jacket, but her purse was in the other room, so she reluctantly walked through the doorway to retrieve it. Cass wasn't anywhere to be seen. Bay's purse lay upside down on the floor along with a smattering of contents: a hairbrush, nail clippers, notepad, a tin of breath mints, and her car keys. Instinctively, she grabbed her wallet, opened it, saw the credit card slots were in order and her cash was intact. She looked accusingly at Minerva, curled up in nap formation underneath the breakfast counter. She gathered her belongings as Barrett rapped on the door and let himself in.

The distressed look on Bay's face registered and Barrett folded her into a warm embrace. "It's going to be okay, LuLu. You'll see. I spent all afternoon with Cass. She's not the same person. Just give her a chance."

Bay broke away and shot a warning glance at her father. "Honestly, Dad…" She stopped short. First things first, and that meant attending this stupid meeting. She touched his arm gently. "I have to go. We'll talk when I get back. Don't let her out of your sight." Bay's instructions seemed hollow since she didn't even know where Cass was. ∎

CHAPTER 2
DISINTERESTED MINORITY

The fifth-floor meeting room in the Humanities department was much too large for the few attendees. Besides Professor McNelly and Bay, the only others present were Stasia Andino, associate dean, and Dean Pamela Foyt. Bay was confused at the dean's attendance since hiring someone as lowly as a gofer for the Literature and Arts department seemed an unnecessary oversight. It ticked her off that nobody was there from music, art, or theater, even though they'd all pledged to support Bay's applicant of choice for the job.

Stasia checked the time. It was five minutes after the hour, high time to get started. "Okay, looks like it's just us, so let's not delay. At our last meeting, Professors Browning and Yoo presented the need for an additional office helper since Trevor had taken on registration and data processing duties."

Stasia's raspy voice indicated boredom. She raised bulging dark eyes around the table for acknowledgement. Bay and McNelly nodded. Pamela looked at her cell phone.

Stasia returned to her notes. "We posted the job and received several applicants. Tonight, we'll hire one of the applicants. I understand both of you have recommendations?"

Bay jumped on Stasia's inquiry to be heard first. "Yes, I recommend we hire Thomas Elkins. Thomas is a third-year English literature major with a music minor—a perfect fit for the department." Bay peered at McNelly, daring him to argue her point.

McNelly stood up, folded his hands behind his back, and strolled to the front of the table where Pamela was perched. Staring upward, McNelly began his sales pitch. "I'm sure Thomas Elkins is a fine person, but I'm suggesting we offer the position to an equally qualified candidate who is in dire need; Diana Poulin. Miss Poulin is in danger of dropping out because of great financial need, which would mean returning home to an abusive stepmother."

Stasia's quizzical expression wasn't lost on Bay. Clearly, this was the first time she'd heard of Diana Poulin and her imminent demise. But Pamela nodded and pretended to look concerned.

Stasia pounced before Bay had the opportunity. "And how has this knowledge come to your doorstep, McNelly?" Her words stabbed the air.

McNelly colored as he brought both hands to his face, tenting them and closing his eyes, perhaps seeking divine guidance. Finally, he stated matter-of-factly, "The girl confided as much to me."

Bay stood up. The long day contained enough pitfalls. She was steamed that her colleagues hadn't bothered to come to the meeting to support her, and she still had to deal with her dad and sister.

"Thomas Elkins will fill our need for greater diversity at Flourish, as a member of the LGBTQ community." Bay hated it that she sounded like a chirpy TV ad.

McNelly dove in. "Diana Poulin is an international student."

"To be fair, she is Canadian." Bay's counterpoint was directed at Dean Foyt. It became apparent the dean was the one she had to convince.

McNelly snorted. "She's French-Canadian."

Bay pointed at McNelly. "He told Ms. Poulin he was a priest. That's the only reason he knows her situation."

Stasia frowned and slapped the table hard. "That's enough song and dance from both of you. This is supposed to be a short meeting. We're trying to hire a damn gofer, not choose the next pope." Stasia's tirade short-circuited due to a coughing attack.

Dean Foyt stood up causing Bay and McNelly to immediately retreat to their seats. Perfectly coiffed white hair dazzled in the artificial light against a high-collared drapey jumpsuit. Pamela dressed like a model and branded herself as a rogue, wearing royal blue and bright yellow despite what some would consider over the top for her age. Bay admired the dean's fearless nature. *But would a rogue kowtow to the likes of McNelly,* Bay wondered.

"Since there are no other supporters present for either candidate, I move to hire Ms. Poulin for the position."

Bay bristled and Pamela stared fixedly at the literature professor. "Hiring a female will balance the office assistants, and Ms. Poulin has an immediate need. Despite the unorthodox way the department was made aware of her circumstances." Pamela cleared her throat and redirected an authoritative stare at McNelly.

Stasia affirmed the dean's decision, and the deed was done.

Meeting adjourned. *Just wait until I see Jennifer Yoo and the other meeting-skippers*, Bay thought. She didn't like office politics or Professor McNelly.

The afternoon rain morphed into evening snow flurries spinning circles that mimicked Bay's thoughts. She absently maneuvered the gray Subaru down College Avenue, left on Grand and back to Windflower Gardens on Hawthorn Way. She pulled up short of the parking ramp, and her jaw dropped. Red and blue lit up the front entrance to her building courtesy of two squad cars idling there, lights aglow.

So, Cass has already violated her parole? So be it. Bay couldn't process why her stomach flipped like the swirling snow illuminated by the Subaru's headlights. Hesitating a moment, she decided to enter the garage and park as normal. The ride up to the tenth floor was too short for Bay to determine her reaction.

What would she say to her father? Would his broken heart ever mend? First mom, then Cassandra. Bay's mother, Penelope, died when Bay was ten. Her leaving created a void as wide as the heavens for Barrett. He tried to be a good father, but mostly buried himself in work, literally in fact, since he was an anthropologist who worked with archeologists all over the world. Sometimes his two daughters lived with him during his field work; more often they lived with Aunt Vee in Chicago.

The familiar ding cut into Bay's thoughts. She gazed at her apartment door for telltale signs of police activity and found none. The key clicked in the lock. She gingerly entered what used to be her peaceful haven. She found Cass and her father seated on the sofa, looking up at her expectantly.

"The police just left a few minutes ago," Barrett began.

Bay plunked her purse and tote bag onto the tile by the sofa table. "Ha! I knew it." She glared disgustedly at Cassandra, who shrunk back in surprise.

Something gave way inside Bay. "What did you do this time? You're out of prison not even one day, Cassandra." Cass's and Barrett's expressions made her pause midstream.

"The cops weren't here for me, Sister. It's you they want to talk to. And they'll be back with a search warrant, so you better get your crap together and get rid of whatever it is they want." Cass spat the words at Bay like hornet spray.

Bay couldn't imagine anything she had in her possession the police would want. She collapsed into the oversized reading chair by the fireplace, head in hands, thinking. Ignoring her sister, she addressed Barrett.

"What did the police say, Dad? Exactly, if you can remember."

Barrett raised his eyes, looking up toward the left, recalling the details. "They asked if you were home. Said they must talk to you. When I said you were at work, they asked to look in your closets. I asked for a warrant, and they left. Officer Downing left his card and asked you to call as soon as you get home." Barrett handed Bay the card from his shirt pocket.

She exhaled a whoosh of air in relief and read the card. "I guess I'll call Officer Downing and find out what this is about." She offered a peevish glare toward Cass. "So, they want to look in my closets. Any chance you stashed something there, Sister?"

Cass shook her head. "I did not. And if I were you, I wouldn't call that officer. Cops can't be trusted."

Of course you would think that, Cass. Bay had no reason not to trust the police. She pulled her cell from her purse, walked into her bedroom, and shut the door before calling.

"Detective Downing."

"This is L.L. Browning. I received a message saying you were at my apartment and wished to speak with me. How can I help?" Bay delivered her practiced mature and professional voice, the one she used to land her job at the college.

Downing wasn't impressed. "Yeah. L.L. Browning? What's the L.L. stand for?"

Suddenly Bay felt like a student with a new teacher reciting roll call. Her first name, Lulabay, was concocted by her dear sister Cassandra, but sounded like a barfing whale when strangers tackled it. Of course, now she was all grown up and had rebaptized herself, no longer living in a fairy-tale world with a sweet sister and darling mother.

"L.L. is the name I go by, if you don't mind, Officer." Bay was displeased that she sounded contrite. Why apologize about her name?

"That's detective, not officer. Ms. Browning, I'll cut to the chase. Did you pick up dry cleaning today at Giorgio's Tender Touch on Grand?"

Bay laughed; she couldn't help herself. She never used the full name of Giorgio's business and hearing it come from a police detective, who had a provocative voice by the way, conjured a massage parlor or something more steamy than dry cleaning.

"Is something funny, Ms. Browning?"

Bay snapped back to the matter at hand. "I'm sorry. Yes, I picked up dry cleaning today around 3:30 p.m. from Giorgio himself." She tried to be precise to be helpful.

"Right. Where is that dry cleaning located right now?"

So that's why the police wanted to look through her closets. "It's actually in the back seat of my car. It's been a busy day and

I haven't had time to bring it up." She pictured the untidy clump in her back seat, likely wrinkled, warranting yet another visit to Giorgio, who believed himself an Adonis.

"You haven't touched it then or removed it from its wrappings?" Downing was pumped now.

Bay affirmed.

"Can you meet us in the parking garage by your vehicle in fifteen minutes?"

Bay agreed, but as soon as she disconnected, she flew to the elevator and pushed the button for the lower level without a word to her father or Cass. She intended to check out the dry cleaning for herself first. ■

CHAPTER 3

DRY CLEANING CLUES

The parking garage was a dim, creepy space, although it was equipped with lighting. Bay walked rapid steps to her car making minimal noise after swapping her heels for slip-on sneakers. She entered the passenger side front door first, located the flashlight she always kept in the glove box, then sat down in the back seat beside the offending dry cleaning. She must open the outer bag and make it appear to the police as undisturbed.

She hung the garment bag on the back seat door hook and examined the top. No way in there without tearing the plastic. Luckily, the bag's bottom had merely been knotted—a shortcut. She fumbled with the plastic knot in her haste but didn't tear it, quite the feat since she'd remembered to put on her driving gloves first.

Bay carefully slid her hands into the opening and removed the first item: a gray herringbone belted blazer and pants—a work staple. She shone the flashlight over the front and back, checked the pockets, and gave both a good sniff. They smelled like dry-cleaning. She quickly draped the herringbone set over the back seat and moved onto the next item: a multicolored cowl neck shirt with attached flyaway vest, her favorite Friday piece since it bordered on casual and was comfortable like a well-worn flannel. The top had no pockets and the print pattern made it difficult to see anything out of the ordinary. Another sniff confirmed it was clean. She laid it on top of the herringbone.

The next item made her smile: a silhouette sheath and matching topper in Christmas red she'd purchased for the holiday party at the college. The style suited her above-average height and accented her well-tended body. Whether she attracted attention from possible bigwigs or lovers didn't matter to Bay—she wore the dress for herself, a statement of her arrival as a scholar. Her flashlight revealed nothing—a relief, since Bay recalled a drip from a wayward meatball had left a small stain. She admired Giorgio's work if not the man himself.

The final item was her coveted lululemon raincoat, a recognizable accessory that branded her as someone of importance. Bay scoffed at the idea of being judged by one's fashion choices, but she lived in a competitive world and played the game as necessary. There was something off about the black raincoat. It didn't pass the sniff test, for starters. It hadn't been cleaned and smelled of something musty mixed with stale perfume. She looked at the label where she habitually marked her expensive pieces with "LLB." The label was blank.

Bay reached into the lululemon's coat pocket and pulled out tissue lint and a bobby pin. She shoved both back into the pocket, but some lint remained on her glove. She checked the other pocket and found a folded paper. "Probably a grocery list," she said aloud and looked around to be sure she was still alone.

She saw headlights rounding the garage corner and her heart beat faster. Was she about to be caught going through the clothes she wasn't supposed to touch? The SUV slid past her to park in the next row, and Bay realized only a few minutes had passed since her arrival.

Tempted to remove her gloves, she swore at her difficulty in unfolding the note. She was successful at last, set it on the seat and held the light to read it.

"Three things cannot be long hidden: the sun, the moon, and the truth. Your mannerisms reflect your reality.

1603–508; Arpino"

The note was typed on plain printer paper. Bay's brain went to work trying to locate the source of the quote from her store of college knowledge. A sudden clatter jolted her back to reality. Her clothes had slipped off the seat back into a heap. Oh figs! She needed to get the cleaning back in order and re-tie the plastic knot. Bay somehow became adept at working with the gloves on, and she wrangled the clothes back into the bag, committed the note to her short-term memory, shoved it back in the pocket and tied the bag.

She felt like a hot mess. She wasn't accustomed to defying authority. Her heart pounded in her chest in a panic, creating a thin line of cold perspiration on her brow. Gloves off, she quickly typed a shorthand version of the note into a text to herself before her memory failed her. If she'd been thinking clearly, she would have snapped a photo of the note before she put it away. She scrambled out of the back, dashed to the front, and was about to replace the flashlight when a squad car slithered into view running with the top light bar off. Her cell phone buzzed. It was

Detective Downing.

"Browning? We're in your garage. Can you hold up your phone with a light on, so we can find you?"

"Sure. You're almost right on top of me. Here." Bay held up the phone and decided to wave the flashlight around as well.

The squad pulled over, close to the Subaru's back bumper, blocking any move Bay might make. Bay absentmindedly tucked one strand of dark brown hair behind her ear and wiped her brow with her coat sleeve. *I wonder if detective spicy pipes has looks to match his voice…*

Downing exited from the passenger side of the car in plain clothes while a second officer emerged from the driver's side in full uniform, hat included. Downing reached Bay first and shook her hand politely.

"Detective Downing, Ms. Browning. Where's the dry cleaning?"

"Driver's side back seat, Detective." Even in the dim garage light, Bay could see Downing was a handsome man, probably in his late thirties. His hair teetered between ash brown and dark blond as best as she could surmise. The modern style parted to the side, longer and tousled on top, with tidy small sideburn tendrils, suggested a carefree spirit that Bay doubted existed. It was impossible to guess the color of his eyes, but his expression was watchful and scrutinizing at once. Pronounced creases descended cheek to chin where light stubble outlined a symmetrical mouth that curved upward toward a rugged nose, not overly large but with a distinctive bump.

Downing's derisive laugh shook Bay out of her reverie. "Are you done looking, Ms. Browning?"

Bay blinked twice, unable to form an answer. The other

officer, who introduced himself as Harris, retrieved a spotlight from the squad and shined it on the dry-cleaning bag that now lay over the hood of the squad.

Bay watched, cataloging the steps in the search process. She knew she could save them some time by telling them what they wanted was in the lululemon, but how could she know that? The other officer removed his hat and both donned latex gloves.

Downing separated each piece starting with the herringbone set. He glanced at Bay. "Is this yours?"

She said it was. Officer Harris ran a UV light over the surface, turned it over and repeated the process. Harris checked the pockets. Downing gestured for Bay to stand beside him. He handed her the herringbone outfit.

"You can put this in your car now. It's been cleared."

Bay obliged and returned to the detective's side as he repeated the method with the blue-printed shirt, then the Christmas-red dress. She watched him closely to see if he held any interest in the dress, maybe imagining what she would look like in it, but his face was inscrutable. She chastised herself inwardly for being foolish, unable to conceive why she entertained such thoughts.

At last, they arrived at the lululemon. Harris confirmed. "This is what we're looking for, right Downing?"

The detective shot a warning look at Harris who didn't catch his drift, but Bay understood that she was supposed to know as little as possible.

"That isn't mine," she offered.

Downing's brows rose curiously. "You don't own a lulu-whatever?" He gestured at the raincoat.

Thankful for the dim light, Bay felt color rising up her chest and neck to her face. How would she recover from her mistake?

"I can smell the stale perfume from here. It's not mine." Bay's cool gaze met Downing's.

He looked away and proceeded to the task at hand. Harris ran the UV light, finding what Bay decided could only be DNA evidence. She wondered if they would search the pockets. They did. Out came tweezers, plastic bags, and other accoutrements for evidence gathering.

The pocket lint went into one bag. The bobby pin went into another. White particles from the second pocket went into a bag, too. Bay wondered if it was coke or another street drug. Finally, Downing pulled out the note with tweezers and placed it in its own bag.

He didn't even open it or read it! If I were a detective, I'd read that note immediately. She scowled, concluding Downing wasn't the kind of detective she read about in crime novels or saw on the big screen.

"Anything wrong, Ms. Browning?" Downing caught the whiff of her disapproval.

Bay had nothing to lose. "You find a note and you're not going to read it before sticking it away in a bag, Detective? Aren't you curious?"

Harris stifled a snort. "What do we have here? An amateur sleuth?" Harris stuck his thumbs through the beltloops below his ample stomach, which bobbed in a chuckle.

Downing remained composed, revealing nothing. "And what makes you think this is a note, Ms. Browning? It could be a to-do list, a receipt, or blank for that matter." One eyebrow cocked in her direction like a volley. It was her serve.

"I guess the only way to find out is to open it." Bay folded her arms across her chest and stamped one foot.

Downing looked amused. "You're free to return to your apartment. I'll be in touch if I have any questions."

Bay sputtered. "That's it? I don't get to know what this is all about? Why you are going through my cleaning, and who sent you here? "

Downing was already at the squad car door. He climbed in and tipped a two-finger salute to Bay. Harris jammed his hat back on, carefully folded the lululemon inside the plastic bag, placed it in the back of the squad and heaved himself into the driver's side. They were gone.

Unsatisfied to be left in the dark, Bay knew a visit to Giorgio on Monday would start her day, and he better be in a talking mood. ■

CHAPTER 4
HOUSE RULES

Back upstairs, Bay stepped into the apartment door, dry cleaning over one arm. Her dad and sister sat on the sofa listening to classical music on the television, *Venus, Bringer of Peace* by Gustav Holst. Bay recognized it immediately, an old family favorite, from a time when she felt like her family was complete. Hearing it now made her bristle.

She carried the clean clothes to her room and hung them in her closet. Hesitating, she considered shutting the door and going straight to bed. She resisted the urge and walked back to the living room.

Barrett, his head laid back basking in the violins' movement, gestured toward Bay to have a seat in the reading chair. Cassandra rose on cue, bringing her sister a tumbler of caramel-colored liquid with a twisted orange slice and dark purple grape on a toothpick.

"Your favorite cocktail, Lu, except you don't have any maraschino cherries so I improvised."

Bay stared at the proffered old-fashioned, took it ungratefully, and set it on a coaster next to her chair. "That's not my go-to drink any longer, but you'd know that if you'd been around," Bay croaked, her voice dry from the long day. "Besides, I don't have any brandy."

"I brought some up from my place," Barrett interjected. "Be nice, LuLu. Cassandra wanted to do something nice. Take a sip. It'll take the edge off."

Bay cleared her throat and took a sip, then another. The brandy descended in a fiery ribbon, warming her insides. She took a third sip. Cassandra was a skilled bartender, among other things.

"Let's get this over with. I'm tired and I want to go to bed." The oboe section joined the suite, Bay's favorite part. She pretended not to notice. Confrontation wasn't her strong suit, but she was learning to deal with it as part of life, certainly as part of her profession.

When Bay had a conflict with a student, she made it her policy for the student to state their case first before she rendered a decision. She knew Cassandra would make a sales pitch no matter what Bay said, so Bay swept her hand toward Cass to begin.

"Lu, I know you have every reason to be disappointed in me. And I know you don't think you can trust me." Cassandra spoke contritely, like a small child sitting with a broken cookie jar and a lap full of shards and crumbs. She waited silently for Bay to unleash a bitter reply. Nothing.

"Please let me prove myself to you. I just need a few months to find honest work, save some money, find a place to live. I promise after that, I'll be gone." Cassandra raised repentant blue eyes, imploring Bay to capitulate. Bay noted the Holst violins swept into a crescendo during her sister's speech.

Bay stood up and clapped slowly. "An almost believable performance, but you're forgetting that I know the real Cassandra, and I'm not buying it."

Barrett stood too and placed a cautious hand on Bay's arm. "Cass is your sister, LuLu. She's family."

Bay exhaled, sat down again with a whoosh, and took a gulp from the tumbler. Her father had played his ace, the "family" argument, the card that always won the hand.

"Let's come to terms then."

Her father and Cass relaxed; small smiles curved upward on their faces. Bay didn't care for that one bit.

"Wait a second. These are my terms." Bay leaned forward and crossed her arms. "First, Cassandra, you are going to show me daily proof of legitimate employment searches. Second, I'm going through your stuff and taking anything that could be used for mischief. Third, I need the name and phone number of your parole officer, who I will be contacting first thing Monday morning. Fourth, I'll be going through your cell phone on a daily basis as well as your online activity. Fifth…"

Bay was running out of steam. She wasn't a parent, so coming up with rules wasn't part of her nature. She taught college students—most of the policies employed with them didn't apply to Cass. She needed to concoct rules for a five-year-old.

"Fifth, sixth and seventh, I'll make more rules as needed." Bay finished, realizing she sounded like her mother and Auntie Vee sounded when the girls were in trouble.

To her credit, Cass sat at attention and nodded at Bay's recitation.

Barrett placed a comforting arm around Cass and pulled her in close. "Make the most of this opportunity, Honey. Please." His voice dropped to a whisper. "Do this for me and for yourself." A tear squeezed from one eye. Barrett was clueless as a parent.

Bay joined the pair, brushed a kiss on Barrett's cheek, grabbed the remote, and turned off the TV. She refused to acknowledge Cassandra's presence. Instead, she went into the spare bedroom, located Cass's duffel, and dumped the contents out onto the bed.

Her sister had very little to call her own. A change of clothes, a long T-shirt for sleeping, and minimal toiletries. Her cell phone was a few years old and would need updates or an upgrade. Bay needed to consider if she wanted to make the investment. Certainly, Cass would need an outfit for job interviews and a better pair of shoes than the sneakers she owned. She confiscated the survival knife kit at the bottom of the duffel, walked through the bathroom that connected the two bedrooms, and locked the kit in her closet safe. She announced a perfunctory good night before shutting the door.

Bay thought about Cass as she prepared for bed. *What am I going to do with her? She has made so many mistakes and makes me so angry. I often give students second chances...does my sister need a second chance, too?* ■

CHAPTER 5
PROBATION BEGINS

After a long weekend, in which the sisters did their level best to avoid each other, Monday welcomed Bay with the blessing of routines. She awoke at her usual five a.m. despite the fact she was still on semester break, pattered to the kitchen to make coffee, changed her mind, walked back to her room, pulled workout clothes from her drawer, and changed her mind again. She knew yoga was exactly what her restless mind craved, but stubbornness won out. There was no way she was leaving her sister alone this morning.

She heard noises coming from the bathroom, so she scurried back to the kitchen. The shutters were still closed from yesterday. She flipped on a switch underneath the cupboards, bathing the coffee corner in soft blue LED lights. Bay automatically grabbed a pebbly green mug from the drainboard and placed it under the coffee machine spigot. A wire basket filled with pods waited beside the machine. She chose a bold Costa Rican blend and let the magic happen.

The aroma helped calm her mind a bit, but agitation returned as soon as Bay started looking for a place to roost. If she sat in the reading chair, would Cass come out and disturb her peace? She didn't want to stand in the shuttered kitchen, and today was not the day for a leisurely coffee in bed reading or playing word games. *Screw this: I'm making myself a prisoner in my own home.* She kicked the bottom trim below the cupboards and instantly regretted it as her toe locked up with pain.

Cassandra walked through the kitchen entryway, yawning. "What are you doing, LuLu? Is everything okay?"

Of course, everything wasn't okay. How could she even ask such a stupid question? "Ha, I've thought of another rule. You may not call me LuLu." Bay gritted her teeth as anger was gaining momentum.

Cass rolled her eyes dramatically. "Really?" She stamped her foot impatiently as only an older sister can.

Bay turned away. She was in danger of being caught up in the past familiarity of Cass being in charge. As a child, Bay followed every move Cass made, eagerly played all the games that Cass initiated, and basked in the love of an older sister who could do no wrong. She was LuLu, the nickname given to her by her parents and doting sister. She was only Lulabay when she was in trouble or in the ditties that Cassandra sang to her at night in the bedroom they shared. She never tired of hearing the story of how her pregnant mother, the perfect Penelope, explained the baby she carried was a special gift coming to Cassandra. Penelope swayed when she sang bedtime songs to Cass, and Cass declared the baby to be a lullaby, except she pronounced the word "lulabay" and declared that to be the baby's name. Cass had gotten her way, like always. Not this time.

Bay spun around to face Cassandra. "Don't, Cassandra."

Managing to look bored, Cass inhaled and twisted her lips. "Okay, I guess I can call you 'Bay.' I hear that's what your colleagues call you."

"No." Bay's retort was sharp, prickly.

Cass laughed and looked at her fingernails. She decided a manicure was in order. "Fine. I guess it's L.L. then?" The abbreviated name sounded foreign coming from Cass.

Resisting the urge to launch her coffee mug at her sister's head, Bay did a five-count inwardly, conscious of her breath. When she raised her eyes to Cass, a sinister smile crossed her lips. "You, Cassandra Selene Browning, may call me 'Professor.'"

She didn't wait for a reaction but cradled the coffee mug in her hands and sidled past Cassandra straight to her private bathroom on the other end of her bedroom. She slammed the door loudly enough to register but not hard enough to knock pictures off the walls, nor it seemed, to disturb Minerva, who was lounging on Bay's bed. She'd forgotten to address rules about a house cat.

The steamy shower felt extra good on this January morning. The damp weather with the temperature hovering around forty degrees would continue another day or so before a frosty plummet arrived. Bay applied the body cream reserved for dry winter skin and dressed in business casual. Second semester was less than two weeks away, and she had plenty to do.

The shared bathroom door was still shut, and Cass was in the shower, but Bay spied a Post-it stuck to the door, eye level. On it was the name and phone number of her sister's parole officer: Kelly Weber.

Bay grabbed a fresh steno pad and pen from her dresser

drawer, sat at the small desk in her bedroom, and tapped the officer's number into her phone.

"Weber," the nonsense free voice answered immediately.

"Good morning, Officer Weber. My name is L.L. Browning. Cassandra Browning is my sister, and she will be staying with me…" Bay felt queasy about finishing the statement. "for a while, I suppose."

"Yes, that's what she told me this morning when she checked in. I'm glad you called, so I can familiarize you with the conditions of your sister's parole."

Bay began taking notes about the expectations, including biweekly check-ins, submitting monthly reports, and paying restitution as outlined by the court. Surprisingly, Cass wouldn't have to wear a monitoring bracelet, but she wasn't allowed to own a firearm.

"Excuse me, Officer Weber, why isn't Cassandra serving parole in Florida where she was incarcerated?" Bay wondered if there was a way out of babysitting her wayward sister. Maybe she could send her packing yet.

Bay could hear pages turning in the background, normally a favorite sound of hers.

"Yes. Judge Daniels ordered your sister to live in a halfway house in Clearwater for three months. After her successful completion of the program, she was given gate money, and permission to travel to Wisconsin, which she listed as her home state. Your sister assured the judge she had relatives to live with."

Bay rubbed her right temple. "What exactly is gate money, please?"

"The state of Florida awards qualifying ex-cons a thousand bucks as start-over money to use for transportation and necessities."

Bay wondered what "qualifying" meant. In Cassandra's case, it likely meant she was able to run a con on the court to get the money. "I see. How much time is she given to find employment?" Bay intended for her sister to find work immediately, giving her less time to get into trouble.

"There isn't an exact deadline. The paperwork states that employment is a condition of parole, however. And she needs to start making restitution payments to the state of Florida on February 1. Hmm. Let's see." Weber tapped a pencil or pen on her desktop. "This document states that automatic deductions will be set up by the employer for restitution."

"I guess that means my sister better get a job as her first priority." February 1st was three weeks away.

"Are you able to help your sister financially? For instance, provide a cell phone, internet, and a work wardrobe?" Weber appeared to be reciting from a manual.

Bay worked to lower her annoyance level before answering. *Isn't it enough I'm allowing her to stay here and disrupt my life?* "She has a cell phone, but it appears to need upgrading. I'll look into that for her. She will have internet access through my account, and as for work clothes, we'll see if she has any of that gate money left."

"You seem skeptical, Ms. Browning, regarding your sister's success. Your role in encouraging her could make the difference," the officer's voice instructed.

"Yes, well thank you for the information and your time, Officer."

"Of course, and I'll look forward to seeing you soon, Ms. Browning. I have your address as 108 Hawthorn Lane, apartment number 1002, Windflower Gardens: is that correct?"

Bay gasped in puzzlement. "Yes, but what do you mean you will see me soon? Are you coming to my home to meet with my sister?"

"A condition of parole is periodic surprise visits to the residence of the offender. That includes surprise inspections of the residence. If you own a firearm, Ms. Browning, I suggest you keep it unloaded and locked away. And, if your sister has any interactions with law enforcement, she must report that within 72 hours of the incident. Even if it's just a traffic violation." Officer Weber disconnected.

Bay noticed the shower stopped running. She rapped on the bathroom door. "Cassandra, I talked to Officer Weber. Did you tell her the police were here last night, looking for me?"

The door opened, revealing Cassandra in her only change of clothes, blue jeans and a Ruth Bader Ginsberg T-shirt. "What did you think of Kelly? She seems strict, but I think I can break her." Cass smirked for Bay's benefit.

Bay feigned indifference. "Give me your cell phone. I'm going to trade it in today. And you didn't answer my question." Bay picked up her purse, gloves, and pulled her jacket off the wall hook, all the while directing a steely gaze toward Cassandra.

"Of course, I didn't tell her the police were here. It wouldn't look good for you or me." Cass jutted out her chin like a puff adder. "What am I supposed to do all day without a cell phone?"

Bay scrawled something on a Post-it and handed it to Cass. "Here's the internet password. Find a job."

She handed Cass the old tablet she'd resurrected during the phone call with Officer Weber. "You can use this to search for work. I created an account for you with Officer Weber's instructions. Any jobs you apply for are stored under your parole file name where she can check them weekly." She raised both eyebrows ominously.

Cass pouted. "When will you be home?" The question seemed innocent enough.

"When I get home." Bay knew better than to let her guard down.

Cass looked down at the floor. "Have a lovely day, Professor," she said demurely. ∎

CHAPTER 6
DUST AND FEATHERS

Bay was about to set her tote bag on the floor in the Subaru's back seat when something caught her eye. She took her phone from her purse and shined its light onto the object; a white feather, like the plume attached to fancy pens at weddings, lay on the floor. She wondered where it came from, and if it was from the dry cleaners, how she had missed seeing it last night. It was damp and matted, likely from the rain that swept into the car when Bay opened the door at Giorgio's.

Should she leave it there, report it to the detective, throw it away?

Bay pulled on one glove, noticing there was still white residue stuck to the fabric. *Better check to see if I missed anything else.*

Sweeping the cell phone light around the back seat, she discovered more white particles clinging to the seat. "What in the world are they?" She spoke aloud, then without gloves, picked up a few to examine. They felt grainy, like little bits of gritty dust. Clueless as to whether they should be preserved or vacuumed up, she brushed them back onto the seat.

"Time to get some answers from Giorgio." Bay looked at the dust and feather. "I guess I'll deal with you later."

Grand Avenue was blessedly quiet. It was an hour past the morning rush, not the typical drive time for Bay, who was accustomed to rising in the dark all winter and being one of the first arrivals at the college office.

Her first stop was her phone provider, whose office was a few minutes from Giorgio's. She chose a basic new model, gave the unenthusiastic salesclerk her account information with instructions to add a line, and left Cassandra's phone for deactivation.

"I might have it ready in an hour or two if you want to check back," the clerk said, shrugging. His words sounded like a question rather than a statement. Clearly, Bay's business was the inconvenience of the day. As if reading Bay's mind, the clerk added, "this is an old phone, so you never know…"

Back at the parking space, Bay opened the passenger door and looked at the white particles in brighter light. They were sprinkled like powdered sugar over the right side of the back seat, directly underneath the bag of clothes Bay had gone through last night. She felt certain the particles must have come from the lululemon coat pocket. She remembered seeing Harris turn the pocket inside out over one of the evidence bags. *Had there been feathers in either of the pockets?*

The empty parking lot at Giorgio's put a smile on Bay's face when she parked the Subaru a few minutes later. She was impatient to get to the bottom of the dry-cleaning mix-up and anxious to shake some details out of Giorgio. She could see him standing behind the customer counter, grooming his dark slicked-back hair and straightening his blue and white polo shirt that matched the building.

"Good morning, L.L. I see you have nothing in your hands, so what can I do for you today?" Giorgio's velvety voice was smoother than grease.

"Cut the crap, Giorgio. You know why I'm here. Obviously, you sent the police to see me about my lululemon. What's the story?" Bay frowned and her dark eyes narrowed.

Giorgio backed away as if Bay might punch him, marring his handsome face. He was Stasia's youngest brother, probably around Bay's age. After attending the mandatory gatherings at Stasia's home the past year, Bay had learned more Andino family facts than she cared to.

He held up both hands, placatingly. "I'll tell you what I know, which isn't much. My niece, Aria, was working on the day of the mix-up. She's in back. I'll go get her."

"Get my lululemon, too, while you're back there." Might as well kill two birds, as they say.

Aria was short and pretty with wide dark eyes and thick black hair pulled into a neat bun on top of her head. She wore the same blue and white polo and hospital-style light blue pants. Bay guessed she was barely out of high school. What was that expression: fear or guilt on Aria's face?

"Good morning, Professor Browning. My uncle is looking for your raincoat." Aria didn't look Bay in the eyes.

Dialing down from accusatory to neutral tone, Bay began her questions. "I understand you were working when my lululemon was switched with the one the police confiscated." No point in lollygagging her way to the matter at hand.

Aria looked down at her fingers, which were drumming

methodically on the counter as if playing a tune on a piano. One hand stopped while the other slowed to a quiet tapping. "Yes. There were three other coats almost identical to yours when he brought in the one the police were after."

Bay registered the information. "Who is *he* that brought the coat in, please?" The girl seemed quite fragile, so kid gloves were in order for this interrogation. Bay was accustomed to communicating with students Aria's age, and she knew the best methods for building trust and rapport.

The finger tapping continued at a leisurely pace. Bay could almost pick out a rhumba beat. Aria continued to focus on her fingers, not looking up.

"He said his name was Chance." She closed her eyes, conjuring his image. "He was wearing a black hoodie but took the hood off to talk to me. He had short dreadlocks swept up to one side and had smart glasses on. You know, his glasses made him look smart." She smiled, caught up in the memory.

It was clear to Bay the boy had charmed Aria, and just maybe she would do anything for him. "Did Chance ask you for a favor, Aria?"

She blushed, then turned a deep red. "He used me..." She choked back tears.

"Yeah, boys are scum," Bay empathized, glaring at Giorgio who had emerged from the back room empty-handed.

The finger tapping quickened as the incident unfolded, from a waltz to a cha-cha, Aria's eyes remained closed during the telling. "He asked me if people brought their expensive clothing here. Like could we be trusted with their stuff, you know. He said he had his mom's lululemon, and he was kind of flirting with me." She paused, thinking.

"I told him we had three of those same coats in the back right now, and they were already cleaned and ready to pick up. I offered to show him, so he would know he could leave his mom's coat here."

Aria stopped tapping and looked at Bay's face where empathy greeted her like a warm embrace. "I didn't know Chance wanted to swap coats until he asked if I could swap one of the clean coats for his mother's dirty one." I figured that he was responsible for getting it dirty, and he didn't want her to know about it.

"So, you randomly chose my coat and made the switch." Bay wanted to sound helpful by filling in details, so Aria's head shake surprised her.

"No. That's when things got weird. He asked me if we had L.L. Browning's coat. He specifically wanted to trade his coat for yours." Aria's dark brows raised question marks at Bay.

Bay was dumbstruck, but she needed to get every detail from Aria to know what she was dealing with. "What else can you tell me about Chance? How did he use you?"

Aria reddened again and looked down at the counter. "He gave me money to make the swap…and his phone number. He said I was cool, and he'd love to hang out sometime."

Momentary excitement rose within Bay. "May I have that phone number, please?"

Aria looked up, anger and embarrassment flooded her face. "It was a fake number."

Bay placed a comforting hand over the girl's. "I'm so sorry. What was Chance driving? How much money did he give you? Did he have any facial marks or tattoos?" Bay's rapid-fire questions must have sounded like police grilling.

Aria held up the quiet hand for her to stop. "He gave me a

hundred bucks and told me it was a practical joke, that his mother and you were friends. I'm so dumb." Tears ran freely.

"You're not dumb, Aria. You're trusting and kind. Nothing wrong with that. Did you see what he was driving?"

"He wasn't driving. He came here on a motorbike. And I don't remember any facial marks or tattoos, but he wore gold hoop earrings and high-top Vans. They were blue and white, and we laughed about how they matched my uniform."

"That's very helpful, Aria. Do you remember anything special about the motorbike?"

Aria shook her head. "I wasn't exactly focused on his bike, if you know what I mean."

Bay giggled. "Sure. Can you remember what day the coat switch happened?"

Aria checked the calendar. Bay had brought in the lululemon sometime between Christmas and the New Year, thinking she wouldn't be wearing it again until spring rains arrived. She habitually took in clothing every two weeks, and usually picked up when she dropped off, but since she had time in her schedule, she picked up this batch on January 7.

"It was January sixth, Professor. I remember Chance saying his mom was getting together with you on the tenth, which is today. I didn't think you'd miss your coat for a few days." Aria colored again with guilt. "I'm sorry about the whole thing. When the police came last night, I was scared and..."

"Okay, that's it. Aria, you've told Professor Browning everything you told the police. Like a good girl. You can go back to work." Giorgio interrupted his niece, casting a warning look with shifty eyes.

Bay couldn't be fooled. "Why didn't you call me Friday to let me know about the switch or the police? You knew they were coming to question me." She darted daggers at Giorgio, who winced and backed away.

"I didn't think you were in danger, or I would have called you. How could I know that the lululemon was murder evidence?" Giorgio quickly clapped his hand over his mouth.

Bay's eyes flew open. "Murder? Murder!" Bay lunged toward the counter while Giorgio ducked. "You better spill it, right now." She flashed her best killer-teacher face.

Giorgio shrugged. "After the police left Friday night, I called my cousin, Dorian. He works at the Madison PD, but he knows people." Bay shook her head, eyes rolling, when Giorgio used a Godfather accent and hand gesture. She waved her hand for him to get on with it.

Dorian's contact at Prairie Ridge said a woman was found murdered in a rental house on Poplar. Get this," Giorgio leaned closer to Bay, lowering his voice dramatically. "Her head was encased in plaster, like she'd been turned to stone!"

Bay gulped, imagining the horror of such a death. "Just her head?"

"No, it gets stranger. Her hand was holding a mirror, raised as if she were looking at herself. The mirror and her raised arm were also plastered."

"Her name?" Bay hoped she sounded as clipped as a cop doing an interview.

"That I don't know, L.L. But I do know the cops were led here by finding one of our tickets under her foot." Giorgio pounded the countertop for emphasis.

Bay looked alarmed. "It was my ticket, wasn't it? So, the police must have my lululemon, too."

Giorgio nodded. "They're calling this the Medusa Murders."

Bay's head jolted upward. "Murders? As in more than one?"

"According to Dorian. But I haven't heard of any murders. In a town like Prairie Ridge, that would hit the news like wildfire."

"Thanks for the info, Giorgio. You're off the hook…for now." Bay didn't smile.

Back in her car, Bay paused to absorb the grisly information and review the note she'd stored in her phone from the lululemon's coat pocket:

> *"Three things cannot be long hidden: the sun, the moon,*
> *and the truth. Your mannerisms reflect your reality.*
> *1603–508; Arpino"*

Bay concluded a couple of things she intended to share with Detective Downing, hoping he would be reasonable enough to give her some inside information. After all, Bay's life might be at stake here.

The Subaru sped down Grand Avenue and turned down Main Street to the police station. She parked in one of the designated visitor spaces and strode through the front door where a reception officer greeted her and asked her to place her personal items in a tub. She proceeded through the metal detector.

"What is your business this morning, Ma'am?" The officer, Shelton, droned mechanically. When Bay looked uncertain, Shelton reworded the question. "Who are you here to see?"

"Oh, sure. I'm here to see Detective Downing."

"Do you have an appointment with the detective?"

"Nooo, but I have information regarding a homicide investigation, so I'm hoping he will have time to see me." Bay couldn't fathom how often her teacher's voice came in handy.

"Your name, please?"

"Professor L.L. Browning." Bay lifted her chin higher when she spoke.

"I'll call upstairs to let them know you're on your way. Second floor, dead ahead is the reception desk. Carol will assist you from there. Have a good day." Shelton nodded and pointed to the elevator.

Carol greeted Bay before the elevator doors closed. "I'm guessing you're Professor Browning?"

Carol's British lilt surprised Bay in a pleasant way. "Yes, I need to speak with Detective Downing."

"Yes. I've let him know you're here. If you could just have a seat. He'll be with you shortly." Carol indicated a row of wooden chairs not designed for comfort. Bay was reminded of every movie with a courtroom scene.

It turned out she didn't have to wait to see if the chairs lived up to their uncomfortable appearance, as Downing's figure paraded down the hallway to greet her.

"Ah, Professor, we meet again, so soon." Downing's sardonic barb wasn't lost on Bay. The pair headed down the hallway, past the detective's office, straight into a small windowless room with a table and two chairs.

"What's this about having some information about a homicide?" Downing played the straight man well. He sat across the table from Bay, holding a pencil over a notepad in anticipation.

"If you're finished with your charade, let's get some things out in the open, Detective." Bay leaned back leisurely, hoping to convey she had the upper hand despite her uncertainty.

Bay stared into Downing's smiling smirk and raised one

hand to tick off her list of grievances against the detective.

"I understand my lululemon is part of a homicide known as the Medusa Murders. My dry-cleaning ticket was found at the scene. I found plaster particles in the back seat of my car, which I assume are evidence connected to the murder. Should I go on, or are you going to level with me?"

Downing's smile disintegrated and he suddenly looked fatigued. "I planned to get in touch with you as soon as some of the details were ironed out. For starters, did you know Virginia Lowe? The victim," Downing added, seeing Bay's puzzled expression.

Bay perused her memory. The name didn't ring any bells. "Do you have a photo of the woman? That would help."

Underneath the notepad was a manilla file folder. Downing pulled out a photo of Virginia Lowe and handed it across to Bay. The smiling woman was dressed in a sophisticated suit, skirt, and colorful stylish scarf. Her auburn hair was expertly styled in an updo, and sparkly chandelier earrings descended to meet the scarf. Bay guessed she was in her sixties based on her makeup and facial lines, but she had no recall of ever meeting poor Virginia Lowe.

"I'm afraid I don't know her. I'm sorry." Bay's apology was genuine. The fact she didn't know Ms. Lowe meant she had no idea how the two of them were connected in the mind of a psycho murderer.

"Can you tell me anything that might help me figure out how I'm connected to this case?"

Downing sighed. "Anything I tell you is strictly confidential. I mean it. You can't tell anyone, not your father, not your closest friends, and certainly not your sister." His voice rose and punctuated the last part.

Bay nodded, inwardly wondering how much background information the detective had already gathered on her.

"Virginia Lowe was from Albany, New York where she was a curator for a fine arts auction house. She was here to view the Vogel collection. Based on the evidence and how the victim was posed, this looks personal."

Bay's thoughts ran rampant now. "My mother was an art historian and professor, but she's been dead twenty years. Maybe she knew the victim? I can ask my father."

Downing's hand shot up in a swiping motion. "No, you can't do that, Ms. Browning. Let the police ask the questions. I'll talk to your father after I look more into the victim's information. What else do you know?"

Bay had to hand it to the man. He could tell she was holding something back. "Did you find any feathers in the lululemon or at the crime scene?"

Downing narrowed his eyes like a predator.

"I'll take that as a yes. Well, there's a feather on the floor of my Subaru. It's matted and damp from the rain, and no, I didn't touch it."

Downing scribbled on the notepad. "Anything else, Professor?"

"Yes, when can I get my lululemon back?" Bay didn't want to leave the encounter empty-handed.

"As soon as the lab is finished processing it. Probably later today or tomorrow. Someone will call you when it's ready." Downing stood up, stuck the pencil behind his ear, and closed the notepad.

Realizing she still had questions, Bay didn't rise. "Just a

minute, Detective. When did you find the victim?"

Downing opened the file folder. "January sixth." He couldn't believe it had only been four days. Of course, he'd slept precious little since the discovery.

"And the first murder victim? Why hasn't anything been released to the public?" Bay could appreciate the need for secrecy in a homicide investigation, but public safety mattered too, maybe even more than keeping the homicide under wraps.

"The first victim is still alive, Professor, but in a mental hospital where they are unable to help much. The connection between the two crimes was only discovered yesterday, since the first victim is from Chicago."

"Oh, I see. Sorry." But Bay didn't actually see anything, given the tidbits tossed her way. She left the small room without a goodbye and asked Carol at reception for directions to the evidence department.

The station's lower level combined tan industrial faux brick walls with flake resin flooring the color of sand. Whisper quiet, humans could move like cats down here, a fact Bay found quite unnerving. She stopped halfway down the corridor in front of a plain closed wooden door, the privacy glass was inscribed "evidence room."

Officer Keene sat behind a high barricade with just a small window and speaker for communication. "Hello. My name is L.L. Browning. My lululemon raincoat is here, and I wish to claim it." After the words fell like mashed baby food from her lips, Bay detected how silly they tracked with the officer in charge. After all, she wasn't at the coat check of the Overture Theatre.

Officer Keene blinked once, twice, three times, a saucy smile playing on her lips. "Who sent you here, Ms. Browning? Do you have paperwork to, ah, what was it, *claim* this item?"

Mortified, Bay shook her head and ran back to the elevator, grateful her running footfalls were indiscernible.

She didn't breathe until she reached the parking lot, where Officer Harris stood waiting by her Subaru, waving an evidence bag. Harris was there to collect the matted feather. ■

INTERFERENCE

Bay tapped one foot while Harris bagged the feather.

"How about these plaster particles? Is it okay if I vacuum them up or did you want to collect them, too?" Bay spoke impatiently, miffed about police procedures that kept her out of the loop and fearful about her personal safety.

"You know we're just following procedure, Ms. Browning," Harris spoke contritely with sincerity. Bay decided the beefy young officer would make a good public relations liaison and wondered why he ended up in homicide.

Bay sighed. "I know, Officer Harris, and I apologize for being disrespectful. I'm just worried about my safety and my father's safety. If we're a target, one of us might be next. You must understand how that feels."

Harris placed a protective hand on her shoulder. "We're doing all we can. You should know there's a patrol car parked at your apartment building to keep an eye on things." He held a finger up to his lips as if the information was classified.

The news made Bay relax a little. "Be that as it may, I'd like to be more involved in the investigation. Maybe you could provide daily updates? Maybe I could help?"

Harris's doubtful expression left an opening for Bay to impulsively add, "I have a friend at Channel 15 News..." she let the remark dangle.

Alarmed at the suggestion of the media, Harris zipped the evidence bag and said a cursory farewell.

Bay planned to ambush Art History Chair Jennifer Yoo, her so-called friend, but when she walked past the outer office, she spied the department assistant, Trevor, entering data at the computer.

"Hey Trevor, how was your New Year's?" Bay was chummy with the graduate assistant, who had proven his value repeatedly.

"Good to see you, L.L. My New Year's was toasty warm, unlike here." Trevor had traveled to Florida for the holidays to see his boyfriend. Their relationship had been rocky at best during the fall semester, so Bay wondered about its survival.

"And just how merry were your holidays? Come on, you might as well dish."

"Not all that merry, really. Brent and I broke up, but it was my idea, so I guess that's something. My sister flew down for Christmas, so I didn't have to spend all my time with my parents. We went clubbing and to the beach."

"Sorry about you and Brent, but I know things weren't all that happy. I hate to sound like a parent, but it's probably for the best."

"Right. What's new with you, L.L.? Did you scoop up anyone at the holiday party?" Trevor grinned and handed her a small envelope with her name hand-printed on the front.

Bay figured it was a thank-you note from someone. She'd given out several small gifts for the holidays. She gave Trevor the side-eye. "I didn't scoop up anyone at the holiday party, but it was a fun time. And since then, let's just say things have been interesting." She stopped short from sharing the dry-cleaning tale ending with a murder victim.

"Not to change the subject, but have you met the new gofer we just hired? I'm not sure when she's starting but it should be anytime. I'm sorry to report that my candidate didn't get the job. Too bad because he's a theater/music double major, and he's awfully cute. He told me he likes to hang at Crossroads…" Bay's voice lifted when she mentioned the popular Madison hot spot.

Trevor smiled for Bay's benefit and filed away the tidbit for a happier time. "The new gofer, Diana, is here. Apparently, she hasn't met anyone in the department except Professor McNelly. She's in the copy room sorting mail if you want to meet her."

"I'll get there eventually. First, I need to see Professor Yoo. Do you know if she's here yet?"

Trevor nodded, pointed toward her office, and resumed data entry.

The English offices sat to the left of the central common area, but Bay headed to the right, where the art history and theater offices were situated, to the last office in the hallway belonging to Art History Chair Jennifer Yoo.

Bay ducked her head into the doorway. Jennifer had a stack of papers front and center which partially hid her small stature as she slumped over one of the documents.

"Better sit up straight or you'll be headed to the chiropractor before the new semester even starts," Bay repeated what she'd heard many times from other professors who spent a lot of time bent over essays and exams.

"Oh, hi Bay. This is the price I pay for taking two weeks off. Even between semesters, the papers never stop." Jennifer, whose hair hung below the shoulders, a cascade of brown with streaks of red and blond peppered randomly throughout, raised light brown eyes toward Bay for sympathy.

Bay noticed her colleague wore a T-shirt bearing the famous Munch painting The Scream, a clear indication of Jennifer's state of mind. Still, she was here for more than a single purpose. First things first.

"Speaking of paperwork, don't forget that I screened all the applications for the new gofer position last month. I happened to notice you weren't at the hiring meeting last night." Bay pursed her lips and leaned over the top of the paper pile.

"I'm sorry, Bay. I had a terrible headache most of the day, probably stress-related." She swept her hand across the impossible stack. "Anyway, I didn't think you needed me to be there. You know, this department really needs to hire more adjunct professors. I'm reviewing my class load this semester and it's heavier than usual."

Bay leaned closer toward her colleague. Jen Yoo was the individual she felt closest to at the college, maybe even a friend. "I counted on someone to support me. Nobody showed up but me and McNelly. His candidate was hired instead of ours."

"Why is that?" Jen stopped reading to give Bay her full attention.

"She had financial need and other special circumstances. If you want to know the particulars, ask McNelly. He's got the lowdown." Other matters were more pressing, and Bay was over the whole business. She plopped down wearily on a nearby chair.

"Hey, I'm sorry about not being there, Bay. I didn't know it mattered that much to you. It's just a glorified gofer job." Jen noticed Bay was staring downward, rubbing her temples. "Is there something else going on?"

The rubbing stopped. Bay had to make a decision to lie, dismiss the topic, or tell at least some of her recent trials. She stood up and shut the office door.

"Wow, this story must be a dilly," Jen said. She moved the stack of papers to one side of the desk.

Bay's words tumbled out like an endless stream of magician scarves. "My sister moved in with me to get a fresh start. Did I mention she's an ex-con? The police questioned me about a dry-cleaning mix-up that turned into a murder investigation. I might be next on the killer's list, by the way. And, I now have a cat living in my apartment." She left out several details to save for later.

Jen's jaw dropped with every sentence, almost landing on the desktop. She got up, went to her closet, and pulled out a pink bag from Sweet Cheeks, the best local bakery in Prairie Ridge. She handed Bay a macaron with Nutella filling. "I have so many questions," she began.

Bay nibbled the macaron, allowing each bite to melt down to sugary syrup and creamy Nutella before the next nibble. Eyes closed, she waited for Jen's inquiry.

"Let's set aside the cat and your sister for the time being, so we can address the elephant. What does your dry cleaning have to do with murder?" Fully cognizant that everyone in the department used Giorgio's services, Jen bit off half of a raspberry macaron and swallowed it without any enjoyment.

Bay explained the lululemon switch, the evidence found in

the pockets, the plaster particles and feather left in her car, how the boy named Chance specifically asked for the coat swap as a practical joke, and that a woman named Virginia Lowe was killed, enclosed in plaster.

"And you don't know her? Maybe she's just some lowlife. Maybe she knows your sister, the ex-con?" Although Jen was trying to alleviate Bay's nerves, she wasn't helping.

Bay raised her hand to stop Jen's speculations. "No, Virginia Lowe is an art dealer for an auction house in Albany, New York. She was here to visit a collector in Madison. And she was killed on January sixth. My sister didn't show up on my doorstep until the seventh."

Bay reached for the pink bag. "May I?" Jen pushed the bag across the desk. Bay peeked inside, happy to see a large stash of macarons. She pulled out a lemon one with strawberry filling.

Jen opened her mini fridge and handed a bottle of water to Bay. "Unless you'd like to get coffee in the break room?"

Bay shook her head, not relishing the idea of running into anyone, including the new gofer.

"This will do just fine." Bay reached into her bag for her cell phone, located the text containing the words on the note, and slid the phone toward Jen. "Read this."

Jen read the note once, twice, then aloud a third time. "How were you able to get this information, Bay? Are you in trouble?"

Bay scoffed. "I didn't take a photo of the note, which was typed, by the way. I turned in the feather and asked about the plaster, so no, I haven't done anything wrong…yet."

Between nibbles and sips of water, Bay shared her theory. "Virginia Lowe was holding a mirror inward to see herself. What's more truthful than a mirror? I think the murder was personal. The killer cares about truth. Whatever Virginia did, it must have been dishonest, at least in the killer's eyes."

Jen chewed the tip of her index finger. "Why plaster?"

Bay shrugged. "She was an art dealer. Maybe it has to do with a sculpture, a fake perhaps?"

"And the feathers?" Jen frowned. Things didn't add up clearly.

Bay sighed. "Maybe they are part of the puzzle, maybe not. I just found out about the feathers and victim today, Jen."

"Do you think the lululemon is symbolic?" Jen's wide-eyed expression held concern for her colleague.

"It seems to be the connection between me and the victim. I wish I had information on the first victim. Maybe Giorgio's contact can wriggle something from the Prairie Ridge police. That Detective Downing is positively exasperating."

As Bay talked about the detective, something about the light reflecting in her eyes gave Jen pause. "Did you try using your charms on the man?" Jen batted her eyelashes playfully.

Bay swatted away the remark, helped herself to a third macaron, and stood up. "Blah, blah, blah police procedures," Bay mocked Officer Harris, pretending to stick her thumbs into belt loops and jutting out her stomach.

Jen laughed. "Be careful, Bay. Those procedures are in place for your protection. Your family doesn't need another convict in it."

Midway down the corridor, Bay stopped in the copy room to retrieve her mail and bumped into the new office assistant, Diana Poulin. She smiled broadly at Bay; her arms full of syllabus copies she'd organized for someone.

"Hello Professor Browning." Diana attempted to extend her right hand for a formal handshake, but the bundle of papers made that impossible. Diana reddened, looking down at her hand peeking out just below the stack.

Bay assessed the girl as if browsing for an outfit at a thrift shop. Diana looked clean, well-groomed, and energetic. She was petite, several inches shorter than Bay, with shiny blond hair cut in a long choppy bob. Sky blue eyes looked sweet and haunted at the same time. The trembling bowed mouth and pale cheeks with crimson glow conveyed the same two ideas—innocence and wariness.

Bay became aware of the toll living with abuse can take, and she felt instantly sorry for Diana and ashamed she'd made such a huge deal about hiring her.

"Here, let me help you with this load. Where are you going with these papers?" Bay took half the stack.

"Professor McNelly's office. He's been so kind to me. And I want to thank you, too, Professor Browning. Professor McNelly said you were the first to support my application for this job." Her smile glided from cheek to cheek.

McNelly said what? That lying goat. Ex-priest my Aunt Portia's plums! Bay sputtered inwardly. Outwardly, she looked curiously at Diana. "Do we know each other? I mean you knew who I was when I entered the copy room."

Diana blushed a second time. "I don't expect you to remember me. I took your Survey of Mythology course last spring. It was a large class."

"Sorry. Yes, those survey classes are usually seventy-five to a hundred students, and with only exams to grade, I'm afraid I don't get one-on-one time with students." Bay only scheduled formal conferences with upper-level students claiming an English major or minor.

The survey course exams were graded by the graduate assistants when possible. Flourish College had a dozen English instructors and one grad assistant, so professors with seniority got first dibs on using the lone GA. Bay might be the department head, but she didn't pull rank when other professors held more seniority. Her position was challenging enough; a thirty-year-old running a department of multiple courses and eclectic personalities.

"Well, here we are." Bay paused, reluctant to go into McNelly's office, afraid she might bite his head off, but she couldn't just hand the stack back to Diana or they'd likely fly everywhere.

Diana briskly entered the office and set the papers on a side table by the wall. "You can just put them here, please, if you don't mind. The professor might be at lunch."

Bay happily complied. "It was nice to meet you, Diana. I hope your semester goes well."

Diana's reply was obliterated by the noisy jangle of Bay's phone. Thankful for the interruption, Bay glanced at McNelly's approaching figure, and ducked into the nearby break room.

The upbeat British accent on the other end belonged to Carol at the police station. "Ms. Browning, your rain jacket is ready to be picked up. And Chief Sessions requests you come to the station today at four-thirty for a meeting. Alrighty?" ■

CHAPTER 8
RELUCTANT ALLIANCE

Bay found it impossible to concentrate on work. She looked at her course schedule, set up office hours, and scanned her class rosters for familiar names. She didn't want to see Diana again or, God forbid, McNelly, so she closed her office door and worked quietly.

The clock stubbornly refused to move, so she packed up midafternoon and stopped at the phone store where she retrieved Cass's new and old phones from a different clerk, who was just as disinterested as the first.

Wisconsin's afternoon sun boasted heat in direct contradiction to the calendar. The Subaru's dash said the temperature was forty-six degrees, so Bay cruised past Windflower Gardens and parked on Magnolia Drive by the empty subdivision where Bay liked to walk to clear her head.

Beginning about a year ago when the development was no more than a cleared field of leftover wildflowers and grasses, Bay could log two miles looping through the packed dirt avenues created by construction equipment.

The street was unnamed at first, so when the sign announced Magnolia Drive, Bay wrinkled her nose and laughed at the inappropriate name. "Magnolias don't really grow here," she'd told a city worker one morning after encountering him at work on a water main. She pointed an accusing finger at the street sign. The worker just shrugged.

Months later, the new sector revealed itself in paved streets, curbs and gutters, and now, a line of turn-of-the-century style lamp posts stood erect along the winding paved edges.

Progress, Bay supposed, but she dreaded seeing the first houses assembled. Where would the sandhill cranes go when their grasses were replaced by bricks and landscape blocks? Would the kestrels that perched on the lamp posts bother hunting the area after the rodent exterminators were finished here?

A crow called loudly in response to her query, bobbing its head in agreement with her skepticism. It stared hard at her from the gleaming black streetlamp, glossy feathers offered vibrancy that couldn't be replaced by metal and concrete.

"All right then, Edgar Allan, can you help solve a puzzle of another sort? Who do you think the Medusa Killer could be?

The crow raised its wings and was aloft in a flash of sunshine. Bay walked on, head bent downward, wondering what the meeting with Chief Sessions would unveil. Maybe a security detail? Even better, maybe they'd caught the killer.

Bay arrived early so she could retrieve her lululemon. She realized she'd acted huffy about getting her raincoat back and wanted to apologize to the evidence room officer. Bay's attachment to the lululemon held sway in her mind. The coat was the first item she acquired after being hired at the college; it was a rite of passage purchase. The fact that her family nickname was LuLu, made the purchase seem serendipitous.

Finding herself at the evidence room counter, Bay greeted Officer Keene with an apologetic smile. "Good afternoon, Officer Keene. I want to apologize for being out of line when I was here earlier."

Keene's stoic expression didn't change. "The lululemon, right?" She didn't wait for Bay's confirmation but proceeded to somewhere in a dark maze of shelves and cardboard boxes to return with Bay's coat, wrapped in plastic.

"It's been cleared of having any connection to a crime, so you may use it as you will." Keene leaned over the counter to shove the coat in stages through the half window, making Bay cringe. Hadn't the coat been through enough?

Bay thanked the officer. "It must be very interesting, working in the evidence room." She encountered a vacant stare from Keene. "I mean, you must know everything about every case with all the stuff stashed here, right?"

Keene blinked. "Have a good day, Ms. Browning."

Upstairs, Bay found Carol to be much more amiable, and she wondered if it had something to do with Carol not being a law enforcement officer.

"Good afternoon, Professor Browning. The chief is ready to see you," Carol chirped, flashing a friendly smile.

Bay looked at the fit watch she always wore. It was 4:20. Carol noticed.

"Chief Sessions is always early. That's his way of being on time. No worries." She spoke over her shoulder at Bay, who followed her to the end of the hallway to his office. At least she wasn't being led to a conference or interrogation room this time.

Vernon Sessions grunted in response to Carol's announcement, and in one motion, he indicated Bay take a seat and dismissed Carol.

"I'm going to make this purty quick, Ms. Browning, before Detective Downing joins us. I'm giving you access to the Medusa case files." He said "access" as if it were two words, then jabbed a brawny finger into the air surrounding Bay's personal space.

"This is for your own safe-tee, and not, I repeat, not for public gossip. This department wants to keep you alive, and you're smart enough to handle some of the par-tick-ulars involved."

Vernon Sessions had a face with character, wrinkled, spotted by too much sun, and ready for retirement, Bay decided. His eyes were slits due to sagging lids and loose bags, but his large nose made up for them, holding black-framed reading glasses. When he stood up, Bay was surprised by his short stature.

Hands on hips, he blew out a puff of air. "Look Ms. Browning, the last thing we need is outside interference in a murder case, so what I'm doing here is off the books, got it?"

Bay nodded, pretending to understand the puzzle box she'd just opened. She had no idea what the chief was talking about or why he was suddenly offering access. Then the door flew open and was slammed shut by Detective Downing.

"What in H is going on, Chief? I heard I'm getting a tail. You mean to tell me it's our Professor Browning?" His ornery smile conveyed amusement and irritation, but his eyes could cut ice.

The chief cut Downing's oration short with a hand slap on the desk. Standing tall and straight, he jutted forward in Downing's direction. "Look here, de-tec-tive. The professor has the right to know a few things. For her own safe-tee."

It was Downing's turn to lunge. "But Chief, this is highly unorthodox and…"

Bay found herself witnessing a verbal fencing match. The detective's argument was immediately blocked by Sessions who parried by folding his arms across his chest and lowering his voice. "You're suggesting this is unorthodox, Downing? You?"

Arms uncrossed; the chief located himself a foot from the detective's face. Despite standing a head shorter than Downing, the chief held the advantage. Downing stepped backward, one hand on the wall to steady himself.

"I get that you don't want to babysit a civilian, Downing. But she might be useful with this mythology hogwash." Sessions's voice rose to full volume in reference to mythology, and Bay wondered how she might be able to help the investigation.

Seeing he'd won that round, the chief spun toward Bay, who was making herself small in the visitor's chair. "I take it you are sat-tis-fied with this arrangement, Ms. Browning. Detective Downing will show you the case files in his office now."

Bay rose meekly from the chair and followed Downing down the hallway, barely breathing, and confused as could be. Before she had a chance to ask for an explanation, Downing pointed to a chair in his office, shut the door, and unleashed his annoyance.

"Who do you think you are, threatening Officer Harris. Just who do you know at Channel 15 anyway?" Downing's eyes moved like hatchets.

Bay stopped in her tracks and inhaled sharply. "That's what this is about?" She found it difficult to believe her insinuating remark to Harris would create such a stir. "I know Charlie…"

"Shortino? The weather guy?" Downing laughed incredulously.

"No, no. Charlie, I mean Charlotte Stone, award winning

investigative reporter." Bay recited the TV promo stating Charlotte Stone's credentials. Bay and Charlotte had been college roommates for a year at UW-Madison.

Downing began to pace in the small office, like a zoo animal. "Sit down. I'm not showing you the case files, but I'll answer your questions."

Within a half hour, Bay naively thought she knew as much as the police did about the Medusa Murders. The first victim was a comic book creator in Chicago, who crafts a mythology-themed series, *Vengeful Venuses*. The creator has a cult following on social media, mostly women-haters and porn lovers.

"How do you know this is the same perpetrator?" Bay had asked.

"Comic book author was found blind-folded, drugged, hands encased in plaster. They're in a coma and may never recover, so it's hard to get answers. The same brand of stucco gun was used on the comic creator as the one found next to Ms. Lowe."

Downing had shown Bay the photos from the Virginia Lowe scene. A stucco spray gun was near her body, and a hunting bugle lay on her lap. "Nobody knows if the bugle is a clue or if it's an art piece the victim acquired here. We've got an art expert looking at it."

"What about the feathers found in the lululemon pocket?" Bay inquired. "Do you know what kind they are?" Photos of two feathers were included in the case file.

Downing pointed to each in succession. "This one is a swan feather. This one an ostrich." Their eyes connected and something inside Bay stirred, making her uncomfortable and warm at once. She looked away before Downing did.

The detective snapped the folder closed and stared hard at

Bay. "Well, what does any of this mean, Professor?"

She was startled by his intensity. "I don't know, Detective, but I promise I'll investigate the mythical angles. I need time."

Downing heaved a troubled sigh. "Can you call me tomorrow or sooner if you have something?"

Driving home in the dark, Bay was lost in a maze of evidence and clues. A phone call coming though her navigation system squashed a tiny thread she attempted to follow. Jennifer Yoo's face appeared in the corner of the screen.

"Hey Jen."

"Bay, can you send me the text of the murder note? I have an idea I want to follow." Jen sounded excited.

Bay laughed at Jen's choice of words. "Sure, as soon as I get home. I'm almost there." Bay turned the corner to Windflower Gardens.

"But you've been gone most of the afternoon. Where have you been?"

Bay relayed a rundown of picking up a phone for the ex-con sister, a walk in the empty subdivision, and a return trip to the police station. She concluded with the news she was being loosely paired with Downing to help with the case.

Jen's hoot on the other end of the call caused Bay to hit her brakes. "What's the matter with you, Jen? It's not that exciting. I could be in danger here, remember?"

"Are you coming in tomorrow? I want to hear all the details, including stuff about the case." She giggled, but Bay wasn't impressed.

"Yes, bright and early. I didn't get much academic work done today, and now apparently, I'll be adding detective work to my repertoire." She paused, thinking aloud. "I don't understand why the chief decided to include me. He forced me onto the case, almost like he'd been threatened."

"It's a gift from the gods, Bay. Go with it. See you tomorrow." Jen disconnected. ∎

# CHAPTER 9
THE GODS HAVE SPOKEN

Bay hesitated before opening the door of number 1002. She dreaded a confrontation with Cassandra following an already-overloaded day. When she pushed the door open a crack, her senses were confounded by a delicious aroma wafting from the kitchen. She stepped forward, dropped her accessories onto the sofa table and peered over the counter that separated the two rooms.

Cassandra wore an apron she must have pulled out of the recesses of Bay's pantry and was stir-frying a variety of veggies in a wok Bay had never used. She could smell garlic, ginger, and something earthy coming from the colorful array of sizzling produce. Another kettle hissed under its cover with an occasional pop.

In spite of the warm welcome, Bay's eyes narrowed. "So, what's this?" She waved toward the stove and the countertop where three individual salads waited, heaped with healthy stuff.

Cassandra was pleased with herself even if Bay was being

pissy. "I thought I'd make dinner for the three of us. Dad took me to the market for groceries. Honestly, Professor, don't you ever eat here?" Cassandra laughed lightly, hoping to change the mood.

"I work a lot," Bay was terse. "When I get home, I don't feel like cooking." Feeling a pang of guilt about her father, she added, "I drop off food for dad all the time." *Do you, Bay, all the time?* She knew she could spend more time with Barrett. During the semester, when Bay often didn't get home until seven o'clock, she figured he'd already had dinner, so she skipped bringing food to him.

Frowning, she turned away from the kitchen, picked up her bag and purse, and strode to the bedroom. "I'm going to change clothes. What time is dinner?" She hated the ungrateful tone she was using.

"About ten minutes, Sister. Dad will be here in a few." Cassandra's voice was forced cheerfulness.

Bay stopped wondering how her sister knew when to have dinner ready. Knowing was among Cassandra's many tricks of confidently acting on hunches, expecting the unexpected, or resigning herself to never being surprised.

Bay traded casual clothes for holey jeans and a gray *Chopin Preludes* sweatshirt with a single red rose against a backdrop of rain and piano notes. Rubbing her hands with extra moisturizing cream, she paused to consider letting Cassandra in on the case information. She immediately chastised herself thinking she could share criminal case evidence with an ex-con. No matter how talented and intuitive said ex-con may be.

She slipped on her house moccasins with the fleece lining and splashed water on her tired face. Before leaving the bedroom, she took Cass's new phone from her tote bag to deliver at dinner. She wanted her father to see what she'd done for her sister. *Catty indeed.*

Speaking of cats, Bay peered around the living room for Minerva. She had yet to locate a litter box, so she opened Cassandra's bedroom door and looked around. No sign of a litter box. Minerva wasn't there either.

Bay re-entered the living room and set the handled bag on the sofa table. Barrett arrived and gave Cass an affectionate hug.

"Whatever you're cooking, I can't wait to eat it." They smiled at one another, father and daughter reunited.

Barrett waved at Bay. "How was your day today, LuLu?"

Hesitating, Bay offered a safe reply. "Oh, you know. Busy. Getting ready for second semester courses. You know what that's like, Dad." Barrett and Penelope had both been college professors for a time.

"Right. It's in your blood, Honey. You'll do fine." It was meant to be a compliment to Bay, but it rang like a dismissal of the topic.

"I see you got your raincoat back?" Barrett nodded toward the plastic bag hanging on the coat tree. "Did the police give you an update on the case?"

Bay pondered how to answer that simple question safely. "They didn't find any evidence relating to the raincoat." Bay smoothed her hair away from her face as she spoke, drawing Cassandra's attention and scrutiny.

"Why don't we eat dinner. I'm anxious to hear about Cassandra's day. Any luck on your job search?"

Cass handed salads to Bay through the kitchen pass-through, which she carried to her small but formal dining table, a seldom used piece of furniture in her apartment. Cass carried out plates piled with fried rice and fragrant stir-fry vegetables.

Barrett inhaled deeply. "This smells divine."

Bay picked at her salad, enjoying the fresh variety of greens, cukes, tomatoes, and radishes made more flavorful by crumbled feta and fresh lemony dressing. "Did you make the dressing, too?"

Cass nodded. "I found a clunky blender in one of your cupboards. How long has it been since you used that ancient thing?" She quickly checked her tongue, even though she meant it as a joke.

Bay frowned. "I'm not sure I ever have. It was a college graduation gift from Auntie Vee, meant to make my life easier. But you inherited all her cooking talents." She offered Cass an appreciative grin.

"I guess that's what happens when you're the older sister." Barrett wanted Bay to understand that Aunt Venus taught Cass everything necessary to keep a house both for his sake and Bay's.

The moment passed as Minerva strolled languidly out of the kitchen to sit under the dining table near Cassandra.

Before she forgot again, Bay pounced on her chance to bring up the subject of the feline. "I haven't seen a litter box anywhere in the apartment. How is that cat, you know…"

"Minerva is toilet-trained," Cass simpered, giving the black feline scratches around her ears and chin. "She came that way."

As if that's an answer. "Speaking of which, where did she come from?" Bay assumed she had a right to know.

"She came with me. I found her in Florida in the alley, under attack by a mongrel. I took her in, tended her wounds, fed her, and loved her." There were tears in Cassandra's eyes.

Bay momentarily saw her sister the same way Cass had seen Minerva. *This is how you get sucked in Bay. Don't let it happen.*

"I didn't have enough money to buy litter and cat food, so I toilet-trained her. I saw it online. Minerva is a wise kitty. She learned right away."

Bay changed the subject. "And how was job hunting today?"

Cassandra beamed. "I interviewed for a job this afternoon for a security position at Outfitters, and two hours later, I was hired. I start training Wednesday night."

Bay looked down at her dinner plate, trying to make sense of what she'd just heard. Outfitters was a chain megastore devoted to the great outdoors. Among the hiking and camping gear was a fair number of weapons in every flavor.

"Does the manager know you're an ex-con? Outfitters sells weapons, Cassandra."

"Duh. Stop acting like I just emerged from an underground bomb shelter."

Bay tried to bury her smug expression. "Well to be fair…"

"The manager has full access to my past. She talked to my parole officer. I'm cleared to work security under supervision. I won't have a weapon. The night guards don't have weapons either unless you count a flashlight and two-way radio." Cass expected Bay to back off.

"Let me get this straight. You applied at Outfitters this morning, interviewed this afternoon, and the manager reviewed your information and hired you within two hours. Pardon my skepticism." Bay folded her arms, elbows on the table.

Cass leaned toward her sister and ignored the imploring looks from Barrett. "Let me educate you, Professor. I never said I applied for the job this morning. I applied last week and had my first interview before I got on the bus headed for this little piece of hell. Today was my second interview after the manager reviewed my records."

Instead of exploding at being bested by her sister, Bay stood up, picked up the phone bag from the sofa table, and handed it to Cass. "Well done. Looks like you earned this."

Sleep had abandoned Bay despite a satisfactory evening with family. Having Cassandra back in her life conjured a blurry past where Bay wandered around in murky memories. From age five to seven, Bay's recollections of her mother were either crystal clear or covered in fog. Penelope's face moved into high definition then morphed into Aunt Venus's face in her place.

Bay remembered an expanse of time where her mother was "on sabbatical", quite the abstract term for a five-year-old to navigate. During her mother's absence, the girls moved several times, jostled back and forth from her father's anthropology work in Turkey, Scotland, and Ethiopia and Auntie Vee's homes in Chicago. Auntie Vee was as much of a vagabond as Barrett.

Bay's past came back into focus at age seven after Penelope returned from her art history studies and the family reunited. For Bay, what followed were a few happy years surrounded by the love of doting parents, but Cass often ruined life by being unruly and disrespectful.

By the time Penelope died from a short viral flu and pneumonia, Cass was well versed in petty crimes and cons, and a couple of years later, she disappeared for months. For the next few years, Cass was like a yo-yo, bouncing in and out of the family when it suited her.

Bay's whole childhood was an incomplete story, and every time she visited the past, she confronted huge gaps she tried to stitch together, but the picture was never complete.

Her father was still too brokenhearted to answer her questions, and Aunt Venus believed mucking around the past was wasteful for the living. So, Bay found herself in the dark again, hungry to know her story.

The next morning, Bay was awake and out the door well before Cassandra. She left her a note, asking if she had any "gate money" left to buy work clothes, which they could shop for that evening.

A dusting of snow fell overnight, prettying up the landscape with a sugar coating. Sugar reminded Bay she planned to stop at Sweet Cheeks bakery to replenish Jen Yoo's macaron supply and pick up fussy coffees for both of them.

The bakery was quiet on this typical winter morning when the world moved slowly. Besides, Prairie Ridge was on pause until the new semester ushered in the hubbub of students, a fact that reminded Bay she had much to do in preparation. Because her mythology course had caught fire, she had three sections for the winter term, easing her load considerably. Teaching repetitive sections meant less prep, and a survey course meant less grading. Her other course was two sections of American Literature from the 19th Century to the Present, a new course for Bay, but she was up for the challenge.

Later, when the elevator doors opened onto the fifth floor, Trevor saw Bay balancing bags, totes, and a drink carrier, and came to her rescue.

"Thank you, Trevor. I didn't want to make two trips but forgot how hard it would be getting on and off the elevator." Bay laughed. Trevor walked beside her down the hallway to her office, cardboard carrier in one hand, Bay's heaviest tote bag in the other.

Bay unbuttoned her long wool coat, then unwrapped her wool scarf and tucked it into one coat sleeve before hanging it onto a hook in her closet. She motioned toward the coffee and pastry bags. "Trevor, that skinny caramel latte is for you, so good thing you decided to come in early today." Bay reached over and opened one of the pink bags. She pulled out a cherry almond scone and handed it to him.

"Thanks, Boss. Anything you need done today? Copies, syllabus prepared, emails answered?"

Unlike some of the department professors, Bay didn't allow Trevor or anyone but herself to read and respond to emails. She considered it unprofessional and a bad practice, period. She wouldn't mind having Trevor revamp her mythology syllabus, however.

"You know what, it would really help me out if I could send you changes to my mythology course packet. Can I share the file with you and have you revise them?" Maybe Bay could be a professor and detective's assistant, too.

"I'm here all morning. I'll look for the doc and changes and take care of them." Trevor backed out the door, coffee and scone in hand. "Thanks for thinking of me. Would you like your door closed?"

"Yes. Can you please let Dr. Yoo know I need to see her as soon as she arrives?"

Behind the closed door, Bay fired up her computer and sipped a dark brew with oat milk creamer, waiting for files to load. She avoided the pink bag, choosing to wait until Jen Yoo arrived, fearful she'd eat them all.

After sending Trevor her mythology course packet, she

turned on some energizing Mozart, then reread the "murder note", as Jen called it. Where to start: mythology perhaps. Maybe rereading Medusa and the Gorgon sisters myth would shake loose a clue.

Bay turned in her office chair to pull a book off her shelf. She couldn't go wrong with Edith Hamilton's *Timeless Tales of Gods and Heroes* and Ovid's *Metamorphoses*, but she grabbed the Joseph Campbell books in case she wanted a deeper dive.

Trying to read the tale with a new perspective, Bay noted that Medusa was one of the monstrous Gorgons, yet the word "gorgon" means "guardian." *Maybe the Medusa killer believes themselves to be a protector of sorts.*

Medusa was depicted with bronze hands and wings. Is this connected to the comic book artist's hands cast in plaster? Bay wrote the question down with her other myth notes.

She couldn't see anything glaring, so she pulled up a search bar and typed in "Virginia Lowe." She didn't want to pay for inside information the police likely possessed, so she jotted down the basics.

Lowe worked at Albany Acquisitions in New York the past three years. Prior to that she worked for the Fennimore Art Museum and Albany Institute of History and Art. She was married to Robert Reginald Lowe, an investment broker in New York City. The two had been estranged for a year. *Blah, blah, blah. How am I supposed to know if something's important, anyway?*

An hour into research, Bay's eyelids already felt like anchors. She jiggled her coffee—empty. She longingly eyed the pink bakery bag. "Better go get more coffee, or I could warm up Jen's." She crinkled her nose. Soy chai latte with a double shot of espresso: definitely not.

Bay opened the door to reveal a smiling Jen Yoo in the doorway bearing to-go cups. "I was just about to knock," Jen's broad grin was the opposite of yesterday's stressed-out expression.

"You're a lifesaver. I was about to go for more coffee." Bay shut the door behind Jen. "I bought you a soy chai double shot, but it's been sitting two hours, so…"

Jen slid the chai toward her and took a healthy gulp. "Tastes fine to me. The college coffee shop didn't get its supply order, so their menu's limited. I had to settle for plain coffees with almond milk creamer."

Bay held up one of the pink bags and jiggled it at Jen. "Macarons from Sweet Cheeks," she sang.

Jen smiled appreciatively but pushed the bag aside. "Later, Bay. We have to talk about that murder note."

Bay moved the notebook to the center of her desk and looked at Jen. "I'm all ears, Dr. Yoo."

Jen was still standing. "Actually, may I use your computer? I need to show you something." She scooted behind Bay's desk.

Bay offered her chair to Jen and stood behind it. "You're the driver."

Jen entered something in the search bar, and rows of paintings filled the screen. "The end of the note included numbers and the word 'Arpino.' I knew there were many artists located in Arpino, Italy, so I did a search. It was too broad, too much to sort through."

"I kept staring at the numbers though. Museums catalog their art by year and ID number. I wondered if 1603 was a reference to the year. So, I searched for Arpino and 1603. That narrowed down the number of paintings."

Bay clapped. "Bravo, Dr. Yoo. You're a genius. So, now we're looking for a painting with a mirror or Medusa or truth?"

"But wait, there's more." Jen pointed at the screen. "I kept turning the words from the note around and around in my brain. I thought if the note is connected to art, then 'your mannerisms reflect your reality' might refer to the Mannerist art period, which was happening in 1603. What you're seeing here is a result of searching for Mannerist art in 1603 in Arpino." She sat back satisfied.

Bay's brown eyes lit up, revealing golden glints that reminded people of tigereye. "Did I mention you're a genius? This could be a breakthrough."

Jen skirted around the desk to the other side again. "Well, this genius is going to have to leave you to it, I'm afraid. I have a date with my own desk and Mount Paperwork." She grabbed the pink bag off Bay's desk and trotted to the door. "Keep me posted."

"Hey, we were supposed to share those!" Bay shouted after her. She bent over and opened the bottom drawer. "Good thing I bought a second bag."

Bay plucked a pair of reading glasses from her tote to magnify the screen of thumbnail paintings. Most of them were religious in subject matter. A few were portraits. She didn't see any mirrors or pieces with 'truth' in the title.

"Well, nobody said this would be easy." Bay sat back and snacked on a vanilla macaron with blueberry filling. She read the note's words again. She looked at her own notes. Then she smacked her forehead.

"Mythology. I need to include that in the search terms." Bay clicked on the bar and perused her options. *Venus and Cupid in the Forge of Vulcan.* No date was listed, but it was in a private collection, so wouldn't be catalogued. Furthermore, it didn't seem to depict anything about the sun, the moon, or truth.

The next painting was promising, Bay decided. *Perseus and Andromeda* showed the hero riding on Pegasus to rescue the chained princess, and he was holding the head of Medusa. "Bingo," Bay whispered, downloading the image to a newly created "Medusa Murders" folder. The painting was part of a collection in Rhode Island. Close enough to upstate New York.

Not one to leave a stone unturned, she wasn't satisfied to choose the second painting without examining the rest. She found more depictions of Venus, but nothing with a mirror, sun, moon, or truth. Then she waded into an infinite pool of Artemis/Diana the Huntress paintings. The Greek moon goddess Artemis, and her Roman counterpart, Diana, must have been a favorite subject of Italian mannerist artists.

Bay spent an hour scrutinizing many versions of the virgin goddess until her eyes crossed. She couldn't have been happier to hear her phone ring.

Without looking, she answered. "Professor Browning. How may I help you?"

"Why haven't you called me yet, Professor?" Detective Downing sounded amused and serious at the same time. Bay found him to be a conundrum.

"Good morning to you, too," she replied, pleasantly. "As a matter of fact, I'm buried in mythology and art history research at this very moment."

Downing's voice held skepticism. "Oh, yeah? Have you turned up anything useful?"

"Maybe." Bay was determined to be methodical in her

dealings with Downing.

"What's that supposed to mean?"

Bay sighed as quietly as possible but stuck her tongue out at the voice. "It means that these things take time, and I'm not going to jump to conclusions. You of all people should know that."

Downing backed down and lowered the temperature in his tone. "How about we grab dinner somewhere we can talk? The Pig Squeal bar at six?"

Bay didn't know if she should laugh or retch. The thought of dinner with Downing at a place called The Pig Squeal seemed ludicrous on a few levels. Did he want to have dinner with her? She doubted it, or he wouldn't choose a bar. But why meet in public about a confidential investigation? Bay couldn't figure out this man.

"Browning, are you there?" Downing's voice returned to impatient.

Bay jolted out of her psychoanalysis. "Yep, still here. Just checking my schedule. I guess I can meet you at six. But I can't promise I'll have anything specific to give you." Nothing but dead air on the other end of the phone. She didn't know if Downing heard her last sentence. ∎

CHAPTER 10
THE PIG SQUEAL

As much as she enjoyed being a bloodhound for the Prairie Ridge police, Bay's courses were sitting on ice with the winter semester starting in eleven days. She had to shelve the art searches for later. At least she could share a couple of findings that might aid the investigation.

Trevor stopped in with syllabus packets run and done and asked for more work, but Bay sent him away empty-handed. She needed to be ready to teach nineteenth century literature and beyond, which meant eleven days of reading and concocting essay questions.

She supposed she could have Trevor call the college bookstore to check on her book order. The bookstore was notorious for lack of communication when it came to books not showing up. *I'm sorry, but we can't get copies of* The Awakening. *Would* Daisy Miller *do instead?* Ugh.

She flew a quick email request to Trevor to call the bookstore and received a thumbs-up emoji in the office chat window. She loved technology for these situations. The stack of books from the American literature class beckoned, so she spent the rest of the afternoon by the sunny office window in her secondhand reading chair, a cushy half-moon affair. A battered copy of Toni Morrison's *Beloved* was her quarry, and although she'd read the masterpiece a few times, she always found something new to highlight or flag.

At three p.m. Jen rapped on the door and let herself in. "I'm here for a progress report." Jen's hair was in a ponytail, and she'd changed into workout clothes.

After sticking in a bookmark, Bay closed *Beloved*. She yawned. "My syllabus packets are ready to go, and I've started on my book stack so I can create essay questions and composition projects for American lit." She pointed to the stack. "There sits eleven days or more worth of reading alone."

Jen smiled in commiseration. "That's good, Bay, but what about the murder case? Did you find a painting that matches the note?"

Stretching her arms above her head, Bay did a combination head shake and nod. "I'm not sure. Let me show you." She walked over to the computer, moved the mouse, and logged back in. The search screen materialized. She pointed at *Perseus and Andromeda*. "See, he's carrying Medusa's head."

Jen twisted her mouth uncertainly. "This is a 1592 piece, not 1603. Did you find anything else?" Over Bay's shoulder, Jen clicked on a tab where a glut of Artemis depictions loitered. "What's all this?" She pointed to the paintings showing the goddess posing with a hunting hound, poised with a drawn bow, and even lying in the nude in repose.

"I'm guessing she was a popular subject in the sixteenth and seventeenth centuries you know, like one of the Kardashians. She's the goddess of the moon, and the note mentions the moon." Bay sat upright. "Hold on. Artemis is a twin to Apollo, the god of truth and light. Why didn't I think of that earlier?" Now she had two mythical entities connected to the note.

Jen frowned. "I see, but how does Medusa fit into the story? Is there a tale that includes all three?"

Bay shook her head. She added Apollo plus mannerist art to the internet search bar. Unfortunately, the more specific her search terms were, the less hits she received. She found one painting that fit the time period, *The Death of Niobe's Children*, by German artist Johann König, no connection to Arpino or Italy. It was the only painting she could find depicting Apollo and Artemis on the same canvas, and it was gruesome. Niobe's crime was bragging about her progeny of fourteen children, making her superior to Leto, who only produced Apollo and Artemis. As such, the twin deities shot all of Niobe's children with arrows.

She closed the tabs and shut down the computer.

Jen patted her on the shoulder. "Rome wasn't built in a day," she chirped. "I've accomplished a lot today, so I'm going to the gym to do a cross-burn class. Would you like to come, too? It might ignite some brain waves."

Bay smiled wanly. "I'd love to, but I have a dinner meeting with Detective Dismal. We're supposed to discuss the case, so you can put away that saucy grin, Jen."

"Where are you dining?" Jen wouldn't be put off.

Bay scowled. "The Pig Squeal. What kind of name is that anyway?" Bay had never heard of the place, but Jen knew it.

She giggled. "It's a cop bar. You know, where cops hang out.

It's pretty much off-limits to anyone outside the force. They have a bouncer who screens customers." She winked knowingly.

Jen's information ruled out dinner being any sort of date, Bay decided.

Bay toyed with the notion of calling her sister to cancel their evening outing, but decided she should check in on her in person.

When Bay entered the apartment, she heard running water coming from the bathroom. She sorted through the class materials she'd brought home, placed *Beloved* and a couple other titles on her nightstand, and looked in the mirror.

I wonder if I need to change clothes. She was dressed in jeans, which she assumed was suitable, but what about her top half? She was comfortable in a blue, green, and white plaid button-down flannel over a navy-blue tee, an outfit deemed appropriate nearly everywhere in Wisconsin during winter.

Bay walked into her closet to browse the wall of earrings hanging there. She picked up three different pairs before choosing medium-sized twisted silver hoops.

The bathroom door opened, revealing Cass, her head wrapped in a towel. Thinking her sister was making an extra effort for shopping, Bay felt a pang of guilt in cancelling.

Cass looked up at Bay, who was standing in the door frame. "You're home earlier than I expected," Cass stated without emotion. When Cass was at her calmest, Bay worried, because it meant something was simmering below the surface.

"Yes, about that, I'm sorry but I have to cancel shopping tonight. We'll go tomorrow morning. I won't be going into the office until later."

Bay grimaced as Cass's towel slipped, unveiling dyed hair.

Bay looked beyond Cass and saw hair dye residue in the sink. She jabbed her finger at the offending dye. "You need to clean that up before it stains the sink. Why did you dye your hair anyway?" Bay wondered if this was the beginning of her sister adopting a new identity. "Something stinks."

Cass laughed scornfully. "That's just the ammonia in the dye. I'm not doing anything illegal, for God's sake—stop glaring at me." She grabbed the cleaner from the lower cupboard and sprayed it liberally on the residue.

Bay cleared her throat. "Why the dark hair dye?" Cass's hair was wet, but Bay could tell it was some form of dark red or even black.

Cass kept scrubbing. "People don't take blond women seriously, and I'm working security. I expect to be treated with a modicum of authority." She sniffed haughtily and giggled. "There, you see, not a trace of hair dye." She waved her hand over the sink basin in presentation.

"Thanks, but I'll be throwing away that bath towel for sure." The light gray towel bore dark-colored streaks.

Cass knew there was no winning against Bay, so she switched gears. "And why can't you go shopping tonight?"

Bay chewed her bottom lip. "I have to speak with the police again. They have more questions for me about the murder." Bay was telling a half-truth, but in choosing her words, she forgot Cass knew nothing about a murder.

"Murder? Who said anything about a murder? What's going on, LuLu?" In her astonishment, Cass forgot the name rule.

"Bugger," Bay blew out a puff of air. "Come on, let's go sit down, and I'll fill you in."

Bay carefully disclosed the basic information. A woman

with the same coat as Bay had been murdered. Bay's coat and dry-cleaning ticket were found nearby. The coats had been accidentally switched. The police want to know if Bay knows the woman. Her words came out pointedly, a stiff list of facts. *If I were Pinocchio, my nose would be a foot long.*

To her credit, Cassandra's reaction showed genuine alarm. "Are you in any danger? I've noticed the cops patrol this area frequently." Not much got past a Browning woman.

Bay presented a brave face. "No, I'm fine. There's nothing to worry about." She couldn't be sure if she said that for Cass or herself. When the sisters' eyes met and locked, Bay could see Cassandra's doubts. Bay looked away.

The Pig Squeal was a former mechanic's garage that squatted on the outskirts of Prairie Ridge. The pole building was a dirty tan color with dark red trim. The overhead door was still intact in front with an overhang on the right side where a burly man with a bald head and thick tattooed arms stood guard, just as Jen had predicted.

The parking lot held several cars, including a few squads, to Bay's surprise. She assumed officers would stagger their dinner breaks and wondered who remained on duty to protect and serve. At the entrance, she encountered the bouncer.

"I'm meeting Detective Downing here at six," she stated her business warily.

Saying nothing at all, the bouncer nodded and opened the door to let her pass.

Bay could smell a hint of axle grease lingering just below the mouthwatering aroma of smoked meat. A long bar took up more than half of the space. A hodgepodge of tables and chairs were stationed along the wall on either side of the overhead door, which was plastered with posters advertising alcohol or quips about drinking.

Downing sat under a weathered tin sign with two large shot glasses and artsy lettering; "Everyone deserves another shot," it read. A full beer mug with a foamy head sat in front of him. He gave the smallest of waves toward Bay to join him.

"Hello Professor. I didn't order anything because I don't know what your drink is." Downing produced a lopsided grin and tapped a server walking by.

The young woman, probably in her twenties, wore a T-shirt imprinted with a large police badge, an opened-mouth pig as the insignia. The shirt proclaimed, "Cops and Pigs: doing business since 2011."

"Hi. I'm Mandy. I don't think I've seen you here before?" It was a query. Mandy's red-blond hair was pulled back in a tight bun, and her posture was perfect. She could have been a server at a fancy restaurant.

Downing spoke before Bay had the chance. "May I present Dr. L.L. Browning, professor of English at Flourish College." He spoke melodramatically and bowed his head in mock deference.

Mandy's eyes widened at the unexpected introduction. "We usually only have cops here, Professor. Nice to make your acquaintance. What are you drinking?" Mandy pulled a pad from her apron pocket.

Bay wondered if they served anything besides beer. She set aside her preferences. "A Corona, please."

"I'll be back with your beer and take your order." She leaned in toward Bay. "Don't be fooled by the atmosphere. The food here rocks."

Downing took a swig of beer. "I didn't figure you for a beer person. I sort of expected something lofty—wine at the very least."

Bay shifted awkwardly in her chair; she didn't appreciate being pegged. "Shouldn't we discuss the case, Detective?"

Downing relaxed a notch. "Nope. We should discuss the menu. Almost everything on it includes pork, so I hope you're not a vegan."

"Nope. I think everything's better with bacon on it." She followed his lead, letting her guard down momentarily. She looked over the menu to study Downing's face. He was a good-looking man and reminded her of the Croatian actor from Timeless, a canceled TV show almost nobody watched. Bay was a huge fan.

Downing's changeable eyes had a disarming effect on her. Tonight, they were the color of a stormy sea, and Bay could only imagine what secrets lay in the fathoms below.

"See anything you like?" Downing interrupted her assessment. "Are you like this with your students—staring at them in an intimidating way?"

Bay wasn't sure if she should be flattered or offended, but she didn't care. "It's just that you remind me of…well, has anyone told you that you look like Goran Visnjic?" Downing's blank response suggested nobody had.

"Just who is that—a Russian poet?"

Bay laughed. "No, he's an actor."

Mandy dropped off the Corona and took their order. Bay noticed uniformed officers coming in to pick up takeout, which made her feel better about the state of safety in the community. People on duty weren't hanging out or drinking, thankfully. She wondered how Mandy and the other servers passed muster to work at the exclusive officers' club.

When Bay turned her attention back to Downing, he was staring intently at her. His scrutiny was unnerving. She lightened the mood.

"Back to your face. Okay, maybe a combination of David Muir and Anderson Cooper." She paused before adding, "They're both news anchors." The detective must watch TV sometime.

Downing snorted. "The media again, great. You seem to admire that type."

"I like to keep up with the world I live in, Detective, don't you?"

"I find it's better to be cautious where the media's concerned. Lots of leeches, Professor." Downing mimed pulling leeches off his arms to Bay's amusement.

"I bet you hate lawyers, too," Bay prompted.

Downing took the bait. "Bottom feeders as the moniker suggests."

"And teachers?"

Downing stroked his chin. "In keeping with the water theme, I'd say teachers are fish."

"Fish?" Bay hadn't anticipated the label.

"They travel in schools," Downing said dryly, pleased with himself.

Bay cocked one brow, her mouth set in a straight line. "You hold the educated in disdain, Detective, yet you're one of us. Or did you learn your profession by osmosis?"

Downing grinned and clinked his beer mug to Bay's. "You're not so easy to pin down yourself, Professor. What's the L.L. stand for?"

"You show me yours; I'll show you mine. What's your first name, Detective?"

"Most people call me Downing. You?"

"Most call me Professor or Doctor. What does your mother call you?" Bay hoped she could corner the man.

"She doesn't." Downing studied Bay's face. "Yours?"

"Same," Bay said. She could be mysterious, too.

Two plates containing pulled pork tacos garnished with cilantro and lime wedges arrived with bowls of salsa and guacamole, pausing the cat-and-mouse game between Bay and Downing. Mandy returned in a flash with a basket of tortilla chips and a dish of fried plantains. "Enjoy. You're going to love this. Another beer, Downing?"

Downing passed. "Could you bring me a Coke, please?"

Mandy nodded and turned to Bay. "Professor?"

The Corona was going to Bay's head, and they hadn't even started talking business. "If you could bring a water with a slice of lime, that would be lovely."

Downing dug in immediately. "Can we eat first, or are you in a hurry?"

Bay smiled, enraptured by the scrumptious smell of her dinner. "It's important to give dinner its due. It would be rude to talk business with this tasty food in front of us." She lifted the taco in a toast and took a less-than-dainty bite. "Delicious."

They ate in silence for a while except for the lip smacks and straw sips. Mandy stopped to check on their progress a couple of times.

Bay nodded in the server's direction in reference. "Just how does someone get hired to work here? The clientele is exclusive, and I'm guessing many confidential exchanges happen here."

Downing smiled broadly, admiring Bay's quickness. "Mandy, and everyone else who works here, has a direct connection to the force. Even the cooks here are retired officers. Mandy's attending the police academy right now. She'll graduate next year."

Bay couldn't hide her surprise that the diminutive, pretty server was toughing it out at the academy. "She's seems too nice to be a police officer."

Downing winked. "You'd be surprised. Can't judge a book by its cover, right?"

Mandy cleared away the clean plates and other remains of dinner and wiped down the tabletop. Bay and Downing pulled out their notes at the same time, plunking them on the table in sync.

"Let's start with the end of the note. Arpino is a city in Italy where many Mannerist and Renaissance artists lived and worked. My friend in the Art History department thinks these numbers refer to the year a particular piece of art was created, along with its museum catalog number." Bay paused for Downing's benefit.

He'd placed a pair of reading glasses on his nose and looked over the rims at Bay. "After I told you not to talk about the case, you shared important details with a colleague?"

Bay backpedaled and crossed her fingers under the table. "I just asked her about Italian Mannerist paintings in 1603."

Downing moved on. "I see, so did you have any luck finding the art or the museum?"

Bay shook her head sadly, thinking she wasn't being very useful. "Sorry, not yet. I found many pieces from the time period depicting mythological subjects. Here's a copy of my list. One includes Medusa's head, done by an Italian painter. But, since the note refers to the sun, the moon, and the truth, I'm inclined to believe the figures of Artemis and Apollo would better fit the case."

Downing reviewed the list. "I only see one piece here that includes both Artemis and Apollo, *The Death of Niobe's Children.* But I don't see a connection to the case." He jotted something in his notes. "Virginia Lowe didn't have any children of her own, and her parents are long gone."

Bay heaved a sigh. "I'm not sure how to connect the note to a painting, but I have a gut feeling that art is the key to solving the note. Why leave a note if it's isn't a clue? Virginia Lowe was an art dealer. The word 'manner' seems connected to the Mannerist period and so is 1603 and Arpino."

"You make a good case to keep looking, Professor. I just don't know if we're there yet. Have you considered the feathers? Swan, ostrich."

Bay shook her head. "Hey, it took the better part of my day just to locate these paintings, Detective. I'm preparing for a new semester, too."

Downing raised both hands in surrender. "I wasn't judging you. Just trying to pick your brain. Any ideas from mythology?"

Bay leaned both elbows on the table, closed her eyes, and imagined her mythology instruction notes. "Let's see. The swan feather could be a reference to Leto. She was the mother of Apollo and Artemis and gave birth in secret to the twins in Delos, which is an island surrounded by swans."

Downing edged forward in his seat. "That's good, Professor. We have a connection between the feather and the twin gods. You said they represent the sun and the moon?"

Bay opened her eyes. "And truth. Apollo is the god of

truth and light. But I don't know any Greek or Roman stories associated with the ostrich. I'll do more research." She wrote notes about the swan and ostrich.

She raised questioning eyes at Downing. "Why a Medusa style of killing, though? It seems like there are easier ways to commit murder."

Downing shrugged. "That's what I'm hoping you'll tell me. We're probably dealing with a serial killer, and they don't follow rules of logic, except the rules they've made themselves."

"Was there a note with the first victim? The comic book creator?" Bay wasn't given access to the entire case file.

Downing nodded slowly. "There was, but it's been evaluated already, so…" He shifted again. "Let's drop this for tonight. I think you've got some holes to poke around in, and I have more digging to do on my end. It's time to call it a day."

He surprised Bay by helping her into her jacket followed by snatching the tab off the table. "This is a business dinner. I'll expense it."

"Thank you. Mandy was right. The food here is way better than the building suggests." She laughed. "I guess I shouldn't judge a book by its cover." She walked out to her car before Downing had a chance to accompany her. She couldn't let herself start seeing the detective as a white knight. ∎

CHAPTER 11
WAKE-UP CALL

Bay set an early alarm to allow herself time for at-home yoga before shopping with her sister. She was still seething about Cassandra's escapade from last night. Bay had arrived home before nine to a dark apartment save for a sliver of bright light shining under the guest bedroom door.

She opened the door to find Cass standing on a dining room chair, paintbrush in hand, filling in a drawing sketched on the wall.

"What in the world are you doing now, Cass?" Bay exploded. "First, the hair dye, now you're painting a mural!" Bay noticed the box of acrylic paints and brushes on the dressing table and remembered her intention to take up painting again one day. Unfortunately, teaching was a harsh master, and she hadn't found the time or inspiration.

"Can you please lower your voice? You're confusing the energy in the room." Cass glared at Bay. "I'm painting my dream." Cass turned back toward the wall and lowered her eyelids halfway.

Bay's mouth fell open. "Well, excuse me sister, but this is a rental," was all Bay could manage in reply.

"I couldn't find a sketch pad. Don't worry, I'll paint over it before you move out. Anyway, your rules didn't mention anything about painting a wall." Cass continued to face the wall in meditation.

Exasperated, Bay turned her attention to the mural. One half was empty, but the other half depicted a woman in a boat. The water appeared to be swirling, caused by two entities on either side of the woman. The entities seemed to depict two varieties of wind.

Bay gritted her teeth, fuming inside for being interested in her sister's dream. "Tell me about this."

Cass spoke in a faraway voice, almost trancelike. "Pandora is in a boat with a broken strand of pearls. She's learned much since she opened the dreaded box, you see. Now she's been given the pearls of wisdom and experience. But the winds of change are rocking the boat and knocking the pearls into the water, where they fall away and disappear. The other half is undetermined. Will a protector emerge, or will a dark force take over Pandora and steal her knowledge?"

Cass began to sway on the chair, losing her footing. Bay instinctively reached for her sister, grasping both of her arms to steady her or catch her, whichever way gravity dictated. At Bay's touch, Cass lunged forward, and her eyes flew open. She fell into a faint, dead weight against Bay's chest. Cass began moaning as images flashed inside her mind, and her body stiffened.

Childhood memories flooded Bay's being. Cass occasionally had similar episodes, always during times of crisis or family stress. She would emerge from them spouting strange, coded messages which would eventually come to pass, but nobody would take her seriously in the moment. The episodes were a source of frustration for Cassandra and a source of fear for her family.

Sitting on the bedroom floor, Bay cradled her sister in her arms until the episode eased. Beads of sweat formed on Cass's brow, and she began to resist Bay's hold on her.

Cass sat up, eyes flashing angrily at Bay. "You lied to me about where you were tonight."

Bay released her hold and began to crawl away from Cass. She stood up, straightened her shirt, and moved away from Cassandra's accusations. *How could she know?*

Cass rose from the floor like a top still spinning in slow motion around the room. She tried to steady herself by grabbing the edge of the dressing table. She thought she might be sick, so she sat down on the dining room chair, nearly knocking the paint tray off in the process.

Bay approached Cass like an injured animal, with sympathy and with caution. She handed her a tissue. "Here, just sit still a moment. I'm going to make you some tea."

Cass laughed, a throaty, doubtful chuckle. "I'm surprised you know where to find tea. You barely live here."

Bay sauntered to the kitchen and opened the cupboard above the stove where Auntie Vee had stocked a variety of remedies, basically an herbal apothecary. Bay suffered from occasional ailments, some as a result of her profession like neck and shoulder pain, some stress induced such as headaches and digestive issues.

She touched each jar in the row as she read the ingredients, finally landing on a jar labeled "Cassandra's blend." Aunt Vee refreshed the pharmacopeia at Thanksgiving, adding the mixture of cat's claw, milk thistle, lavender, and valerian into a jar and tucking it into the cupboard.

At the time, Bay raised a curious eyebrow at her aunt, who smiled warmly at Bay, patted her head lovingly, and said, "Wait and see. You may need it."

Bay brought a steaming mug of the stuff to the bedroom and set it in front of her sister. Cassandra inhaled the steam deeply, once, twice, three times. "Auntie Vee must have been here recently. She left this for me, didn't she?"

Bay scoffed and plopped down wearily on the guest bed. "The Charming women strike again. You, Auntie Vee, Mom, Grandmum—you all inherited the Charming ways. I guess I'm a Browning through and through."

Penelope and Venus, whose family name was Charming, had lived, for lack of a better term, charmed lives. Grandmum Althea and Grandpop Hugh Charming were wildly imaginative dreamers, who indulged their children and grandchildren in exploration of both the known and the fantastical world at their leisure.

Hugh was an inventor of strange and amusing devices but dabbled in any number of odd jobs to make money. Althea, the quiet matriarch in their relationship, ran a greenhouse and secret apothecary. She was as skilled as a doctor but lacked the necessary certification and license. In their small central New York community, nobody cared. People went to Althea for help with all varieties of complaints.

Cass finally relinquished a small smile toward Bay. "Oh, never underestimate the power of the Charming genes. There may be more to you underneath that lofty exterior." She thanked Bay for the tea. "And for catching me when I was falling."

Now in the predawn hour, Bay sat cross-legged on her mat, trying to meditate after replaying both chapters of the evening before. She couldn't erase her conversation with Detective Downing, the elements of the Medusa Murder case, her questions, Cassandra's dream and accusation.

Maybe she owed it to her sister to tell her the truth. Maybe she should make sure not to touch her sister again. Maybe she needed to break into the detective's office and look at the comic book creator file. Maybe.

Fingers of light were making their way through the living room drapes casting rose-colored stripes across the furniture and floor. Not one to miss out on a sunny winter day, Bay left her mat to pull open the drapes, letting in all the available light.

Her eyes scanned the horizon for the promised sunrise, looked upon the black skeletons of the bare trees in the park, and descended lower to the stone wall that separated the park from Windflower Gardens property. She gasped when she caught sight of a figure in black running away from a freshly graffitied wall.

She scrutinized the artwork, unable to blink; tears formed in her eyes from staring so hard. She ran to her bedroom to grab her jacket and cell phone. As she descended in the elevator, all Bay could think of was to examine the graffiti, take a picture of it, and decipher the message that was certainly meant for her.

The outside air bit into her face, making her cry from its iciness. She ran across the courtyard to face the wall. She clicked a widescreen shot, then individual close shots that broke the artwork into sections.

Spray paint cans had been left behind. The artist was probably wearing gloves, and the paint could be easily purchased anywhere. Among the colorful waves and splats, a large hand mirror stood front and center on the right half of the design. An Egyptian eye occupied the center of the mirror, indicating watchfulness, or so Bay supposed. Her Egyptian mythology was rusty.

On the left side of the work, the head of Anubis, the Egyptian god of the dead, had been painted on a backdrop of feathers with a set of scales beside him. The jackal-headed god had green eyes narrowed in a hard stare, and a scarab of blood red was the centerpiece of his headdress.

An arc of black letters formed the word "vengeance" as a bridge between the two halves. Carried along by the colorful waves of the graffiti, Bay's eyes began to swim. They landed on one upper corner where a large letter A was emblazoned in dark red. The revelation made her eyes travel to the lower corner where the letter I lay on its side, a jagged black knife. In the opposite lower corner, a chunky R squatted, its elongated foot stretched out to trip an innocent bystander. The top left corner revealed a decorative S sporting a snake's head.

Bay looked again and again, trying to see more letters, even scanning the graffiti in a line-by-line fashion, like reading a paper. She couldn't see any other letters, no matter how hard she tried to will them to appear.

A loud screech from a hunting hawk jolted her out of her trance. Someone's dog was barking down the street. She could hear a car engine thrum to life. The neighborhood was waking up, and she didn't know how long she'd been studying the wall.

Too frozen to function properly, Bay gave up trying to place a call to Detective Downing. She blew on her fingers but was barely able to bend them back to straightness. She dashed across the courtyard to the welcome warmth of her building.

Once in the elevator, she pressed her floor, then swiped through her contacts until she found Downing's number. He picked up on the first ring.

"Downing."

"I'm sorry for the early call, but someone painted a message on the wall outside my apartment building. I think it's a clue." Bay shuddered. "Or maybe a warning. I don't know."

Downing swore a blue streak. "I'm sending a squad now and I'll be on my way shortly. Are you home, Professor?"

Bay shivered. "I'm home, yes." The elevator dinged loudly, and she could see her door.

"What are you doing in the elevator?" Nothing got past Downing. "Aw come on. You went outside to look at it, didn't you? Stay in your apartment and lock your door. I'll be there soon."

It would be bad enough to face the reprimand of Downing, but Cass stood in the living room and offered Bay a frosty stare when she walked through the door. Pointing out the window where she must have seen Bay, Cass sputtered, "You're going to tell me the truth, or so help me gods…"

Bay felt defeated. It wouldn't be fair for safety's sake not to tell Cass about the case. Once Downing arrived, Cass would find out anyway, and Bay would have to live with her wrath.

"Would you like it standing up or sitting down?"

Cass stayed rooted to the spot while Bay added details about the Medusa murder she'd conveniently omitted the day before. Minutes later, both women saw a squad car pull up in the courtyard followed by an undercover car, announcing Downing's arrival.

"You're going to hear more once Detective Downing gets here. He's going to come up to question me." Bay suggested Cass might want to trade clothes for the long shirt she wore to bed.

On her way to change, Cass tossed last night's accusation at Bay. "I knew you were lying to me, and we're not done here."

A sharp rap on the door was quickly followed by a shout. "It's Downing, Professor."

Bay opened the door and ushered Downing into the dining room. "I'm having coffee, would you like a cup?"

"Dammit, this isn't a social call, Doctor, Professor. What the H is your name, anyway?" Downing was rattled, surprising Bay.

She went to the kitchen and pressed the coffee machine into action. "Do you take cream, sugar?"

When Downing shook his head, she set the cup in front of him. "I'm thinking you could use this," Bay said. "I know I could."

Downing opened his notebook to a fresh page. "What time did you see the graffiti?"

"It was right around sunrise, so seven-fifteen, maybe. I was up early doing yoga and when I saw the light coming through the drapes, I opened them up to get a better look."

Downing's quizzical expression, half smile, and pen tapping made Bay stop talking. "Go on. You were about to tell me why you opened the drapes." His smile widened.

Bay's withering expression wasn't lost on him. "I have a nice view of the park across the street. I like looking at nature, Mr. Downing."

When he didn't comment, Bay continued. "I noticed a dark-hooded figure running away from the wall."

Downing sat up straighter. "You saw the tagger? Are you sure?"

Bay was sure. "I saw them toss away one of the spray paints, so I must have caught the tail end of their activity. Before you ask, I didn't see their face. I'm not sure if the person was male or female. From up here, they looked thin and short. I don't have a good perspective from ten floors up."

Downing picked up the sequence. "So, you went outside for a closer look?"

Bay didn't see any reason to lie. "I did. I wanted to study the wall, take pictures, look for a message."

Downing swigged his coffee. "Enlighten me, Professor."

Bay faltered. "I need time to think about it. The word 'vengeance' is obvious, but the letters in each corner don't appear to spell anything specific. I'm certain that graffiti out there is meant for me, and I'm going to get to the bottom of it."

Downing dropped the pen and took Bay's hands in his. "Look at me, Professor. I appreciate your help, but you need to be careful. I don't like this, not even a little."

Bay dropped Downing's hands when Cass walked into the room.

"Detective Downing, this is my sister Cassandra. I believe you met her the other night when I wasn't home."

Downing's inscrutable expression met Cass's fiery glare. "Cassandra. Well, at least one of you has a name."

Cassandra lurched toward Downing and stood above him, the posture of a hunting lioness. "I assume your department is going to provide protection for my sister here and at work."

Downing sighed, blinked, sighed again. He didn't move an

inch, refusing to give Cass an advantage. "We're a small police force, Ms. Browning. I don't know that we have a security detail to offer the professor. But there will be a patrol squad posted out front 24-7."

Cass huffed. "That's not good enough, I'm afraid. If you can't do better, we will just have to deal with this our own way." She cocked both brows meaningfully.

Downing laughed derisively. "Just what does that mean?"

Bay shut down the chess match. "Never mind. I'm sure the police will do everything they can, Cassandra. Meanwhile, Detective, I assume you will keep me informed." Bay's wide-eyed glance and nod at Cass told Downing there was something amiss between the sisters.

Downing rose. "Thanks for the coffee. We'll be in touch soon." ∎

CHAPTER 12

SNAKE EYES

Winter retail hours dictated that breakfast precede shopping. At Cassandra's insistence, Barrett was invited to meet the daughters at Sunrise Café, a favorite dining spot of Bay's and Barrett's.

"Explain to me again why it's a good idea to involve our father in this investigation?" Bay asked.

"Credit card, please," Cass said sweetly, as she knocked on the car window. They had stopped for gas on the way, and Bay instructed Cass to do the pumping, saying it was the least she could do in exchange for room and board.

Eyebrows narrowed, Bay retorted, "Don't you have any gate money left?"

When Cass glowered at her sister, Bay tallied a point on the imaginary scoreboard she was keeping.

"If I spend it to fill your gas tank, I won't have money to buy clothes." Cass proclaimed, wearing an expression of victory. Cass's victory was erroneous, however. Bay only suggested she buy gas to determine if Cass had any money. Bay didn't intend to be a bottomless purse.

Bay handed Cass a bank card through the window. "Oh, all right then. I'll buy gas and breakfast. You can buy your own clothes." Her tone was huffy as if paying for gas and breakfast was a consolation prize.

When the sisters stepped into the cheery diner, Barrett was already sitting at a quiet corner booth away from foot traffic and other diners.

The server brought a pot of coffee and two more cups for Bay and Cass. They ordered quickly, and Bay began relaying the information about the murder and the wall art.

Barrett rubbed his knuckles and stared at his wedding ring, looking decidedly worn and older. "Your mother could have known Virginia Lowe, I suppose. They're about the same age, but the name means nothing to me."

Cass, who sat next to him, took his hand in hers comfortingly. "It's okay, Dad. We're actually hoping you can help with the graffiti art, since you did anthropology work in Egypt."

Barrett squeezed Cass's hand and ran the other hand through his soot and ashes hair, which he kept long over the collar where it landed in soft curls.

"It's been a very long time since I worked in Egypt. You two were so young." He looked lovingly at Cass, remembering. "You must have been around ten. I can still see you with your long braids running around the dig site, chasing your sister."

He patted Bay's hand across the table. "Remember that bucket hat you always wore? You said you were an archaeologist, too."

Bay giggled. Her childhood memories had many gaps and

blurs, but she recalled happy images of keeping company with Gasira and Amon, two archaeologists in Egypt who took Bay under their wings. Gasira had made the bucket hat for Bay from one of her nylon and mesh vests. Bay could recall sleeping with the treasured hat like a teddy bear.

Bay slid her cell phone across the table to show Barrett the photo of Anubis, the jackal-headed god. "This is a close-up of one piece of the graffiti. I wasn't sure if you'd seen it this morning." Barrett's apartment faced the other side of the street.

Barrett grinned. "Not a bad depiction of Anubis, Egyptian god of the dead. In fact, I'd dare say the artist knew something about the subject." He picked up the phone to study the photo more closely.

"How so?" Bay asked, ready to write down anything of interest.

"Let's see. In ancient Egypt, Anubis was viewed as the god who restored order in the cosmos. He judged the dead before guiding their souls to the afterlife. The artist included the scales and feathers, Anubis's tools of the trade. Each soul was represented by an ostrich feather, you see. Anubis placed the feather on the scale to determine the worth of the individual in life."

Bay gasped upon hearing the reference to the ostrich feather. Another connection was made to the case. Is it possible the killer didn't find Virginia's life worthwhile? She scribbled down everything her father had just said.

Bay took the phone and scrolled to the photo of the eye and mirror. "This is the eye of Horus, right? It represents protection from evil?" Bay recalled a tidbit from her studies.

Barrett took the phone and immediately shook his head

no. "It's a common mistake, LuLu. This is the eye of Ra, not Horus. This is a right eye. The eye of Horus is the left eye. Ra is associated with the sun, while Horus is associated with the moon. The protective power of Ra comes from fear and violence." Barrett shuddered and handed back the phone.

Bay gazed at the eye, noticing that the curled extension from the eyelid formed the head of a snake. She dropped her voice to just above a whisper. "Dad, is it possible the killer combined Greek and Egyptian snake symbols? You know, Medusa with her head of snakes."

Before he could answer, Cass nabbed Bay's phone and pulled up the photo of the letters painted in each corner of the graffiti. "Look at the letter 'S'. It has a snake head, too." She shoved the photo under her dad's nose.

"Ureaus." Barrett swept his eyes from Cass, who blinked unknowingly and Bay, who nodded, concentrating.

"Well, who is Ureaus?" Cass impatiently stamped her foot under the table.

"Ureaus is not a who but a symbol of the serpent, most commonly thought of as the cobra. It's part of the pharaoh's crown because it later came to represent royalty." He raised his index finger dramatically to make a point.

"However, before the pharaohs took to wearing it, the ureaus was a symbol for Wadjet, the Egyptian cobra goddess whose magical powers included poison and fire against her enemies. And if you want to go further down the rabbit hole, the ancient Greeks viewed the power of snakes as a dichotomy: the power to heal and the power to kill. Of course, immortality cannot be ruled out either."

Barrett was on a roll, and Bay waved a hand in front of

him to stop. "Information overload. I'm afraid this case is too complicated for me to solve. They need an expert."

Cass jumped to her sister's defense. "LuLu, you are an expert. An expert puzzle master, at least. Besides, the three of us together can solve this case in a hot second."

Bay snorted. "What do you mean by the three of us? No way am I involving you two any more than necessary." Bay stabbed two fingers across the table at her father and sister.

Before Barrett and Cass could protest, Bay checked her watch and announced the end of breakfast. "Sorry, Dad. We have to get going. Cass needs to find new clothes, and I need to get to the office."

Bay snatched the bill off the table and strode to the cashier's station. "Breakfast was delicious as usual," Bay purred for the cashier's benefit before she even had the chance to ask.

The shopping trip was successful, and the sisters enjoyed spending time together. The excursion reminded Bay of their preteen years when the two would romp around the mall, trying on outlandish or fancy outfits for kicks. Cass used most of her gate money to buy two pairs of pants and two tops. Bay sprung for what she deemed a "dressy outfit" just in case the occasion called for it and two new pairs of shoes for her sister. Cass would be given at least one work uniform tonight as part of her orientation, so the new clothes were for her off-duty life.

Bay called Downing after dropping off Cass and her shopping bags at home.

"Downing. What's up Professor? Everything okay?" Downing's voice had taken on an edge ever since the graffiti incident.

Bay tried to sound nonchalant. "Of course, everything's okay.

I'm on my way to the office, but I have some information that might be helpful. I just texted it to you. It's a copy of the notes I took after speaking with my father."

"Your father?" Downing spit coffee down his shirt and swore. "Look, L.L., just how many family members do you intend to involve in this? I can't protect all of you."

Bay cut him off. "My father is an anthropologist. He studied ancient cultures, including those of the Egyptian and Greek variety." Her tone was sarcastic and boastful at the same time.

Downing was caught off guard and it perturbed him. "For God's sake, I hope you're not texting and driving," he managed a counterstrike.

Bay giggled. "Not me, Detective. Let me know what you think or if you have questions," the teacher's voice kicked in. She disconnected before the detective did.

The fifth-floor elevator door opened just as Professor McNelly walked past, intimately conversing with the new gofer, Diana. Bay snarled in their direction.

Instinctively, McNelly turned toward Bay. "Well, well, well. Good afternoon, L.L. You must have had an exceedingly busy morning." McNelly's weaselly smile made Bay's stomach flip. He drew nearer, and she could smell man-stink covered by a menthol-based cologne.

McNelly leaned in, speaking quietly enough that Diana couldn't hear. "Stasia's been looking for you. I hope you're not in trouble."

Bay stiffened and moved away, but not before Diana could offer a cheery greeting. Responding with a perfunctory wave, Bay continued down the hallway to Jen Yoo's office.

"Bay, it's about time you got here. All hell's breaking." Jen noticed Bay's grim expression. "What's going on?"

Bay shut the door. "So much. I don't know where to begin. Wait. Am I in trouble? I heard Stasia's been looking for me."

"I don't know about that, but you missed the police takeover. There were cops crawling around the place this morning like grasshoppers."

Bay blinked. "You mean ants. The cops? They were crawling around like ants."

Jen's eyes narrowed in consideration. "No, grasshoppers." She leaned forward, lowering her voice. "One guy asked me questions about you. How do I know you and what do I know about you."

Bay sucked in air suddenly." "You didn't tell him that you knew about the case? That I told you about the note left in the lululemon. Did you?" She began to imagine being locked up in a jail cell, just like her sister.

Jen patted her on the head reassuringly. "Of course not. Do you think I'm crazy? I only told them about us working together and all."

Bay wondered what 'and all' meant but didn't pursue it. She rethought her original idea of sharing the graffiti incident with Jen, instead giving a benign explanation for coming in late. "I went to breakfast with my dad and took my sister clothes shopping this morning."

"Your ex-con sister?" Jen punctuated the term. It must be a novelty for her to know someone related to an ex-con.

"Yes, Cassandra's the only sister I have. She's starting a new job tonight, so that's good. But she needed some clothes and shoes."

Jen seemed to share Bay's positive attitude about Cassandra being gainfully employed. "You're lucky to have a sister. I have two brothers, so my parents always focus all their criticism on me. The way I dress, why I'm not married, why I eat too little, why I eat too much. You get me?"

Bay was lucky her father never criticized either of his daughters. She wondered what life would be like if her mother were still alive though. "We'll talk later, Jen. I better get my butt in my office."

Bay managed to take three steps before crossing paths with Stasia. Stasia's arms were folded, and a disapproving frown graced her face. She looked more troll-like than ever, especially in her chosen garb of the day. A clingy olive-green cable knit sweater over a dark green corduroy skirt cut Stasia in half, giving the short woman the appearance of a hummock in a bog.

"I'm glad you're finally here, L.L. Let's go to my office, shall we?" Stasia gestured for Bay to go in front of her, lest she escape down the stairs.

Stasia's office was an explosion of Greek tchotchkes against a backdrop of a large woven cloth in blue with white Hellenic symbols hanging behind her desk. Bay sat down as indicated, curious about the opened file folder front and center. Stasia followed Bay's gaze and closed the folder with a sharp snap.

She looked over gold wire frames and smiled a toothy grin. Whether or not she was admiring Bay or about to devour her was uncertain. Stasia took a deep breath, then gulped something from a Trojan horse mug.

"Now, L.L. I want you to know that you're doing a great job here. Your students have nothing but praise for you." Stasia's voice deepened and her hands met, fingers drumming against each other, calculating.

"The police were here this morning; I suppose you know

about that."

Bay wore her best quizzical expression. "Well, I…"

Stasia interrupted. "They asked me questions about our security here. They wanted your work schedule, which I gave them. They asked if you have any enemies, which I said no, I don't think so. I told them your classes have become popular, and that you get along with everyone here." She leaned forward, her beaky nose almost touching Bay's. "That's right, isn't it? You get along with everyone in our department."

Bay thought Stasia would make a fine hypnotist or influencer. She suddenly felt like one of Pavlov's dogs. Was Stasia indirectly referring to McNelly, the one person in the department Bay disliked?

Stasia swiveled around in her chair and picked up a bronze statue of Athena from her shelf. Facing Bay, she set the figure in front of her. "I've always liked Athena the best of all the Greek gods. She is so wise," Stasia's accent had become curiously more pronounced.

"I want you to have this for your office, L.L. It's perfect for you, teacher of mythology." The toothy grin returned.

Bay examined the trinket. Poor Athena. The goddess was dressed as a warrior, but someone had given her Madonna-like breasts and the flowing long hair of a fashion model. The owl perched on her wrist had its wings spread, ready to fly away, and no wonder, Bay thought. She reached out and lifted the statue from the desk. It was light, made of resin but painted to appear like metal. Bay was speechless.

"I just want you to know that my brother Giorgio and my niece are in no way involved in this murder. Giorgio—he didn't even know that Aria switched coats. And Aria, she's just a child.

I hope you don't think either of them would associate with a murderer." Stasia spit into the air, gesticulating. "Apapa!"

Comprehension began to dawn on Bay. Stasia thought her family might be in trouble with the police, something that would never do in her world. Bay let out a long breath of air she didn't realize she'd been holding.

"Stasia, of course I don't think your family is involved in the murder." Bay reassured her. "I'm sure the police don't want to leave any stone unturned. I was worried you might think I'm a liability to the college."

Stasia stood up and placed her hand aside her face in contemplation. "Hmm, well, I know you'll do everything in your power to make sure that doesn't happen. We don't want people to be afraid to come here. But, of course, we want you to be safe, too. Do you really think you're next on the killer's list?"

A rock sunk in Bay's stomach, and she regretted suggesting she might be a liability. "No, I don't think I'm on the killer's list, if there even is a list. Don't worry, Stasia." Bay set the statue back on the desk. She didn't need a bribe or whatever Stasia thought she was offering in exchange for her family's good reputation.

Stasia snatched the Athena and returned it to the shelf behind her. "Very good, then. I think we understand each other." The gruesome troll expression settled back on her face.

Bay didn't appreciate Stasia's intimidation tactic, especially since it was unwarranted. "I do hope the media doesn't bring Giorgio and Aria into the public eye. That wouldn't be good." Bay left without a backward glance. ∎

CHAPTER 13
DISCOVERIES

At the end of the day, Jen Yoo waited for Bay by the elevator. "How about the Tipsy Cow for a drink? We can catch up. I have something to share with you."

Bay checked the time; she wanted to chat with Cassandra before her eight p.m. shift. "I can't stay long. How about we go somewhere less hip, like The Crow?"

Jen shrugged. "Okay. Meet you there."

The Crow had been in business for decades, and it looked like it, too. Located in the original part of town, there was only street parking for patrons. The interior was dark; ripped black barstools with marred chrome lined up at the drink-stained Formica-topped bar or circled around the high-top tables. When Bay pulled out one of the stools to perch on, it stuck stubbornly to the worn vinyl floor.

"Why in the world did you want to come here, anyway? This isn't exactly a social escape," Jen complained, trying to decide where to safely place her designer bag. She settled for the stool beside her, situating the bag to keep it from tipping over.

Bay laughed. "Now I know another reason I don't own a fussy purse." She pointed to the Coach bag. "I wanted to come here because it's quiet and we can talk safely. You said you had something to share?"

A scruffy bartender around fifty or so shouted over the bar. "If you want somethin', you can order it up here. We ain't got a waitress today."

Jen blinked and inhaled sharply. "I don't suppose I can get a Cosmo." Bay's glare and pursed lips confirmed Jen's suspicions.

"Right. I'll have whatever red wine they carry."

Bay laughed and held up one hand. "Just stop. Rail drinks. You don't want wine from a place like this. It will only lead to disappointment. I'm having an old-fashioned."

Jen wrinkled her nose. "Do you think they can manage vodka and tonic?"

Bay ordered from Scruffy, handed him a twenty and told him to keep the rest. He smiled, minus a full set of teeth.

"Comin' right up," he said.

"Here, just for that, you can have some bar nuts, too." He handed Bay the drinks and a dish of opened nuts sprinkled with spices.

Jen raised her brows at the peanuts, but declared her drink was passable. "I did more research on the possible artwork from Arpino. You know, from the murder note." Her voice dropped to a mysterious whisper on the last words.

"And?" Bay hoped Jen's expertise resulted in a new connection.

"The bulk of mannerist paintings have religious subject matter, so there were fewer pieces for me to study with mythical subjects." She dug her cell from the Coach bag and pulled open a downloaded image entitled *Diana and Actaeon* by Giuseppe Cesari, 1603. The painting showed the goddess Artemis or Diana, the Roman counterpart, bathing nude with her entourage. The hunter, Actaeon, is shown as he arrives on the scene with his dogs and discovers the goddess bathing in all her glory.

While Bay studied the details, Jen presented her findings. "Cesari was from Arpino and the date matches the number in the note. Diana is the moon goddess, and the moon is mentioned in the note, too. And, didn't you say the victim was found with a hunting bugle in her lap?"

Bay's thoughts did a rewind. She remembered seeing the bugle in the police file, but had she mentioned it to Jen? She couldn't recall and chastised herself for not keeping better track of the information she shared.

"I guess this is a possibility. As you said, the date and location match the note. I just wish there was a piece of artwork that included the sun, moon, and truth in it." Bay's frustration was wearing on her.

Jen reached across the table to grab her friend by the wrist. "This case scares me, Bay. It seems like the murder note may have a clue to the first murder and more murders to come. Maybe the other pieces are supposed to help the police find the killer before they kill again."

Bay shivered, but wondered if what Jen said was true. "You may be right. I've heard true crime stories where serial killers want to be caught. Part of them knows what they're doing is wrong." Her insides froze at the prospect of being the next victim.

Bay gulped the rest of her cocktail, which slithered down her throat in a fiery rivulet. She steeled her nerves, determined to figure out the note and the graffiti. "Thanks for taking the time to research this. I'll pass it along to the detective."

She jumped topics. "Are you ready to start your new classes? Only a few more days." Bay herself was far from ready.

Cassandra was cooking up something delightful in the kitchen when Bay dropped her usual burden of tote bags. "You didn't have to go to the trouble of making dinner when you have to work tonight," Bay said, grudgingly.

Cass smiled slightly. "I'm always going to be working nights, and we both have to eat, so…"

Bay walked into the kitchen. "Can I help with anything?"

"It's a pretty simple meal. We're having a spinach quiche with a winter fruit salad. If you want, you can bring out plates and silverware."

"Is Dad joining us?" Bay looked over her shoulder as she pulled dishes from the cupboard.

"Not tonight. He's playing euchre or something like that somewhere. He said it's his Wednesday night ritual. Didn't you know that?" Cass pulled the quiche from the oven.

Embarrassment and guilt reared inside of Bay. Of course, she should know her dad's routine. "I remember him mentioning playing cards, but I guess I didn't know it was a weekly thing," she stammered. She set the plates on the counter next to the flatware.

Cass didn't look at her sister while she sliced bananas on top of individual bowls containing apples, pears, orange sections, and grapes drizzled with honey. "Dinner's ready. Help yourself."

Without their father, the two women didn't sit at the dining table, choosing to eat standing at the kitchen counter, alternating between quiche and fruit.

"Can I pick your brain, Cassandra?" Bay hoped to get her sister's take on a few details of the case.

Cass eyed her warily. "Is this about the murder case, because I thought you didn't want me involved in that." She wasn't about to make it easy for Bay.

"Since Virginia Lowe is a dead end for now, I wondered if you heard of the comic book creator who draws the *Vengeful Venuses* series." Usually not one to stereotype people, Bay had heard the comics were popular prison fare.

Cass shrugged. "Lots of comic books float around prison, Professor. I don't want my parole officer to see a search like that, so if you want me to take a look, could you pull it up online?"

Bay had to hand it to Cass. Being difficult was her specialty, but Bay couldn't argue with her this time. If Kelly Weber was monitoring Cass closely, a search for "Vengeful Venuses" would raise suspicion. When the search hit on the series, along with some steamy porn sites, Bay selected the comic book result and tapped on the images button. Covers popped up revealing voluptuous women clad in next to nothing, most of them wielding some form of weapon or tool. Many of the weapons were phallic designs.

She handed the phone across the kitchen island to Cass. "Here you go. Have an eyeful." Bay made a distasteful face.

Cass snorted in recognition. "Oh yeah, I've seen these babes circulating around the cell block. Some inmates trade for them, so I've heard the wheeling and dealing going on during chow time or in the yard."

Bay adopted a haughty tone. She still couldn't accept the

seamy side of life Cass had chosen. "I'm interested in knowing more about the creator. I only saw a glimpse of the case file, and I've come up empty searching for their name. I'm wondering how this case connects to Virginia Lowe's, and and…"

Cass dismissed her sister's disapproving airs in view of what Cass determined was fear for herself. "You think if we can figure out the connection between comic book writer and Virginia, we can find a trail that leads to you."

Bay swallowed a hard lump in her throat. "That is the general idea, yes."

Cass began discriminately picking grapes from her fruit salad, popping them inside her mouth as if they were stress bubbles. "This series is hard core, Professor. The creator is extremely private, writes under a pseudonym, and has never been interviewed or done live appearances. Where I was living, the comics were known as VV, sometimes just by making the letter V with two fingers. The series is contraband, dark, mostly created for the S&M crowd or worse." Cass shuddered as faces of certain inmates rose in her mind; the women haters.

Bay noticed genuine fear mixed with disgust on her sister's face. "What is it?" she asked softly.

"Women who hate women are worse than men who hate women. You never know for sure who they are and how they might get to you." Cass shook off the memory and returned to discussing the case.

"One common denominator is mythology, or maybe it's art, or both. Comic books, paintings, graffiti are all types of art. And we also know the comic series includes mythical characters, and many paintings do, too." Cass continued in thought.

"And the Anubis and eye of Ra on the wall graffiti are

mythical." Bay was pacing the length of the countertop. Minerva, who hadn't been seen for a day or so, paced right beside her. "I guess my mythology course could be a link. So maybe the killer is a disgruntled student."

Cass scooped up the black cat to save her from being kicked or crushed by Bay's sudden turns around the kitchen. Minerva protested though, leaped away from Cass, and sauntered off to another room.

"Can you look back through your student rosters and grades? Maybe a failing student, someone who stands out because they're starving for attention? Someone who may have had a crush on you?"

Bay heaved a long sigh. "Someone who's watching me and knows where I live?" Bay's voice rose in emotion. "Knows where Dad lives."

Cass picked up an apple slice with her fingers, taking small, thoughtful bites. "I wonder why the killer didn't succeed with the comic book writer. Medusa only took away the comic creator's hands but left the creator drugged and alive."

Bay finished the last bites of fruit, staring off in space. "Medusa took away the comic creator's life by destroying their hands and robbing them of their mental health. Sometimes torture is more effective than murder."

"Yikes, you have a sinister mind sometimes. But I suppose you're right. It doesn't explain Virginia Lowe's murder, though. Unless Virginia is connected to one of your students."

Bay paused, searching her memory about the case file. "Downing said that Virginia had no children, but I guess she could be connected to one of my students another way. Her murder was personal, I'm certain of it. She suffocated in plaster, holding a mirror so she could look at herself. The hunting bugle, the lululemon coat switch, and the note all point to careful planning."

Cass set her dishes in the sink. "I'm going to get ready for work and hit the bus stop. You should try to get some sleep, sister. You look wrung out."

"Bus stop? You know I can drive you to Outfitters." Bay wasn't sure public transportation at night was the safest idea right now.

Cass shook her head. "I'm very capable of fending for myself, as you well know, Professor. It's early enough to take a bus, and it will be almost daylight on the way home from work. You should make friends with Minerva tonight. She loves your reading chair."

Bay did indeed begin the night by reviewing William Faulkner's *Absalom, Absalom!*, but she cast it aside after an hour, deeming the family tragedy was too much for her current state of mind. Instead, Bay took her laptop out of one of her tote bags and set it on the dining table to resume case research.

Minerva delighted in her change of fortune and made herself at home in the warm spot on the reading chair.

With the benefit of a larger screen, Bay studied the details of the Cesari painting of *Diana and Actaeon*, the unfortunate hunter who saw the bathing goddess. She'd forgotten to call the detective, so she clicked on his name in her phone's contact list.

A tired voice acknowledged the caller. "What you got for me?" Economy of words seemed to be Downing's specialty.

"Well, good evening to you, too," Bay sniped. "I'm going to muddy the waters, maybe. I have a new painting that could be the reference point in the note. I texted you a link to it before I called. The work is a mannerist piece from 1603 by Cesari, an artist from Arpino."

Muffled movement came through the line while Downing pulled the link up on his computer. "Tell me what I'm looking at."

Bay presented the highlights. "Actaeon, the hunter, saw the moon goddess in all her naked glory while she bathed with her friends. He was punished for peeping—torn to pieces by his hunting dogs. You can see his hunting bugle hanging by his side."

"That's it? A hunting bugle and a naked moon goddess with a grudge; not much to go on."

Downing's skepticism brought Bay's mood to a new low.

"No, I agree. I wish I had something more specific to offer you. The Medusa is playing with you, with us, really. What did you think of the notes from my dad about Anubis and the eye of Ra?" Bay tried to sound hopeful.

The tired voice resumed. "It's kind of a mythology stew at this point. No neon sign pointing in one direction."

Bay agreed with Downing. "I bet your crime board looks like a labyrinth." She paused but all went quiet on the other end. She wondered if Downing had fallen asleep.

"Hello—you still there?"

Downing emitted a loud yawn. "Yes, sorry. Labyrinth—ha ha. Seriously though, I want to remind you to keep any information to yourself, even if it doesn't amount to anything. We need discretion here." He paused, adding louder than necessary, "The more people involved, the bigger the risk. Got it?"

"I understand. Believe me, I don't want anyone in my family to get hurt, but more importantly, we need to get this psycho off the street." Bay's insistence carried tremors of fear. "I want to help any way I can. Tomorrow I'm going to review the student rosters from the past two mythology courses I taught."

"Smart idea, Professor. The department already has those rosters, by the way. We're looking for students with any prior history or connection to the victims. But you probably already knew that."

Bay stiffened. "Yes and no. My associate dean told me the police came by to interview people in my department and that she'd given them my course schedule. She didn't say anything about the rosters, though. Isn't that confidential information?" Her delivery was pricklier than intended.

"Oh, you're something else, Ms. High and Mighty. The police handle confidential information all the time. It's literally part of the job. What's beyond protocol is sharing confidential information with outsiders. Good night, Ms. Browning."

Downing disconnected, leaving Bay to feel foolish and lonely. She padded to her room, changed into her favorite comfy pajamas and fleece scuffs, and walked into the kitchen to make one of Auntie Vee's remedies for a stress headache. The steeping concoction of lavender, bergamot, and lemon balm aroused Minerva, who strutted into the room and sat on Bay's feet.

Bay bent to stroke the cat, who produced a purring motor as a reward. *"I guess you plan to win me over no matter how much I resist."* After several more minutes of petting and purring, Bay brought the mug of tea to the dining room and awakened the computer.

The letters on the outside wall by the courtyard kept arranging and rearranging themselves. AIRS. A reference to someone lofty, too superior for their own good? Is that a reference to Virginia, the fine arts dealer? RISA, SIRA, SARI,

ARIS. One by one, she searched the words for mythical or art references.

"Aris could be another spelling for Ares, god of war." She continued reading aloud, then laughed hysterically. "Aris means the fleshy part of the butt." After multiple searches, giddiness was overtaking her.

The more inquiries she made, the more she discovered mythical or mystical associations with every arrangement of the letters. Removing one slipper, she began stroking the sleeping Minerva with her foot. "Maybe that's supposed to be the message. Everything's connected. There isn't one specific clue." She yawned doubtfully and rubbed her sleepy eyes. She checked the time, just past midnight.

Bay closed all the tabs to run a scheduled update on her laptop, cleared away her mug and tea caddy, and plodded wearily to her bathroom to brush her teeth. When she slid under the covers, she felt a forlorn twinge inside at the emptiness of her apartment. Dismissing the feeling as silly, she turned to face away from the door leading to the guest bedroom and curled her arm under her pillow. When Minerva leapt on the bed to nest at Bay's feet, she didn't protest. ∎

CHAPTER 14
DAYLIGHT REVELATION

Minerva kneaded at Bay's pillow and rubbed her head against the top of Bay's head. The physical contact abruptly awakened Bay, and she pushed away the cat, who would not be deterred. Bay logged the time as six a.m. The notion she hadn't heard Cass come home startled her. How easy would it be for an intruder to enter her apartment and hurt her?

Before scuttling to the bathroom, Bay, phone in hand, crept out of her room and paused at Cassandra's doorway. The bedroom was empty. Fear and worry held hands and flooded Bay's insides. Was it too early to call the police to check on Cass? What time did her shift end? Bay admitted, selfishly, she didn't know the answer. Her skin prickled; a loud thump knocked inside her ears. She didn't know how long she had stood immobilized looking at the empty bedroom, but the sound of the front door opening brought her around.

"Cass, is that you?" Bay's squeak barely left her personal airspace. She could hear someone setting things down on the sofa table and the exhalation of a leather couch cushion being squished.

Bay rounded the hallway, just poking her head around the corner. "Cass?" She spoke normally this time.

"Did I wake you up? Sorry about that." Cass stifled a yawn, but Bay observed that her sister looked radiant.

Bay sat on the floor below the couch. "How was the first day?"

Cass smiled mysteriously. "Surprisingly good. I didn't realize working at a real job would feel this rewarding. It's nice to have somewhere to go where I'm expected, you know?"

Bay nodded, resisted the urge to pat her sister's knee, and rose instead. "You didn't wake me up, by the way. But I'm going to take advantage of the early hour and get caught up on my work. I expect you're going to sleep soon?"

Cass stretched, Minerva-like. "I think I need to unwind a little, but then I'm going to try. It'll be a hard adjustment to change sleep routines for a while." Cass grabbed the remote control off the side table. "May as well watch some mindless TV. That should help. Did anything interesting happen last night? Any visits from Detective Snarly?" She watched carefully for Bay's reaction to the topic of conversation.

A snappy chuckle danced across the room. "Ha, that's a good one. No visits but we talked on the phone. Let's just say it didn't end well. I stuck my foot in my mouth and managed to piss him off." Bay's voice held regret.

Cass's head snapped to attention. "Wait a minute, you actually like him, don't you?"

"No, not the way you think. I respect him. He's quite good at his job, Cassandra."

Cass was in too good a mood to argue about the pitfalls of consorting with the police, so she shrugged instead, and made a shooing motion at Bay. "Go about your business. Seize the day and all that. I need something mindless."

With her sister commandeering the television, Bay skipped morning yoga, showered, dressed, and scooted out the door and down to the parking garage.

As usual, she didn't wait for the heater in the Subaru to blow warm air, and the interior wouldn't warm up to bearable until she arrived at the college. She pulled out and around to the courtyard side of the parking lot, facing Elfenham Park, to take another look at the graffiti art.

Bay could hear her mother's advice: "perspective is everything whether viewing art, reading a book, or having a heated conversation." The memory made her insides ache a little, but she smiled at the sky as a small thanks to the universe in reply. She left the car running and stood front and center staring at the wall. Closing her eyes to refocus her energy, she opened them again to drink in the artwork in its entirety.

Boom, a light sparked to life in her head. "Why didn't I see it before?" she said out loud. The corner letters, Bay decided, should be read from left to right at the top, then again at the bottom. The letters formed "SARI", and Bay concluded they were meant as a reference to the painting by Cesari, the Mannerist artist from Arpino. Satisfied she was on the right track, she climbed back into her car, which was now blessedly warmer from having idled awhile.

The fifth-floor offices at Flourish College were dark and empty when Bay arrived; nobody was in the reception area either. Bay's first stop was the break room to make coffee.

Although she spoiled herself at home, indulging in single serve fussy espresso from her machine, she knew how to use the office coffee pot.

Once the coffee maker hummed to life, she stopped at the mailbox, stuffed its contents into her tote bag, and proceeded down the hall to her office. She deposited her scarf and coat in the closet, patted her hair to smooth away the static, and set the pile of mail on her desk. She sighed, seeing the stack of mail she hadn't yet opened from earlier in the week.

"I'm not tackling you on an empty stomach though," she scolded the mail stack and rifled through her selection of eats in the cupboard behind her desk. "Thank goodness for breakfast bars," she sang, waving the package at the mail pile. She opened the bar and took a couple of bites, then looked at her fitness watch and decided to check the coffee's progress.

A light was on in an office across the hall from the reception area. "Excrement, it looks like McNelly is here." Bay forced herself to tiptoe the rest of the way to the break room, but her stealth was for naught. McNelly stood by the percolating pot, mug in hand, looking like a bear fresh from hibernation. Standing behind him, Bay noticed the man's unkempt brown-black hair made his head appear double in size, and she wondered if he intended to visit a barber soon. McNelly made impatient grunts and huffs at the coffee maker, but barely flinched when Bay tapped him on the shoulder.

"I didn't know anyone was here. Good morning, L.L. You're early." He glanced over his shoulder, bleary-eyed.

Bay rolled her eyes and puckered her lips in disgust. "Just who did you think made the coffee, McNelly?"

The professor waved his hands in surrender and stood

sideways as the coffee pot emitted a final gurgle. "After you, by all means, Dr. Browning."

Bay stepped up, mug in hand, and poured a cup, then politely moved over to let McNelly take a turn. She opened the fridge to see if anyone left any free goodies for the masses, but only saw marked containers. She closed it, ready to retreat to her office again.

"L.L.?" McNelly waited for Bay's attention. "Do you have a minute to talk? It's business."

Bay hesitated. "I don't know. I came in early because I have a lot to do."

"This won't take long, I promise." McNelly waved Bay through the door and followed behind her.

Bay sat at her desk, placed the coffee on a coaster and dug out a second coaster for McNelly. She eyed the opened breakfast bar longingly.

"By all means, eat your bar, L.L. I myself had a full breakfast before I came in." McNelly's wide smile was surrounded by a bushy mustache and beard.

Bay didn't believe for a minute that McNelly had eaten unless he decided to forego all grooming in favor of food. She pulled a granola bar from her stash. "Here. I don't make a habit of eating in front of others."

McNelly shrugged, opened the bar, and ate it in three bites.

"What's this business you want to discuss?" Bay enjoyed a soothing gulp of coffee.

"I'll get right to it then. I think you should spend some time with Diana."

Bay almost spit out her coffee. "Diana? Our new employee?" she sputtered. "Why would I do that?"

McNelly leaned forward and placed his hands in prayer position on Bay's desk. "She needs someone to take her under their wing, and I see how you and Trevor interact…so I thought you might be just the right person to do it."

Bay's anger flared; she didn't appreciate McNelly's insinuating comment about her and Trevor. She stood up but stayed on her own side of the desk. "For starters, don't jump to conclusions about me and Trevor. He's a great guy and hard worker, and he's not my student, and we're not involved, if that's what you think." The last thing Bay wanted was for Trevor to get into trouble.

McNelly raised his hands for the second time that morning. "Whoa, whoa, whoa. I'm not suggesting any such thing. I just mean that you have a good rapport, so I thought you could use your people skills on Diana."

Bay laughed in scorn. "Oh yes, my people skills are well-honed. That's why you and I get along so well."

McNelly smiled to himself. "Can't argue with you there, L.L., although I'm not sure what you have against me. I'm not so bad once you get to know me." He reached over the desktop for her hand, but she pulled it away.

"I just thought you might chat with her, get to know her better. Diana's been through so much, and she could use a positive female role model in her life."

Bay sat back down. "Why me? She's not an English major. Isn't there anyone in criminal justice you can bother?"

McNelly picked up the antique decanter from Bay's desk and turned it in his hands, admiring its iridescent patina. "This is quite a nice piece. It reminds me of glassware I've seen at the Vatican."

Bay screwed her face into a half-puzzled, half-annoyed expression. "Please be careful with that. It's from a dig my father worked on in Sardinia when I was a child. It's from the second century." Roman glass was Bay's weakness—it's blue-green colors reminded her of the Tyrrhenian Sea between Sardinia and Italy.

Wistfully, McNelly turned his pale green eyes toward Bay. "I would love to see Italy again. See, we have something in common after all. Now, would you please take time to talk with Diana here and there?"

Bay frowned. "All right, I guess I can chat with her. Just why do you care so much? Be honest."

He shrugged and set the decanter back on the desk. "I told you. The kid's had a tough time of it. She needs to acquire a spine, and you are one of the grittiest women I know." McNelly downed the rest of his coffee, picked up the mug and left without Bay noticing he had his fingers crossed.

With McNelly out of her hair, Bay tackled the first pile of mail on her desk. She removed the junk first, an easy task. She read through the invitation reminding her of the upcoming potluck. The department held social gatherings of some sort every month. This month would be a kickoff to the spring semester on the last Saturday of winter break in the Atrium of the Luxe Art Museum on campus. The food sign-up sheet hung on the break room bulletin board. Bay committed to making baked ziti, a dish she'd shared on multiple occasions.

Several official forms were next on the pile, including a survey about the work culture at the college that came from the HR department, year-end statements for her 401K plan, and a list of upcoming enrichment workshops to choose from as part of her job requirements.

She placed the 401K statement into a folder marked "taxes" and jammed the workshop list into her tote to take home. She decided she could complete the survey during their next useless department meeting.

The giant budget packet for next year loomed large in front of her. She checked the deadline for submission and marked it on her phone calendar for March 1. When she moved the thick packet to place it in her budget binder, something fell out. It was the small envelope Trevor had handed her the other day.

"L.L. Browning" was printed in neat script on the cream-colored envelope. She opened it and unfolded a single sheet of parchment paper. At the top, someone had drawn a cobra in striking position. Just below the drawing, the heading read "Justice and Truth." What followed was a verse of sorts:

"One's wings are clipped: they fall.

Weighed and measured, Two descends to darkness.

Worthless work, Three must drown if Time wills it.

With the new moon, Four and Five will be relieved of duty."

Everything was typed and the numbers were delineated in bold capital letters.

Bay stared at the cryptic message, reading it over and over. She looked at the handwriting on the envelope, but she didn't recognize it. As soon as Trevor arrived, she planned to ask him who dropped off the envelope. It was Diana's first day of work and she was sorting mail, so she'd be sure to speak with her, too.

As sure as she was sitting there, Bay knew the note came from the Medusa Murderer. Reading it again, she wondered if one of the numbers was designated to her. Number Four maybe? Acid rose from her stomach to her throat. Of course, she had to call

Downing immediately.

Jen Yoo stood in her doorway, rapping lightly on the frame. "Good morning, Bay. Is this a bad time? You look kind of off."

It seemed to Bay that Jen was her only friend in the department whom she trusted, so she waved her in. "You called that right, Jen. My stomach is acting up. It's this murder case. Honestly, I know I'm a target." Bay slipped the note back into its envelope and tucked it into a drawer. She had to call Downing before talking about it with anyone.

Jen gasped. "How can you be sure? What does the painting have to do with you? You're not an art dealer or instructor. Is this about the lululemon switch? I don't think…"

Bay raised one hand. "Slow down a second, Jen. I appreciate your reassurance, but I haven't had the chance to show you this." She handed Jen her cell phone photo of the graffiti wall.

Jen stared at it, trying to make sense of the depiction. "I'm afraid I don't get this. I won't pretend to be a graffiti expert."

"This is the wall across from my apartment complex. The wall that I see every day when I look out my living room window. I think this message is meant for me if I could figure it out."

"Oh my God, Bay. Do the police know about this?" Jen grabbed Bay's hand as Bay nodded.

"My dad reminded me of the Egyptian mythology surrounding the eye of Ra, Anubis, and the ostrich feather. Remember, there was an ostrich feather at the murder scene and in the coat pocket? And look at all the snakes in the letters, the eye, and background? Another connection to Medusa."

Jen's eyes widened with fear. Bay continued. "See the letters in the corners. If you read them left to right, they spell 'sari' like

Cesari, the artist from Arpino. I think this was painted by the murderer."

Jen swallowed hard before speaking somberly. "I stopped by because I wanted to show you something else that came from my research. It seems like this case won't let me rest either, so I spent some time looking at things last night. May I?" Jen headed to the other side of Bay's desk to the computer.

While Jen typed and clicked, she explained, "My mind kept going back to the note and the three things that cannot stay hidden. The moon seems to reference Artemis, but we don't know how she's connected to Medusa. The sun is still a mystery. But the truth is such a common subject in literature and art. It got me thinking about the unit I teach on allegory, so I took home my unit files and found this."

Bay read over Jen's shoulder at the caption under a painting, entitled *Allegory of Justice and Truth*. The artist was Giorgio Vasari, an Italian Renaissance Master. The title alone sent a shiver down Bay's spine. "Justice and Truth" was the heading on the note she'd just opened.

"Can you make heads or tails out of the painting? It's crowded with so many things that look symbolic." Bay was glad to have Jen's help.

"You could spend hours studying and discussing this piece; it's so loaded with iconography. But let's get to the highlights. The half-nude woman represents justice. You can see here that her arm rests on an ostrich."

Bay gasped. "An ostrich. The ostrich feathers. Anubis weighs the souls of the dead with an ostrich feather to determine their worth."

"But in this painting, the ostrich symbolizes patience in

facing a challenge. Because Justice herself must rely on patience. It takes time for justice to be meted out."

Bay soaked in this new revelation. "The ostrich has more than one connection to the murders. The killer thinks they mete out justice, one victim at a time."

Jen nodded. "That may be correct. Look at Justice's left hand. She crowns this woman, who represents Truth, with laurel, a symbol of victory."

Bay interrupted. "Wait a second. How do you know this woman represents Truth?"

Jen pointed to a figure of a bearded man with an hourglass on his head. The man is shown offering the woman to Justice. "The bearded man here with the hourglass is Time. Time presents Truth to Justice. The artist is saying that in time, the truth is discovered and will result in justice."

Bay nodded uncertainly. "Why is Truth holding two doves?"

"The doves symbolize innocence. The Seven Deadly Sins are represented in the painting, too, but most interesting are these two." Jen pointed to two men being crushed under the feet of Truth.

"They represent falsehood and slander, which are defeated by Truth," Jen explained.

Bay sucked in a gulp of air again. "The first victim. The comic book creator slandered women in the *Vengeful Venuses* series. I wonder if Virginia Lowe lied about something, something big."

"Could be," Jen said. "One more thing. Vasari was an artist, but he was famous for writing a book about the lives of the artists he knew. Vasari himself described this painting and its meaning in that book."

"So, there's really no mystery in interpreting it correctly

then," Bay observed.

"Right, but don't you see, Bay? The graffiti art with the letters that spell out 'sari' could just as easily refer to Vasari, or maybe both artists," Jen was breathless with excitement.

Bay held onto the back of her office chair to steady herself. It seemed like some of the pieces were falling into place. "Thanks, Jen. It's good to feel like we're getting somewhere. But there's still so much to figure out. I need to call the police right away."

Jen stood up and hugged Bay. "You're my friend, Bay Browning, in case you don't know that, you do now. Don't get killed, okay?" Bay hugged her tightly, too choked up to speak.

Bay took some deep breaths, trying to meditate away her anxiety. She contemplated lighting her favorite candle, but remembered she wanted to see if Trevor was in yet, so she could ask him about the note. She inhaled deeply and counted to six, then exhaled fully and counted again. A few rounds of measured breaths and she was ready.

Trevor sat at his post, tapping away on the computer next to a stack of papers waiting to be entered. Bay was thankful that she didn't see anyone else around the area, so they could have a private conversation.

"Good morning, Trevor. I see you're hard at it." Bay attempted to sound cheerful.

Trevor looked up, beaming. "Good morning. I'm glad you stopped by. I went to Crossroads last night and met Thomas. We've got a date this weekend. So, thanks for thinking about me."

"I thought you two might hit it off. Word of advice, Trevor: proceed with caution. Don't dive into the deep end of the pool until you test the water." Bay raised her brows as she spoke.

Trevor saluted, comprehending. "Hey, you look sort of gloomy this morning. Anything wrong? Is your sister driving you crazy?"

Bay shook her head and bit her top lip. "I suppose you were here when the police were asking questions yesterday? Did they ask you anything about me?"

"No! I mean, yes, I talked to them, but they didn't ask about you. They wanted to know my schedule, security procedures in the department, and they showed me a drawing of someone and asked if I'd seen him around here."

Bay wondered if the drawing was of the mysterious lululemon swapper, Chance. "Do you remember what the drawing looked like?"

Trevor opened his desk drawer and pulled out a copy of the drawing. "The police left this with me in case the person showed up or in case I saw him anywhere around campus. Why? Have you seen this guy?"

Bay had not, but she'd also seen the drawing, probably rendered from Aria's memory at the dry cleaner's. "So, you haven't seen him, then? And do you know who dropped off that envelope for me that you gave me the other day, the one I said was probably a thank-you?"

Trevor shook his head. "No to both questions. The note for you was sitting in my in-basket when I got to work that morning. Why? Do you think there's a connection?" Trevor's voice held concern for his favorite professor.

Bay laughed too easily. "No, of course not. Just wondering. I don't recognize the guy in the drawing either."

Changing the subject lest she disclose something she shouldn't, Bay asked, "Is Diana here today? I'd like to see her."

Trevor pointed to the mail room. "She's in her usual spot, sorting mail, running errands off the gopher pile." The mail room included a basket where department professors placed work orders of odds and ends that used to be Trevor's job. He affectionately referred to the basket as the gopher pile.

Bay entered the mail room and found Diana sorting through the gopher basket, checking the dates, and prioritizing the needs of the staff. She jumped when Bay walked over. Bay noticed a large stack of orders requested by McNelly, which made her frown.

"Good morning, Diana. How's the job going for you? Looks like you have a lot to do." Bay feigned concern.

Diana sighed. "Good morning, Professor. I'm only approved for fifteen hours a week, so I have to prioritize these work orders."

Bay felt guilty for not talking to Diana sooner. The girl needed some guidance and a backbone. "Diana, can I offer some advice?"

Diana nodded eagerly.

"Do not let anyone in this department walk all over you. You're right about prioritizing the work orders. Can I help you do it?" Bay needed the distraction from her own reality.

"Sure, that would be great. I'm not sure how to decide what's more important."

Bay looked through the requests. McNelly apparently wanted Diana to be his own personal assistant; he asked her to organize files in his office, go to the bookstore to pick up his orders for the semester, create a syllabus for three courses, and create a slide show for his new course in ethics—"Everyday Morality."

She kicked the table leg and borrowed a Shakespearean

profanity. "That fustilarian!"

Diana jolted and peered wide-eyed at Bay.

Bay took a breath. "Look Diana, I know Professor McNelly supported your application for this job, but that doesn't mean he can take advantage of you. Professors in this department are expected to make their own class materials, so forget about these orders."

She set them aside and passed the other requests under her nose. "It's up to you if you want to pick up his bookstore orders, but if I were you, I'd ask the associate dean about organizing his office files. There's bound to be confidential information, so I doubt she will approve."

Diana swallowed a hard lump in her throat. "I'm sorry. I didn't know."

Bay patted her shoulder. "It's okay. You're learning. Let me just take a gander at the rest of these." Most of the orders were for bookstore pickups, and the theatre department asked Diana to help organize the costume room whenever she might have extra time during the semester. Bay herself didn't have any work orders in the basket.

"These look standard to me. But, if the deans ask you to do anything, you probably should take care of their needs first. At least if it's reasonable."

"Thank you, Dr. Browning. What do I do with Dr. McNelly's orders that you set over here?" She pointed to the offending requests.

Bay smiled deviously. "I'll take them back to his office. I need to see him anyway." It would give her great pleasure to return the work orders to McNelly. Before leaving the mail room, Bay remembered the day she received the note was Diana's first day of work.

"Diana, did the police speak with you yesterday? Show you a drawing?"

Bay's inquiry made the office gofer jittery.

"The police asked me questions, but I couldn't be helpful. I just started working here, and I didn't recognize the man in the drawing." Diana looked away nervously.

"One more question. On your first day here, I received a note in a small envelope, the size of a thank-you or invitation. Do you remember if someone gave the note to you or if it came in the department mail crate?" Bay realized it was a long shot. Mail went in one hand and out the other, so she probably wouldn't remember any particular piece.

"Well, nobody handed me any personal mail, that I do know. I'm not sure if something came in the mail crate, but if it was in your mailbox, then it probably came in the crate. Or, maybe from someone in the department." Diana answered matter-of-factly, and Bay was satisfied.

"Thank you, Diana. Please stop by my office if you need anything, okay?" Bay meant it sincerely this time.

Work orders in hand, Bay walked down the hall to McNelly's office, knocked on the door, and swept into the room before receiving an answer. She slapped the work orders under his nose and spun toward the door.

"Wait, what's this?" McNelly asked.

"I followed up on your request and spent some time with Diana this morning. We sorted through work orders. I'm returning the ones she won't be completing." Bay leaned over McNelly's desk to get in his face.

"You wanted to be part of arts and humanities. In this

department, we do our own course work and confidential filing. She's not your personal employee, Dr. McNelly. Have a nice day." Bay shut the door quietly on the way out. ∎

CHAPTER 15

DIGGING IN

Back in her office, Bay paced back and forth like a zoo animal. Should she call Downing to be sure he was there or just show up unannounced with the note? A phone call seemed tedious, especially with the complicated amount of information she needed to share. Of course, Downing would want to see the note firsthand, so she may as well just drive to the station.

Bay stared regretfully at the course files on her desk. When would she ever get her prep work done for the new semester? The logical part of her brain said it was a priority to find a killer, especially if she was a target.

On her way out, Bay stopped to tell Trevor she would be going to the police station in case anyone important was looking for her.

Trevor raised worried eyes toward her. "The police station? I suppose you can't talk about it, but please be careful, and if there is something going on, make sure you let me know where you're going to be. I've got your back."

Bay appreciated Trevor's chivalry but doubted he'd be very useful if she were in harm's way. She imagined she'd have to rely on the gnarly detective for protection, and that idea presented an obstacle for the independent Bay.

At the police station, Bay greeted Carol pleasantly. "Good morning, Carol. I'm here to see Detective Downing if he's available."

Carol grinned all the way up to her eyebrows. "You're becoming a regular around here, aren't you, Professor?"

Bay shuddered inside, wishing her life to go back to normal, but smiled weakly. "I guess I am whether I like it or not. As long as I'm a regular as you say, please call me Bay. That's what my friends call me. But do me a favor please? Don't tell Downing my name."

Carol laughed and winked. "Your secret's safe with me. We women must stick together. I'll phone his office to let him know you're here."

Downing hurried down the hallway to greet Bay. To his credit, he seemed fresh, like he'd gotten some sleep or maybe had a lead in the case. Bay could only hope.

"What brings you down here? You usually just call, Professor." Downing ushered her into his office and closed the door. Officer Harris was sitting at a table in the corner, pouring over case files. Unlike Downing, Harris looked disheveled.

"G'morning, Ma'am," Harris mumbled. He took a swig from a half-empty two-liter of cola.

"Good morning, Officer Harris." Bay indicated the soda in amazement. "Do you normally drink that much at a time?"

Harris smiled despite his fatigue. "Only when I pull an all-nighter. I'm about to end this shift though."

"If you're working on the Medusa files, you may want to see what I've brought in."

Harris turned his chair around to face the desk as Bay pulled the envelope from her purse and passed it to Downing.

Downing and Harris exchanged knowing looks. Downing's grim face met Bay's quizzical one.

"Where did you get this?" he asked quietly.

Bay's face traversed from surprise to fury. "You've already seen this note, haven't you? How could you keep this from me?"

"Apparently, I couldn't. Where did you get this?" Downing repeated.

"Some unknown person dropped it off at the reception desk in my department. I asked Trevor and Diana, our office workers, but neither one knew where the note came from. And I guess you should know I've had it a few days. It was in my mail stack, and I just opened it this morning."

Downing swore, slapped the desk, glared at nobody in particular, and turned sorrowful eyes on Bay. "I'm sorry. Sorry this is happening to you and sorry that we couldn't share the information."

Bay backed down and resumed breathing normally. "Can you share now? Where have you seen this?" she pointed to the note.

Downing gestured to Harris, who opened a file, pulled out a copy of the same note, and handed it to the detective.

"We found this pinned to the comic book creator. You can see it's the exact same note."

"So, I guess Medusa is ready to go after victim number three, if it hasn't already happened. What number do you think I might be, Detective?" Bay's silky voice filled the room with spite and dread.

Downing stood and ran his fingers through his parted hair, messing it up. "We're trying to prevent another victim. We've got extra plainclothes people on the ground. It's damn frustrating, Professor."

"It sure is. I know I can't concentrate or think about anything but this case, so could you please give me something to do? I need to be useful. I've got skin in the game." Bay pleaded her position.

Downing looked at Harris, who nodded. "I'm going home to get some rest. Professor Browning could look through the case files with fresh eyes. Maybe something will trigger a memory," Harris suggested.

Downing cleared his throat loudly but nodded his agreement. "Doctor, you're green-lighted by the chief to assist, so have at it. I'm going to order lunch from Ellie's Deli. Let me know if you'd like something." Downing slid a menu in front of Bay.

She couldn't resist jabbing the detective. "What, no Pig Squeal food today?" Too late, she saw Downing open his drawer, produce a super-sized bottle of Tums, and chomp a handful. Clearly, the case was not agreeing with him either.

Between bites of a Greek salad with grilled chicken and slurps of iced coffee, Bay reviewed the comic creator's case file, then Virginia's. When nothing obvious struck her, she carefully studied Virginia's long list of family members. The art dealer had been married four times, three times to men and once to a woman. She had no children of her own but had several stepchildren. Most notably, Virginia's only sibling, a brother, had died in prison.

Downing interrupted her third reading of the case files. "See anything?"

Bay could understand how frustrating detective work must be. "Virginia's got a long list of connections to her name. But I'm curious about the brother. What was he in prison for?"

"He was a disgusting pedophile. After several small stints in prison, someone on the inside took care of him for good." Downing's face indicated he didn't have any sympathy about the man's death. "I can't find anything that indicates Virginia and her brother were close. They lived in separate areas of the country most of the time. Of course, Virginia did move a lot."

Bay's stomach turned when Downing told her about the brother's crime. "Could the person who killed Virginia's brother have killed her, too?"

Downing shrugged. "The brother was found hanging in his cell. These crimes don't fit, especially if you consider the comic creator."

"What about her exes? She had four of them."

Downing nodded. "We're still looking, but two of them died before her. Her current husband would be the obvious suspect, so we're investigating. He's a well-known New York broker, so he's lawyered up and isn't talking to us."

"Stepchildren?" Bay asked.

"Yeah, we're looking for them. We've found three, but no luck finding the other two. The three we found don't seem suspicious. Two of them have solid alibis. None of them have had contact with Virginia in several years. But…" Downing was formulating an idea.

Bay watched as he scrunched up his face, contemplating. Finally, she couldn't stand it. "What? You have an idea, what is it?"

"Something about our interview with one of the stepsons

bothers me. We have it on video, since he lives in California. I've sent it to a consulting psychiatrist, but maybe you'd like to see it?"

"Why me? I'm no psychiatrist!" Bay protested.

"Exactly why I'd like you to look at it. No offense to the pros, but sometimes they go overboard."

Bay sat in front of a police station laptop in another room and watched a female officer interview Virginia's forty-three-year-old stepson from her second marriage. After watching the interview three times, Bay wondered if the psychiatrist would confirm any of Bay's observations.

Since the office blinds were closed, Bay rapped on Downing's door. He was working in silence in low light. "I've got a headache, sorry," he explained.

"I watched the interview three times," Bay began.

"And?"

"The stepson fidgets every time Virginia's name is used in a question. And, he also looks away from the officer when she asks questions about Virginia's brother, whom he admits to knowing. He has a nervous tick, too. If I had to guess, I'd say he may have been a victim of Virginia's brother." Bay felt nauseous thinking about it.

"Bingo. I think so, too. The shrink will give us a formal report, so we'll have to see." Downing was agitated.

"Did the stepson have an alibi? I mean, being abused by Virginia's brother could be motive. But how does the comic book creator fit in?"

Downing slammed his hand against his thigh. "The stepson has an ironclad alibi, and the comic creator doesn't fit at all."

Bay wasn't surprised. "I think the Medusa is a woman. It fits with the method of killing and with the motive of vengeance against the comic creator making art that objectifies women. But we need to figure out the motive against Virginia and, well against me, I suppose."

Suddenly lunch wasn't sitting so well in Bay's stomach. She turned to another line of questions.

"Did you notice anything in my class rosters? I've only looked at two of the three, and nothing stands out to me. No confrontations. No stalkers. No failing students."

Downing nodded. "We didn't see anything unusual either. I wish we could find Virginia's other two stepdaughters."

"What's the hold up?" Bay wondered.

"Canada. They were raised there. Both of their real parents are dead, and they probably have different last names now, so there's no trail. Let's just say some local Canadian offices do not cooperate too well in these kinds of matters." Downing frowned.

"Well, I'm ready to call it an afternoon. I need to stop back at my office and take some work home. Thank you for letting me do something, even if it wasn't helpful." Bay smiled as Downing helped her into her coat.

"Oh, one more thing. I found a different piece of art that might be key to figuring out the note left with Virginia. I'll send you a link to it and a few more notes. Can't you get a better expert than me on this case, though?" Bay didn't feel equipped to decipher whatever messages were in the notes and wall art.

Downing shrugged. "We could, but for some reason, the killer wants you to be involved. So, Professor, we're in this boat together." He smiled as brightly as he could given the circumstances.

As Bay drove back to the college, a fleet of squad cars

blazed past her, and a line of vehicles pulled off to the shoulder. Normally, Bay would think a bad accident had just happened, but this time, a feeling of dread welled up inside of her.

When she saw Downing's unmarked car amid the squads, she was certain the Medusa had found her third victim. ∎

CHAPTER 16
VICTIM THREE

Downing and several police officers stared at the display tank at Capital Aquarium as emergency medical techs tried to breathe and pound life back into the man wearing concrete shoes. When Downing arrived, police tape already marked the tank area in the aquarium's main room.

Two divers in wet suits had pulled the man from the tank, then dove back in to carry out the plastic sign that had been strapped to the man's hand. Madison police were combing the area for the perpetrator, and the Prairie Ridge officers joined the search upon arrival.

Because the aquarium had a Madison address, the local police responded first, but someone quickly tipped off Prairie Ridge that this victim could be another Medusa kill.

Downing recognized one of the two Madison detectives and wormed his way through the bystanders and cops to join in on their interview with the aquarium manager. Detective Rodriguez nodded at Downing in recognition, mid-question.

He was taking the lead on the case with the much younger detective at his side who was learning the ropes.

Rodriguez raised his hand to pause the interview. "Ms. Gladwell, if you'll excuse me a minute. Detective Hawkins, could you please stay with Ms. Gladwell?" Rodriguez was over the top in gentility for a detective.

"Downing, how are you? I figured you'd be along once I saw the victim." Rodriguez shook Downing's hand firmly.

"Catch me up, Rodriguez." Downing wasted no time on pleasantries.

"Nina Gladwell, the Aquarium's manager, called it in. One of the aquarists saw the man standing at the bottom of the tank when it was time for the afternoon feeding. The worker radioed Ms. Gladwell immediately, and she called 911."

Downing scribbled like a madman. "Okay. Next."

Rodriguez watched Downing, looking puzzled. "You can have a copy of my notes, Downing. There are no secrets here. We've only spoken with Nina Gladwell. The aquarist is in the break room waiting for us."

Rodriguez pointed down a hallway, and Downing started walking determinedly.

Rodriguez smiled. "I guess you'll take the lead on this witness then."

The dapper Madison detective trotted alongside Downing to keep up and pulled on his shirt sleeve when he passed the break room door.

The pair encountered the aquarist, a young man barely out of college, face buried in his hands.

"Hello, we're Detectives Downing and Rodriguez, and we need to ask you some questions about what happened here, Mr.

ah…"

"Mr. Vaughn. Jeremy Vaughn." Rodriguez provided the answer, adding, "We imagine this is quite a shock for you."

Jeremy Vaughn looked from Downing to Rodriguez, then down at the notebook where he had written down everything he could recall about the incident while he waited for the police.

Downing took a breath, trying to quell his impatience. "Why don't you start at the beginning, Mr. Vaughn. What time did you arrive at work today?"

"My normal shift is from seven until three. I do the morning and afternoon feeding in the big tank."

"Tell me everything you can remember about finding the man in the tank today."

Jeremy Vaughn took a gulping breath and let it out, steeling himself for the retelling. "I went to the cooler and loaded food into the buckets. There's more than one type of food used for the big tank because we have many different animals in there. Just like always, I climbed into the boom with the buckets and tossed the first bucket into the top of the tank."

"Do you always do the feeding alone?" Downing interrupted.

"Yes, unless someone is job shadowing or interning. But we won't have an intern again until summer."

"Okay, go on please."

"I was watching the food descending and watched for the fish to come up to eat. That's when I noticed Maggie."

Downing's eyes widened and glanced over at Rodriguez. "Wait, who's Maggie?"

Vaughn smiled sweetly. "Maggie is my favorite manta ray. She was caught on the man's shoe at the bottom of the tank. I was worried she might be hurt."

"You weren't concerned about the man in the tank?" Downing scoffed.

Vaughn nodded. "Of course. At first, I thought it was some sort of prank. A crazy person wanting to dive into the fish tank to be one with the fish or something. He was wearing scuba gear, so I figured he was all right. But then I noticed he didn't seem to be moving, and I saw his shoes didn't look right. That's when I radioed Nina."

"Do you have any emergency medical training? Could you have dove into the tank and tried to rescue the man?"

Vaughn's voice became agitated. "Yes, I can dive into the tank if necessary. I never have, though. Only the marine vets dive into the tank. It's not part of my training, Detective." Vaughn looked down at the black waterproof overalls he still wore. "Especially in these. They weigh a lot and I'd drop like an anchor if I dove into the tank."

"I assume these are your normal work clothes?"

"Yes, it keeps the fish food and water off my regular uniform."

"What did you do after you contacted Ms. Gladwell?"

Vaughn was ready to cry. "Exactly as she told me. She said to stop feeding, come down the boom and wait in her office. She said help was coming." Vaughn's voice broke into pieces. "It was awful. Waiting. Wondering if anyone was going to come save the guy in time. Knowing." His voice dropped to a whisper.

Downing leaned forward. "Knowing what, Mr. Vaughn?"

Vaughn raised red-rimmed eyes upward to meet Downing's. "Knowing it was too late. He's already dead, isn't he?"

Rodriguez walked to the other side of the table to place a reassuring hand on Vaughn's shoulder. "The paramedics are still working on him. They'll do everything they can."

Vaughn looked down at his lap. "I recognized him, the man in the tank." Vaughn's face held guilt and helplessness. "He comes here often, always at the same time. He told me once he loved the saltwater tank. It relaxed him."

"Did you see anyone strange or new around here today? Anything different about today in any way?" Downing's intuition suggested Vaughn might have more to offer.

Vaughn tried to think. Instinctively, he shook his head no. "I've worked here a year and I know everyone."

"Do you have any recently hired workers? A custodian? Office worker? Gift shop cashier?"

"You can check with Nina for sure, but I haven't seen anyone new here in months. I don't think the guy in the tank worked here, Detective."

Downing didn't think so either. "Thank you for your help, Mr. Vaughn. If you think of anything, even the tiniest detail, call me right away." He handed Vaughn his business card.

Rodriguez stopped to pat Vaughn's shoulder. "I know you did everything you could, Jeremy. This isn't your fault."

The two detectives headed back to Nina's office without exchanging a word. To their dismay, Detective Hawkins and Nina were engaged in a detailed back-and-forth about the workings of the aquarium.

Hawkins stopped her furious scribbling at the opening of the door. She looked up at both men as red color deepened from her neck to her cheeks.

Before Downing had the chance to fume, Rodriguez sat down next to his charge. "I think we will take it from here, Hawkins."

Hawkins rose and stood behind Rodriguez's chair and

Downing plopped down next to Rodriguez.

Nina confirmed there were no recent hires and gave a glowing report about Vaughn and the other aquarists on site. She offered her complete cooperation to the officers.

"You should understand though, the Aquarium owners are going to want as little publicity as possible. The news stations are already here. They're going to expect me to put the best face on this, and they're going to want the aquarium opened again ASAP. The saltwater tank is the main attraction, you know." Nina's complete-cooperation face had been replaced by business-as-usual.

A scowling Downing returned to the scene where only one paramedic remained filling out paperwork on the victim.

"Well, what can you tell me…" he looked at her name tag. "Roberts," he recited.

"Good evening, Detective Downing." Roberts apparently went through the same civility training as Rodriguez had.

She paused, seeking acknowledgement from Downing before proceeding. He nodded impatiently.

"The victim's body is being transported to the Madison morgue. Your people bagged his shoes, the plastic sign, and other stuff the divers brought up from the tank. They're looking for you, by the way. You'll find them behind the building or in the storeroom. That way." Roberts pointed.

So much for specifics, Downing grumbled to himself. He wondered where Rodriguez and Hawkins were, and he quickened his pace toward the storeroom. They were already there, standing around the feeding boom, asking questions of the officer in charge.

The Prairie Ridge officer dusted the surface of the boom for fingerprints and other DNA signatures. He looked at Downing when he spoke. "I've got a few bags to process. I found two hairs on the boom, a couple prints, and partial handprints. The fish feeders don't wear gloves, so the prints are probably theirs."

The back door opened revealing Officer Harris, called back on duty to the aquarium. He motioned for Downing to come outside. Rodriguez stayed behind but waved Hawkins out the door to tag along behind Downing.

"What did you find, Harris?" Downing stood by him at the dumpster, hands on hips, blocking Hawkins's view.

Harris held up a wallet and office badge, already bagged for evidence. "I took pictures of these IDs, and grief officers are going to the man's office and his home to see about a morgue identification."

Downing nodded, rolled his eyes to indicate Hawkins, and held a finger to his lips. "Good work, Harris. Did you find anything else unusual in the dumpster?"

Harris shook his head. "Trash, broken down cardboard. I went through the employee equipment earlier. Every person who works in the tanks has assigned scuba gear. Vaughn's was missing. The scuba gear on the vic is bagged in the trunk." Harris pointed to the parked squad.

"Do we still have people inside interviewing the other employees?"

Harris nodded. "We can reconvene at the station later. Might as well go back, log evidence, and see what we're looking at so far, huh?"

Downing spun around to face Hawkins. "Good night, detective. Our office will take it from here. I expect you'll pass along your station's info tonight. Here's my card. Email address is on the bottom."

Instead of walking through the aquarium, Downing sidetracked around the outside of the building to the front. He was surprised to see that only the Prairie Ridge squads remained along with his nondescript black sedan.

Downing pounded his fist against the steering wheel hard enough to hurt. During the short ride back to the station, he fought to keep his anger in check. He didn't know if he was angrier that Madison was on the scene or that the Medusa had another victim. He slapped the steering wheel again. God, he hated this case.

Downing walked up the back steps of the Prairie Ridge station, glad he wasn't the grief officer going to Psychologist Paul Johnson's front door and asking his wife to come identify his body. ■

CHAPTER 17
BAD NEWS AT TEN

A large rap on the office door jarred Bay awake. She looked around, surprised to find herself face down in her office, lights still on. She jumped at the second knock and jangling keys at her door.

"Hello. Professor Browning. Are you in here?" Bay recognized the voice of Rich, the night custodian.

"Yes, come on in, Rich," came Bay's sleepy reply.

Rich unlocked the door and poked his head inside. He prided himself on keeping a close eye on the building and was detail-oriented, so he noticed when lights were left on when they should be off and checked it out.

"I don't usually see you burning the midnight oil until grading time. The new semester hasn't even started yet, Professor."

"You're right, Rich. I'm a little behind and haven't been sleeping well lately. So, you caught me taking a nap. What time is it anyway?"

"It's almost ten o'clock. Are you going home soon? I don't want to scare you away, but you know there's a killer on the loose, and I wouldn't want any harm to come to you." Rich was a gentle giant, and Bay doubted he'd be very useful if a killer came calling.

"You're right. I need to go home. I'll just shut down my computer and pack up."

"I'll be working on this floor for another fifteen minutes or so. Why don't you come find me when you're ready to go, and I'll walk you to your car."

Considering the circumstances, Bay decided to take Rich up on the offer.

Before shutting down the computer, Bay noticed multiple lines of the letter "J" on the document she'd been working on before dozing off. The Js went on for three pages before she shifted her chair over to lay her head on the desk.

Bay suspected she dozed off less than an hour earlier, and she'd accomplished a large percentage of her course preparation. It was a respite from thinking about the Medusa files, and a relief to catch up somewhat.

Rich walked her to the lighted parking lot where Bay's Subaru sat, frosted over from the moisture on this heavy night. Rich suggested she lock herself in while she waited for the defrosters to do their best. She obliged and waved him off.

Bay turned on the radio just in time to catch breaking news about a third murder victim, found in the saltwater tank at Capital Aquarium that afternoon. Psychologist Paul Johnson of Madison drowned in the tank wearing cement shoes… another victim of the Medusa Murders.

Bay shivered, wrapped her scarf more tightly around her

neck, and cranked the defroster to high. She watched Gale Hall swallow Rich, leaving her feeling more alone than ever and wanting to go home. Her eyes darted around the parking lot and the dark trees and gardens beyond. She saw moving shadows and statues that seemed to float in the strange light as paranoia settled in.

She shoved hard on the wipers and pushed the washer fluid button. Blue slush formed on the windshield, leaving delicate patches of frost in spots. She didn't care how well she could see; she was leaving. She wondered if she dared go to the police station where she imagined Downing was bent over the evidence and files, looking for answers.

Bay told herself she would drive around until the Subaru warmed up with the excuse it was better for the engine than to make a short trip. The main shopping district of Prairie Ridge was alive with action. The Tipsy Cow's parking lot was more than half full as was the superstore's lot.

Bay had half a mind to check on Cass at Outfitters, where she saw two cars parked. She rejected the idea, feeling foolish. Besides, she was still angry at Cass for being Cass.

Bay turned on her street, intending to drive past her building to look for the patrolling squad car that was supposed to protect her and her family. There it was, making a turn down the parking garage side of Windflower Gardens. Then she saw the plain black sedan at the front entrance, engine running. It could only be Downing's.

Her tires emitted a small screech as she made the last-minute turn into her complex. Instead of driving straight to the garage, Bay pulled up to the entrance, directly behind the black sedan and almost tapped lightly on her horn.

Downing was already climbing out of the car, so Bay did the same, right into his wide-open arms. She laid her head on his shoulder, and he pulled her into him more firmly, both frozen in the moment.

They let go simultaneously and both took an awkward step backwards. Downing cleared his throat twice, and Bay eased the tension.

"Thank you. I needed that." She spoke simply and honestly.

Downing surprised both of them by saying, "I think I needed that, too."

Bay glanced toward the front door. "Would you like to come up? I can make you something to drink, and you can fill me in." Her voice sounded more normal than she felt inside.

"Yeah, I can do that."

They rode the elevator silently. Bay unlocked the door, and Downing insisted he enter first and check the premises. Bay padded into the kitchen directly behind him and opened the tea cupboard.

"Make yourself at home in the living room. Is tea okay?" Bay called.

Downing stood in the kitchen entryway. "Dammit Doctor, can't you wait until I call all clear?" Downing sounded more upset than he looked.

Bay laughed, more out of release than for any other reason. "Sorry. Old habit. I'm used to taking care of myself. So, tea okay?"

Downing nodded and left to sit in the living room, staring into space. Minutes later, Bay came into the bright room and walked around to dim the lights to something more bearable. She handed a mug to the detective. "This is a special blend from my aunt. It's supposed to bring you to zen mode."

Downing scrunched his nose skeptically but took a sniff and decided it smelled okay. Bay went back to the kitchen and returned with her own mug and a plate of apple and orange slices. Since Cass moved in, there always seemed to be food in the place, one small bonus.

"Thank you. I don't suppose you have any antacids hanging around?" Downing was on a steady diet of chalky tablets and aspirin ever since the Medusa Murders landed on his desk.

"Just a minute." Bay went to the bathroom and retrieved two brands of antacids. She'd had intermittent stomach issues her whole life, so she kept remedies on hand. "You know these don't always do much good. I have just as much luck drinking baking soda or eating dill pickles."

Downing laughed heartily as he took a few tablets from each bottle and washed them down with a gulp of tea. "Dill pickles? That's a new one on me."

"You should try it sometime. There's nothing to lose."

Bay sat in the chair next to the couch where Downing was perched, sitting nervously on the edge of the cushion.

"Where were you tonight, anyway? I came up to your apartment and when nobody answered, I decided to wait out front. Didn't you know about the third victim?"

Bay colored, embarrassed that she hadn't paid attention to the news when she'd seen the fleet of squads heading south together. "I'm sorry. I know I need to be more careful. I just have so much work to do before the new semester, so I went to work. I ended up falling asleep at my desk."

Downing blew out a breath. "That's understandable. Neither one of us has been getting much lately." Seeing Bay's amused expression, he quickly added, "sleep, that is."

Between fruit slices, Downing told Bay as much as he could about the third victim. "It didn't take long to ID the guy because his wallet and work badge were in the dumpster outside. I guess the killer needed to be sloppy, committing this kind of murder in broad daylight."

"What did the sign say that Dr. Johnson was holding?"

Downing gasped. "Was that on the news? They weren't supposed to divulge any details, just the preliminary cause of death and his identity."

Bay placed her hand on Downing's arm. "I didn't hear it on the news. You told me about the evidence you found, remember?"

Downing stood and ran one hand through his wavy hair. "Damn, I hate this case. Sorry, I guess I'm tired." Downing pulled out his work phone and opened it to the file photos. He handed it to Bay. "Here's the sign. The writing was done in permanent marker, nothing special about the sign or marker, just the words."

Bay read it out loud. "Time is running out for this Bottom Feeder. Let him sleep with the fishes." Below the writing was a drawing of a trident with snakes wrapped around the staff. "More snakes."

She handed the phone back to Downing. "It sure doesn't look like the victims were chosen randomly. Not just because of the planned list on the killer's note. These murders are personal. I bet the doctor was the killer's therapist, and he couldn't help her. Can you find out?"

Downing raised tired eyes toward Bay's enthusiastic plan. "That would be so simple, wouldn't it? But you're forgetting about doctor-patient confidentiality. We can't just barge in and ask for all of the man's records. Without knowing the name of the patient, we wouldn't have a leg to stand on in court."

"But he's dead," Bay protested. "What's going to happen to his records?"

"The clinic will forward each patient file to the next shrink. Psychotherapy goes on."

"Let me try another angle. Doesn't a therapist have to let the police know if one of their patients is a criminal or about to commit a crime?"

"It's complicated, Professor. A therapist must break confidentiality if their patient shares an exact plan to commit a crime, but if the patient says they've committed past crimes, the therapist has to keep that under wraps. There are other specific instances, too, on both sides of the issue. We have no idea if Doctor Johnson knew anything."

Bay sat further back into the chair, willing herself to fold up into a ball as she lamented the state of things. She suddenly felt ten years older and no wiser than a week ago.

"Before you get too discouraged, take a look at this." Downing took a small piece of paper from his jacket pocket, a photocopy of a business card. He handed it to Bay, who sat up at attention.

"The Fabulous Fiona. Hypnosis. Meditation. Super Empathy." Bay noticed the card had both a Chicago address and web address. "What's this supposed to mean?"

Downing took the card and slipped it inside his wallet. "It's another sloppy or intentional mistake by Medusa. I think this one's sloppy. Harris and I pried the plaster from the doc's shoes so it could be analyzed and compared to the other cases.

Fabulous Fiona's card was stuck to the bottom of one shoe."

Bay cocked one brow at the detective, and Downing asked, "Would you like to take a field trip with me tomorrow night?"

Cass wandered the expanse of Outfitters, shining a flashlight purposefully. She'd seen a rodent on her rounds in the men's clothing department and was determined to rid the store of the critter. During her term of confinement, she'd seen an abundance of mice and rats running around the prison, and she'd become adept at cornering them and stomping the life out of them. It afforded her a modicum of control over her environment.

Day two and Cass was tired of reading the manuals and watching the training videos already, so while Jason took his second dinner break, Cass decided to get some exercise. She mischievously undressed one of the mannequins in the men's section and decked it out in a lacey ruffled skirt and white eyelet yoked blouse. She topped the plastic man's head with a pink cowboy hat trimmed in spangles and placed matching pink cowboy boots where the mannequin's feet should be.

As she set down the boots, she noticed movement nearby. A medium-sized rat scuttled under the clearance rack and disappeared. Cass assumed stealth mode, flashlight in one hand, night stick in the other. The Outfitters manager issued the night stick to her when she arrived at work that day. Clearly, he wasn't concerned about her ex-con status.

Being on the prowl in a dark store raised her adrenaline level and reminded her of pre-prison days when she would occasionally take part in breaking and entering if she was desperate for a job. She cautioned herself about the addictive side to adrenaline rushes as her rehab days trained her to do.

"Cassandra, are you down there?" Jason shouted from the

mezzanine overlooking the men's department.

"What a fool," Cass muttered under her breath. If there was a burglar in the store, that guy would never catch them.

"Cassandra?" Jason repeated.

In response, she flashed the light beam directly in his face, blinding him. "Yes, I'm down here chasing a rat."

"Oh, well, let it go. There're traps around the store for that. You need to get back upstairs. We're not supposed to leave the security office unattended." Jason's voice indicated boredom rather than chastisement.

Cass reluctantly left the chase and climbed the stairway slowly back to the office.

"I didn't leave the office unattended, by the way. Where's Phil? He was here when I left to go to the ladies' room."

Jason yawned as he scrolled through his social media account. "Oh, Phil got called home. His daughter had another night terror and I guess his girlfriend couldn't handle it by herself."

Cass loaded another training video into the computer queue. She wondered how many more hours of training were required, and if there was something she could do to make the time pass more quickly. This video focused on the electrical grid configuration in the megastore, what to do in case of a power outage, and location of the exits. Now here was a video Cass found fascinating. When she was doing B & Es, she studied electrical grids so she could bypass alarms and turn off power. The adrenaline began to flow once more.

"Oh my God," Jason vaulted from his seat to stand by Cass's desk. "Look at this! Someone drowned at the Capital Aquarium. It was murder. The guy was wearing concrete shoes."

Cass grabbed Jason's phone to read the story. An icy chill flooded her body. "Excuse me a minute. I need to call my sister."

Bay jumped when her cell phone rang before she had the chance to answer the detective's question.

"LuLu. Did you know there was a murder at the aquarium?" Cass sounded like she was gulping air. "Are you okay?"

"I'm at home and Detective Downing is here." Bay paused, thinking about how much to say to her. "He's filling me in on whatever details he can share about the victim."

Cass blew out an audible sigh. "I'm just glad you're home. I'm glad someone is there with you. See you in the morning." She clicked off the call before Bay could thank her for calling.

"My sister, checking in with me. She saw the news." Bay sat back down to steady her body, which became shaky during her call with Cass. She'd allowed herself to think about the third victim with emotion, and it left her reeling.

"You okay?" Downing asked.

Bay nodded. "Field trip tomorrow night? I take it we're going to Chicago to see Fabulous Fiona." Downing affirmed.

"And you're not going to take Harris? Why me?" Bay hoped she didn't sound pitiful.

"I have other things for Harris to do. You're the perfect person to come along. For one thing, you're a woman, so that will be a good balance for the conversation. And another thing, you're less skeptical about this hocus-pocus than I am."

Bay stood up, indicating she was ready for Downing to leave. "All right. I'll go. I think we both need some sleep, so I'll say good night. Thank you for checking in, Detective."

Barrett sat in darkness in his first-floor apartment. He'd just finished his third cup of tea and considered switching to something stronger to encourage sleep. His worries for LuLu and Cassandra occupied his time. He wondered how he could make himself more useful in catching the killer before it was too late. His mind turned repeatedly along the same corridor. He couldn't stand it any longer. He picked up his phone and scrolled to Venus's number.

Accounting for the time difference, it would only be around seven p.m. there.

"Good evening, Barrett," the breathless, melodic voice of Venus sang through the airwaves like a symphony.

"You sound good—happy, Vee," Barrett wondered if he could disguise his discord.

"Uh-oh, what's wrong Barry? I can hear it all the way across the ocean." Venus didn't miss a beat.

"I never could fool you. There's trouble here, Vee. The girls. I wish you'd come for a visit." The choppy sentences tumbled out.

A sharp inhalation of breath jumped through the phone. "So, Cass and LuLu are together again. There's bound to be fireworks with those two. They're adults now, Barry. They'll have to sort things out on their own."

Barrett sat in stillness, uncertain what to say, what not to say. Venus had been his rock during tough times without Penelope. She'd given his daughters something he could not give—stability. Hadn't Venus earned a life of her own after all these years?

"I can hear you thinking," she said skeptically. "Is there something else?"

"No, Vee. How are you? What are you up to?" Barrett sank back into the chair cushion and sipped his fourth cup of tea, an herbal concoction from Venus.

"I think I might stay in Kauai forever, Barry. I'm teaching

meditation and yoga on the beach. I even learned to play the ukelele thanks to Marty. He's amazing." Venus giggled in delight.

"You're the amazing one, Vee. You sound great. I'm happy for you." Barrett summoned his acting skills for the delivery.

Venus clucked softly into his ear. "There, there. Everything's going to be okay, Barry. It will sort itself out. I'll come for a visit in the summer—with Marty. You two will get along famously. Bye for now." Venus made a smoochy noise and was gone.

Barrett walked into the bedroom, lifted the pillow from the other side of the bed, and inhaled deeply. He wept into Penelope's scent. Her favorite perfume lingered on her pillow. Wild Things reminded him of her; the salty ocean breeze, fresh lemonade, and something from the forest floor. Years ago, when he'd heard the fragrance was discontinued, he sought out every bottle he could find, just to have Penelope's company.

"What should I do, Penelope? Can you help me save our daughters?" ∎

CHAPTER 18
MUDDY WATERS

When Cass arrived home from her shift, Bay was dressed for work following a long yoga session in the living room.

Seeing Bay nonchalantly holding a mug of coffee, working a word puzzle in her favorite chair caused Cass to stagger, overcome by a sudden wave of emotion. Without thinking, she went to Bay's side and put her arms around her in a tight embrace.

Bay was surprised, but even more stunned by her own reaction to hug her sister tightly in return.

Cass broke free moments later and Bay wondered if her sister was trying to read her, fishing for information or betrayal.

Cass turned her back on Bay and walked toward the bedroom. "I'm glad to see you looking fresh for the day. Can you tell me what your plan is?"

Bay smiled quizzically. "Are you trying to big sister babysit me?"

Cass folded her arms and frowned. "Like it or not, I am your sister, and nothing's going to change that fact. Maybe you could humor me."

Bay glowered. "You're on shaky ground with me, in case you've forgotten. You check in with me, not the other way around, Cassandra."

Cass stomped her foot. "Maybe we could call a truce until the murderer is caught?"

"Maybe." Bay hesitated, wanting to say something snarky but biting her words back instead. "I'll be at the office all day. I only have one more week before the new semester. After work, I'm going with Detective Downing to interview a potential informant."

"Getting pretty cozy with Detective Downing." Cass batted her eyelashes flirtatiously.

"Oh, please stop. You know the police are using me as a consultant on the case. For some reason, they think I can help because I'm a mythology professor. Between you and me, the Medusa isn't following a specific myth story. I really don't know what I'm doing, Cass."

Cass swept her gaze somewhere distant. "Don't doubt yourself, LuLu, I mean Professor. I felt something powerful in you. I can't see it, but you have answers that will solve this case. I know it."

"Aha! So, you were trying to tap into me. That was the reason for the hug." Bay pursed her lips and rose to collect her work bags. She was out the door leaving Cass behind in an emotional drift.

"That's not why I hugged you. Not at all." Cass whispered to the apartment walls.

Bay lugged her tote bags and haul from Sweet Cheeks bakery

past the reception area to her office. There was no way she planned to face a long day of reading and project preparation without the largest latte she could find with a triple shot of espresso. That, and pastries from the best bakery in town.

Once she settled in place, she returned to reception with a drink carrier and bakery bag.

"Good morning, Trevor. TGIF. Here's a coffee for you and lemon cream cheese Danish." Bay looked around the area while Trevor smiled with gratitude.

"Where's Diana? I brought her tea and a scone. I saw her drinking tea the other day."

"Oh, she called in. She won't be here today." Trevor glanced around the area to make sure there was no one within earshot. "She called Dr. McNelly. Mighty strange if you ask me. I have to notify Stasia or one of the deans if I'm not coming to work."

Bay frowned, picked up the tea and wrapped scone and paraded to McNelly's office. She charged through the door like a lioness, rapping on the desk to announce herself.

McNelly was dozing at the computer, snorted, and sat bolt upright when Bay knocked on his desk.

"Good morning, L.L. Sorry, I didn't hear you knock." McNelly's disheveled bushman appearance matched his shaggy brown sweater.

She set the tea and scone on the desk, far enough away from McNelly that he wouldn't assume it was an offering. "Diana Poulin. She called you this morning. Why?"

McNelly scratched one ear and leaned across the desk, head lowered, inviting a tête-à-tête.

"Diana was a patient of that murdered psychologist, Paul Johnson, poor fellow. She's distraught and in no condition to come to work today."

Bay gasped, disbelieving. "You're kidding! Did Diana report this to the police? Did you report this to the police?"

McNelly shook his head. "Why would I? Why would she? The therapist had many clients. You can't expect them to voluntarily call the cops to what—check in!"

Bay realized how silly her suggestion sounded. "No, of course not. I was just…I mean, a murderer on the loose is frightening. I'm just hoping that anyone who knows something will come forward to help catch them."

It seemed there was nothing else to say, so Bay rose, and slid the scone and tea across to McNelly, who produced a friendly smile at the gesture.

"I brought these for Diana, but since she isn't in today, maybe you'll enjoy them." Bay spoke crisply.

"Thank you just the same," McNelly said, "maybe you could call Diana, check in on her? I'm sure she'd like to know someone cares."

Bay wondered how she could make that call without digging for information. Could Diana be another piece of the puzzle to solving this case?

Bay scuttled to her office and shut the door, then called Downing.

"Downing," he answered without registering the caller.

"Hi. It's Professor Browning," she said tentatively. "I have information that might be useful."

"Good morning, Professor. Go ahead, shoot."

"We have a new employee in our department. Her name is Diana Poulin and she was just hired a couple of weeks ago as an officer helper." Bay swallowed a lump of anxiety. Maybe she was out of line here.

"And? Go on, Professor."

"It's just that she didn't show up to work today because she was too upset about the latest murder victim. You see, he was Diana's psychologist."

"I imagine the man had many patients. What makes this one so special?" Downing's calm demeanor coaxed Bay's hunches to the surface.

"Diana is Canadian and has an abusive stepmother. That's why she was hired. One of the professors here knew about her circumstances and that she was about to lose her financial aid to stay in college." She paused to let Downing connect the dots. "I know it's a long shot, but maybe Diana is connected to the case."

Downing searched through the Virginia Lowe file while Bay spoke. "I'm looking here but not seeing a stepdaughter by that name. There is a Diana with a different last name, listed in Montreal. This says she's a grad student at Concordia there…" He continued shuffling.

Bay felt foolish. "I'm sorry. I imagine there are plenty of wicked stepmothers in Canada." Bay laughed to lighten the mood.

"No, no. It's good information and worth a conversation at least. But I'm not going in guns blazing. If she's Johnson's patient, she's dealing with enough trauma for now." He changed subjects.

"I called Fabulous Fiona. She agreed to meet us on the north side of Chicago tonight at nine. Can I stop by at six to pick you up?"

"Yes. Thanks. I need to get back to my real job now. See you." Bay disconnected, feeling at loose ends. She gathered herself over a second coffee and blueberry lemon scone and dismissed

Diana Poulin from her mind.

Cass was surprised to see her father at the apartment door.

"Hi Sweetheart," Barrett kissed his daughter's forehead and squeezed her shoulders. "I know you need your sleep, but I was hoping to catch you before you went to bed."

Cass had changed to sleepwear and was sipping a cup of chamomile tea, slowing down her brain to prepare for sleep. "Mind if I keep the lights off and the drapes closed?"

Barrett nodded and sat down on the sofa. "Did you see your sister this morning?"

Cass nodded. "Would you like something to drink, Dad? I suppose you saw the news about the latest victim at the aquarium?"

Barrett shuddered. "I'm worried about the two of you. I know you can take care of yourself, but I'm not so sure about LuLu. I don't want to lose either one of you."

Cass sat next to her father and handed him a cup of tea. As always in her life, the spotlight of concern shined upon her younger sister. "You know, I've been thinking about these murders. If LuLu is a target, we should help any way we can."

"No, Cass. We're not going down that road. We promised." Barrett stared into the tea.

"You promised, Dad. There's no we in this story," Cass said flatly. "I've been keeping this secret for far too long. LuLu is an adult, for God's sake."

Barrett shook his head as if it was filled with bees. "No, Cass. No, no, no!"

Cass stood up. "Dad, what if the Medusa is connected to our past? It would be completely unfair not to tell LuLu the truth. Can't you see that?"

Barrett sobbed into his hands. "We can't tell her the truth. She will never forgive us. Never!"

Cass stormed out to the kitchen with her teacup and slammed it on the counter. "You're letting LuLu hold onto a fantasy about our life. Or are you trying to hold onto it, Dad? Because I'm not."

"Cass, come on. Come here please. Let's talk about this."

Cass pointed to the door. "I'm sorry. I need to go to sleep, and you need to do whatever it is you do. Please think about this, Dad. This secret was never meant to be kept. It's a lie." ∎

CHAPTER 19
THE FABULOUS FIONA

Like a gentleman coming to call, Downing picked up Bay underneath the apartment building entrance. He laughed when she climbed in the dark sedan, carrying her winter jacket.

"What's with the getup?"

Bay laughed, too. "I didn't want my professional appearance to get in the way of a good interview, so I chose something more relaxed." A floral bohemian peasant blouse flowed over wide-legged pants. The tropical colors suggested vacation, especially since Bay wore lemon yellow clogs, atypical of winter in the Midwest. A long scarf of the same blouse fabric twirled in and out of Bay's dark long ponytail.

Downing stared too long in his assessment, and she looked away.

"I think I like this new Professor Browning look. Much more carefree." He nodded, admiringly.

"Maybe those carefree days will return once the Medusa is out of commission," Bay said.

A mixture of pebbly snow and sleet splatted across the windshield on the sedan. The wipers rhythmically thrummed to fight the mixture. Bay and Downing sat in silence while the detective added their destination into the GPS. Bay concentrated on putting her gloves on, then taking them off again when she decided the car was plenty warm.

"Are you nervous, Doctor?" Downing kept his eyes on the road.

"Bay." She paused. "It's not going to be very convincing for you to introduce me as Doctor or Professor to the Fabulous Fiona. My closest colleagues call me Bay."

Downing's eyes widened and he ran one hand through his hair. "Well, this is unexpected. Where in hell did you get that out of L.L.?"

Bay took a deep breath and looked at the rivulets running down the passenger window. "My first name is Lulabay. I know, you've never heard that one before. I've had the same response my whole life. My middle name is Laurel. L.L. seemed like the best choice for a professor. Keeps people guessing."

Downing glanced sideways. "Kept me guessing, that's for sure. All right. Turnabout's fair play. Name's Bryce. Almost nobody calls me that except family or next to family. I prefer Downing."

Bay turned back to look at Downing. "Okay. Fair enough. Tell me where we're going."

Downing blinked a couple of times. This woman continued to surprise him. "Scarlett's Hidey Hole. It's off 94 on Glenwood, if you know where that is."

"Not exactly. I lived in Chicago on and off during my childhood with my aunt. She preferred the city to the burbs.

We lived off of North Halsted near Lincoln Park for a time, then on Dickens Avenue in Bucktown." Bay hadn't mentioned her Chicago life to anyone for ages, but now talking about it seemed as easy as chatting about the weather.

"Besides the Lincoln Park Zoo, Aunt Vee took us to most of the museums, outdoor concerts, and gardens. Her favorite place was the Art Institute, and it became mine, too. Her enthusiasm for art and music was contagious. She taught us how to appreciate a sonata as well as bebop or smooth jazz, and we loved that music as much as new wave." Bay stopped, lost in her memories.

"Sounds nice," Downing said. "Very eclectic."

"What about you? Where did you grow up, Detective?"

The answer was stuck somewhere inside, and Downing cleared his throat to unstick it. "Dodgeville area, on a farm."

"That must have been nice. Such beautiful countryside there." Bay prompted.

Downing stuffed his story inside, away from her, and resumed looking straight ahead where the headlights met the roadway. "It was quiet. Real quiet."

Downing tuned the radio to a classic rock station, ending the awkward conversation. Bay didn't take the gesture personally. She understood all too well how painful or confusing the past could be. She was pleasantly surprised when Downing sang along quietly with some of the tunes or kept time tapping on the steering wheel to others.

Traffic moved along at a steady pace interspersed with miles of empty roadway. More vehicles were headed north away from the city than south, until they reached the suburb exits where signs of life were abundant on a Friday night.

Downing turned off the Tri-State Tollway onto the Edens Expressway and in no time, they were on Glenwood, parking a block away from The Corner Bar. The cream brick bar faced two streets in a wedge shape, and the pair noticed the small wood-front diner tucked around the corner on the side street. A hot pink neon sign flashed "all night diner" above an antique-style sign with flourishes and curlicues. Scarlett's Hidey Hole stood out in bright red dimensional letters, looking like an ad for burlesque entertainment.

The Corner Bar was busy, a sharp contrast to the nearly vacant diner. The door jingled when Downing and Bay entered and the two spotted a single customer in a corner booth, chatting with a server. Downing and Bay scrutinized the pair and exchanged curious glances. Certainly, neither of them could be The Fabulous Fiona.

The female customer had dark hair, cropped very short, and she wore no makeup. Her clothes were ordinarily plain, a pair of faded jeans and a black rock band T-shirt. Bay guessed she was in her sixties. The server, on the other hand, was flamboyant, radiating sexuality with her tight black and red satin uniform and lacey black apron. Her hair was a mass of black curls, too perfect and shiny to be real, and her large feet were jammed into high heels covered in black sequins.

Downing gently elbowed Bay and leaned in to whisper, "I've seen that look before. I suspect this is a hangout for cross-dressers."

Bay had seen plenty of diversity in Chicago and other places in the world, so she wasn't uneasy, but the long drive made her want to get down to business.

"Which one of you is Fiona?" Bay's voice echoed loudly in

the empty space.

Both women stared at Bay and Downing, as if noticing them for the first time. The unembellished woman in the booth raised her hand.

"That's me. I'm so sorry. You must be Detective Downing and his associate." Despite her appearance, Fiona had a captivating, commanding voice. She waved them over to the booth. The server curtsied rather clumsily and dropped a couple of menus on the table.

Fiona held out both well-manicured hands in greeting across the tabletop. She grasped both of Bay's hands in hers and examined them, then looked into her eyes.

It's nice to meet you…" Fiona paused for Bay to fill in the blank.

Bay noticed Fiona's long sapphire blue fingernails, every other one adorned with a clear jewel. "Lu Browning, Ms. Fiona. The pleasure's all mine."

Something sparked in Fiona's dark eyes causing one eyebrow to twitch sideways and back again. She turned to Downing and picked up both of his hands, turning them over three times as she clasped them.

"Ah Detective Downing, you are clearly a man who loves hard work. Your work is mostly in your office, but it is the land, the outdoors, that draws you in. The land is your lifeblood."

Downing pulled his hands away but smiled leisurely at Fiona. "I imagine your work is mostly designed to trick people, convince them to believe something is real when it's not."

Fiona sat up a little straighter and pulled her shoulders back as she lifted her chin. "Do you mind if we order something? Scarlett…," she indicated the server who was sweeping behind the counter, "Scarlett doesn't appreciate squatters."

"Pardon me for saying so, but you're not what I expected. You don't look like a performer in your line of work. I thought you'd look more mystical." Bay spoke matter-of-factly.

Fiona threw her head back and laughed, displaying a large set of radiant teeth. "I'm not working right now, so I'm not in uniform. But here, let me show you how I usually dress." Fiona's cell phone showed photos of a woman wearing a long auburn wig, a crown of white and turquoise cabochons, and large glittery eyelashes. Fiona wore heavy makeup, a billowy genie-style outfit, and brocade slippers. That was more like it, Bay thought.

Scarlett arrived to take their orders, winking dramatically at Fiona when Downing ordered a foot-long hot dog, Chicago style. Bay and Fiona decided on BLTs with fries, and Bay splurged on a vanilla Coke, reminiscent of a childhood treat.

"We're looking for someone who might have taken one of your classes, Fiona. Have you heard of the Medusa Murders? Medusa did a number on a comic book creator here in the city." Downing paused to fashion his setting for questioning.

Scarlett brought drinks to the table and leaned over Fiona. "I think he's talking about the *Vengeful Venuses* creator, a real swine, if you ask me."

Fiona nodded. "You won't find a lot of sympathy for that one, but it sounds like Medusa's been busy."

Downing pushed aside the sugar and cream and took a sip of coffee. "Murder isn't exactly the flavor of the day in a community like Prairie Ridge. When I found your card stuck to the bottom of the third victim's shoe, let's just say I'm hoping for a break here."

Fiona was intrigued. "I'll help if I'm able to. Understand that I offer courses every six weeks with up to thirty students. I've had a lot of classes since the comic creator was mangled."

Bay leaned toward Fiona. "Does this mean you think it's possible one of your students is the Medusa? How could that be? Can you explain it to us?"

Conversation stopped momentarily when Scarlett slid plates of steaming food in front of them.

Fiona took a large bite of BLT followed by a few fries and washed it down with a gulp. She pushed her plate to the side and pulled a medallion from her purse. It was about double the size of a silver dollar, prismatic on both sides, silver and gold. She held it at eye level between thumb and middle finger and began to turn it from side to side.

"This disk is commonly used for hypnotism. But this little baby won't hypnotize someone all by itself. The hypnotist is the master. The medallion is just one tool used to gain access to a person's mind. Some people are easily hypnotized, and part of the trade is to be able to mark those people."

"You expect me to believe that mind control is possible, that you can make someone do something they don't want to do? Spare me, Fiona." Downing scoffed and turned away.

"That's not what I'm saying at all, Detective. I teach people to use hypnosis for their betterment, maybe to lose weight, break a bad habit, or even feel more confident. I don't teach mind control. However," she looked directly at Downing, "I can't control how my students utilize the craft."

"I said this coin is just a tool. I also teach meditation and help people discover their capacity to read others, to learn from their body language and emotions. The more you discover about someone, the more you can help them—or hurt them."

Downing shut down the discussion quickly. "Yeah, well. Can you tell me if you've had any memorable students these past months? Maybe someone who was more zealous or argumentative. Or someone manipulative, asking you questions about other ways to use hypnosis."

To her credit, Fiona grew thoughtful, then reached into her purse for a wad of folded papers. "I took the liberty of bringing along my student lists from the past year. I never forget the face that goes with each name."

She studied the list, sometimes pausing to smile at the memory of one student or another.

When she finished, she refolded the papers and tucked them away, then pulled her plate over to resume her dinner.

"I'm terribly sorry, but none of these students conjure anything strange or negative, I'm afraid. Sometimes people only see what you allow them to see. I don't need to know my students personally to teach them about hypnotism."

Bay calculated there was much more to Fiona below the surface, and wondered what she might be playing at.

"I'd appreciate it if you'd continue to think about your students and call me if anything new comes to mind." Downing handed his card across the table.

Scarlett returned to the booth offering refills. Downing asked for the check for all three of them.

Bay raised concerned eyes toward Fiona. "How on earth does Scarlett make this place go? There's nobody in here on a Friday night? Even though the bar next door is busy."

Fiona genuinely liked Bay. "Don't fret about Scarlett. This place will be packed from midnight until six in the morning, just like every other day."

When Bay raised her brows to points, Fiona added: "It's the clientele, Dearie. They come in after they've finished working the clubs for the night."

Bay understood. "I have one more question. Your business card says *super empathy*. Could you explain what that means."

Fiona's eyes sparked with some unknown pleasure yet again. "I think you might have it, Miss Lu. Being an empath means you can sense someone's feelings or mental state. You can read people, sometimes to the level of knowing what they will do or even their deepest secrets."

Bay was intrigued but doubtful. Cassandra and Aunt Venus were the empaths in the family. Not Bay.

"What a lot of malarkey," Downing mumbled into his coffee.

"For example, Detective, I know that Miss Lu here is no beatnik or free spirit. She's some kind of professional woman in disguise. And she carries a heavy burden even while trying to look carefree."

Fiona looked slyly at the two across the table. She picked up one of Bay's hands and held it between her palms. "Be careful of your sister, my dear."

Bay's hand stung with a burning tingle, and she pulled away from Fiona. "How did you know…"

Downing left the two sitting in the booth and took the check up to pay. Bay stared at Fiona, but the spell was broken.

Fiona pulled a scrap of paper from her purse, wrote something on it and slid it across to Bay.

"Phyllis Levine. That's my name. Fabulous Phyllis doesn't have the street cred Fiona carries." She laughed and patted Bay's hand. "I thought you deserved to know, especially since you let me pick your brain."

Bay grinned. "To be fair, I didn't let you. It just happened. And my name is Bay, not Lu. You deserve to know that, too."

Fiona wagged her finger under Bay's nose. "You're wrong, Bay. You let me pick your brain. Those things don't just happen. The giver has to allow the person in there." Fiona pointed to Bay's head.

Then Fiona reached back into her bag again. Grabbing Bay's hand, she placed the medallion in her palm and closed her fingers around it. "Keep it as an artifact or play with it. The detective may be a skeptic, but you have an open mind."

Bay placed the medallion in her purse while Downing was chatting with Scarlett at the register. Downing called back to Bay that it was time to go.

"It was lovely meeting you, Fiona."

Outside, the quiet street shut out the music from The Corner Bar except when the door opened to admit or expel a customer. The sky had finished its sleety tantrum and allowed the half-moon to make a milky appearance.

Bay shivered in Downing's car, her body shaking hard enough that he reached into the back seat for his extra jacket. It was fleece-lined, and she gratefully laid it across her legs like a blanket.

"Well, what did you make of Miss Fabulous?" Downing let the car idle a bit to warm the engine.

"I think she's intuitive, and I think she remembers at least one student who might use hypnotism to kill people." Bay suspected Fiona was holding something back from them, willingly or unwillingly, she wasn't sure.

"We agree on the second part, Professor. I could see it in her eyes, on her face. She came across a name that made her afraid. You know how I know that? Years of experience interrogating people. There's no hocus-pocus about that."

Bay brooded in silence for a time. She wondered where the case was going next. Had Downing already investigated Fiona? Would he attain Fiona's student lists and research them one by one? What about the drowned psychologist—was there any way his patients could be tracked and investigated? Just exactly what was she supposed to do to help? She felt trapped as the repetitive questions orbited her mind. She dozed off in retreat. ∎

CHAPTER 20
UNEXPECTED DELIVERY

Bay rose early Saturday, did a round of yoga before dawn, then dressed in winter leggings and layers to take a brisk walk through the subdivision in progress. She left Cass a note, since her sister would be home from work soon and trotted into the frosty sunrise.

The sky showed off rosy and lavender, offering Bay sensations of hope. She jogged two streets over to Magnolia Drive where a large sign boldly proclaimed "Morningside Grove, Community of Good Neighbors: Lots for Sale."

Three crows perched on the sign called out to Bay when she entered the neighborhood. She immediately noticed a gatehouse in the final stages of completion beside a bank of numbered mailboxes, sixty in all.

Bay turned her face toward the sun, welcoming its radiance, even in the freezing temperatures. She skipped the side streets for the time being to stay in the sunbeams, picking up the pace whenever she felt cold.

Finally, Magnolia wound into Crabapple Way, where Bay proceeded with the sun beside her, casting light onto the street edges. She was surprised to see a few construction workers digging a basement on one of the lots. Construction companies took the chance to work outside when possible, so temperatures in the thirties meant developers and homeowners were itching to get their projects going.

Bay waved in their direction, but the workers didn't notice her. The noise of an approaching vehicle made her turn around as she moved over toward the curb. She figured it was another construction truck, so she was startled to see a motorbike heading down the empty street.

The bike pulled up, and the rider leaned one foot on the pavement to steady it. The figure was dressed in jeans and a black jacket and wore a helmet, which he didn't remove when speaking to Bay.

"Can you direct me to Flourish College? I have a delivery to make." The voice sounded like a young man.

Bay could see an insulated carrier strapped to the bike's back. She wondered who would order delivery this early on a Saturday. She was going to the office herself that morning to lead an English department meeting.

"It's pretty early for delivery on a Saturday," Bay found herself speaking aloud. She drew a mental map with her hands pointing left, right, and straight to the college from the subdivision as she relayed directions.

Suddenly, she noticed the rider's shoes, a pair of blue and white high-top sneakers. Her eyes narrowed as she studied his helmet and spied a wayward dreadlock poking out on one side. Dumbfounded, she whispered, "Chance?", then repeated the name louder.

The rider jolted forward on the bike, revved the engine, and sped away, leaving Bay frozen in place for a flash before another vehicle pulled up beside her. Downing.

He rolled down the window. "What in the hell are you doing here walking alone?"

Bay sputtered, pointing down the street. "Chance. Go after him. There was a guy on a motorbike. He took off. He's heading to Flourish College."

Downing was trying to make sense of Bay's words, but Bay stamped her feet and kept pointing down the street. Finally, she got in the car.

"Just go that way. Go! I'll explain on the way."

By the time the two reached the end of Crabapple Way, the motorbike was out of sight. They looked over toward Magnolia, but figured the bike was out of the subdivision, so Downing headed toward Flourish.

On the ride to the college, they kept a sharp eye out for the motorbike while Bay said she was sure the bike driver was the same guy who swapped her lululemon at the dry cleaner's.

"He fit the description with the shoes and dreadlocks, and he took off the instant I called him Chance. That's the name Aria gave me at the dry cleaner's.

Downing pulled up at the entrance to the main building. "I don't suppose he said where he was delivering?"

Bay shook her head. "There can't be many people around this early besides maintenance. Maybe they ordered food."

Downing rang the night bell at the main building by the campus security office. A guard came to the door to speak to Downing.

"Security didn't order any food. The guard said there wasn't a motorbike here this morning, but delivery drivers could come in any one of the three main entrances to campus. I told him we're going to drive around and look."

Downing patted a gloved hand on Bay's arm. "Take a breath. You're pretty smart. Do you think this guy was really making a delivery to the college?"

Bay shook her head. "Why would he be driving through an empty subdivision unless he'd been following me? And for what—just to scare me? It doesn't make sense, Detective."

Bay paused, thinking, trying to steady her racing heart. "I spooked him by calling him Chance. But he must have known who I was. He just didn't expect me to know him. Still, if he wanted to hurt me, that was the perfect opportunity."

"Which is why you can't go walking there by yourself. Who is this motorbike guy? He doesn't fit the Medusa profile." Downing turned down the street where Gale Hall, the Humanities Building stood, its gray stone tower blotting out the sun.

Bay held her breath, but they didn't see the motorbike out front or in the parking lot behind.

"Maybe the motorbike guy is the Medusa's assistant." Bay doubted that was true, based on what she knew about serial killers. Still, a killer needed a hand sometimes, just for little things. "He could be the Medusa's gofer. I mean, I'm guessing Chance doesn't know the killer is a killer."

Downing grunted. "Maybe. I think the guy was supposed to deliver a message to you, but you scared him off before he could finish the job. So, be careful. I mean it, Professor."

Bay nodded her agreement. "Could you take me home, please? I have to work today, starting with a department meeting

I'm running in about an hour."

Downing dropped Bay at Windflower's entrance with another warning to stay vigilant.

Cass was asleep when Bay entered the apartment. She quietly showered and changed into professional clothes, dressing as a department chair should, she believed. The only thing she hated more than meetings was leading meetings.

She hurried to the college, barely noticing the scenery and buildings passing by. She despised being rushed and hated being thrown off her game; the events of the morning had thrown a wrench into her plans.

She looked forward to riding the elevator solo so she could take some meditative breaths, but that wasn't meant to be, and she shared the ride with the professors known as the theater bros, who were chatty as ever.

"How's it going, L.L.? When are you going to send the new office helper upstairs to our department?" Desmond Carver, the witty head of performing arts, enjoyed bantering with Bay on occasion.

Bay wasn't in the mood for banter this morning. Besides, she hadn't forgotten Desmond's absence at the hiring meeting where he was supposed to support her candidate. "You know I'm not in charge of Diana, right? As far as I'm concerned you may have her help anytime you wish." She bit off the urge to say Diana might not be there for a few days.

"Ew, someone's touchy this morning. Let me guess: you're quitting caffeine? No. You're not ready for your new classes? No wait. Stasia is driving you mad. That's got to be it." Leo Avery, the head of theater tech and Desmond's partner in most productions, was more annoying than charming. Bay didn't understand how Desmond could stand spending so much time with Leo.

Blessedly, the elevator doors opened on five, allowing Bay to escape, but not before Leo's parting shot. "God forbid, don't tell me you're giving up alcohol!"

Leo should have been an acting coach, Bay thought. She grimaced, seeing Stasia strolling past the elevator with the new English instructor, whom Bay had just met. Stasia glared at Bay in the name of decorum.

"Sorry, Dean Andino," Bay decided a fair amount of butter must be applied here. "You know what Leo Avery is like." She let the comment settle without further explanation.

"Mm-hmm. I'll be dropping in on your department meeting later, just to be sure everything is running smoothly." Stasia didn't wait for Bay's reply before moving on.

Bay flopped her daily workload on her desk with a loud ugh. She checked the time, happy to see she still had fifteen minutes to set up the meeting in the conference room. Thankfully, she'd tapped Trevor to pick up her bakery order, and he happily agreed.

Bay set meeting agenda copies and handouts around the conference room table. Besides Bay, there were six other instructors in the department; three were part-time adjuncts and three were tenured. Admittedly, Bay didn't have much competition from the tenured professors when she applied for the department chair.

Vivian Rossi was seventy and the deans were enthusiastically pushing her toward retirement. Most of Vivian's headspace was in the clouds, so poetry seemed a good fit for her instruction, and she also shared multicultural literature courses with Bay.

Vivian encouraged Bay to establish the multicultural curriculum to her preferences, while Vivian was content to go with the flow.

Simon Devane, a contented linguistics professor in his sixties, had no designs on the head position. He delighted in the studies of linguistics and rhetoric and didn't want to be bothered by administration or management. He only wanted to instruct serious English majors, so he was happy to take a part-time load.

The third tenured professor, Gerald Fendley, specialized in British literature of all periods, which filled his roster every semester. Fendley had vied for the department head post, but the deans decided on Bay, even though she'd only been teaching three years at the college level. Perhaps they wanted a woman at the helm, or maybe they thought she could be managed more easily than the opinionated pompous Gerald Fendley. Truth be told, he had sulked during Bay's first year in charge, but he came around since Bay gave him free reign in selecting his course content.

The adjunct instructors taught all the first-year students in composition and introductory literature. Bay knew two of them, but a new adjunct was coming aboard for the spring semester, which would give Bay more supervision and mentoring duties.

Ninety minutes later, the meeting was wrapping up without any fuss, making Bay breathe easier. Stasia had poked her nose in long enough to wish them a "fruitful" semester and abscond with two pastries from the treat tray.

Bay walked confidently back to her office and shut the door to work in peace. There were no messages waiting for her, so she guessed Downing had nothing new to convey. She silenced her cell phone to concentrate on finalizing her plans for the American literature course. If she had that ready to go, the rest of the week would be smooth sailing before classes started the next Monday.

Shortly past noon, Cass knocked on Bay's office door and breezed in, carrying take-out bags.

"Hey sister, I thought we could have lunch together since it's Saturday and I'm not working again until Monday night. I brought food from Chicken Salad Chick. Remember how much we liked that in the old days?" Cass's smile beamed a little too brightly to convince Bay it was real, and she wondered what her sister's motive was.

"Just give me a few minutes. I'm almost done with this document." Bay had already placed a lunch order, but figured she would share it with Cass when it arrived.

"Sure. Which way is the restroom?"

Bay pointed down the hallway toward the break room. "There's a restroom next to the break room and there's another in the back of the break room. Take your pick."

Cass left, wandered to the end of the hallway and glanced into Stasia's office, which was empty but open. She'd hoped to get a reading on the associate dean who seemed to control the department with a lot of personal demands.

She looped behind the break room to the other side of the hallway and nearly collided with Gabriel McNelly. Cass recognized him from an image Bay inadvertently communicated when Cass had brushed against her before she left for the college one day. The image was memorably negative, and Cass guessed Bay was disturbed by this man.

Cass pretended to stumble so she could bump into him, and McNelly reached out to catch her.

"Whoa there, everything okay, young lady?" McNelly applied

some charm.

Cass grew dizzy from McNelly's energy and held on tighter to keep from swooning. She needed to break away from the man, so she took a step backwards and grabbed the wall to right herself.

"Everything's fine," Cass said, breathlessly. "I just need to use the restroom. Thank you." She moved away quickly, her body leaning against the wall for support.

Cass was cognizant that Bay didn't like McNelly, and though she couldn't understand why, she felt the same. There was something duplicitous, something clandestine in the man's aura that was cringeworthy. She wondered if he meant Bay harm.

In the restroom, Cass splashed some cool water on her face and patted it with a paper towel. She closed her eyes and took a few cleansing breaths, decided that Bay must be ready for lunch by now, and opened the door to leave. As she was going out, Diana was coming in and the two collided perfectly in sync. This was Cass's second unexpected contact within minutes, and her body wasn't prepared for the reception.

The pair staggered, trancelike, and almost fell into the bank of sinks along the wall. Cass's eyes jolted open, and she tried to pry Diana's fingers from her arms, but Diana sank onto the floor like a wet rag.

Cass broke free, grabbed a paper towel, wet it with cool water, and began to pat Diana's face. *Who was she, anyway?* Cass was unnerved staring at the girl, wondering why she was familiar. Had this woman been involved in her past, maybe part of a con Cass ran?

Diana slowly came around, but Cass sprang away from her reaching hand. Instead, Cass placed a paper towel in her right hand and held it out to the girl to grab onto when she helped her up.

"I'm sorry to run into you. Are you okay?" Cass put on her best normal act.

Diana looked warily at Cass, the way a person regards a spider. "I think so. I'm sorry, too." Diana grasped the sink and hung her head forward in sudden throbbing pain. Drops of blood slid into the sink bowl from her nose.

Cass swore under her breath. "Here let me help you. I'll get some cold water." Cass ran cold water onto more paper towels. She placed a wad on the back of Diana's neck to stop the nosebleed and handed her a few more.

"Thank you. I don't know what's happening. I didn't bump my nose or hit my head. I feel very strange." Diana's eyes searched Cass's face for answers.

Cass couldn't just abandon her in the restroom, could she? "Come on. Let's take you to the break room where you can sit a while." Cass lightly touched Diana's sleeve to guide her the short walk to the break room.

"Thank you for your help. I haven't seen you in the department before. Are you new? I'm Diana, one of the office assistants." Diana sounded more clearheaded.

"Good to meet you, Diana. I don't work here. Just visiting, and I need to get going, so…should I find someone to help you?"

"No thank you. I'll just sit here a few more minutes. I'm feeling better."

Cass ducked down the hallway to Bay's office as fast as her feet would travel. When she sank in the chair, Bay turned from her computer in bewilderment.

"You look like you've seen a ghost or were running from a

mugger. What's going on, Cassandra?"

Cass stood at a crossroads, weighing how much she should share with her sister about McNelly and Diana. She decided to practice restraint until she could sort it out in her mind. She needed to decompress after an encounter, and she couldn't do that here and now.

She swallowed hard. "I ran into the new office assistant in the restroom. She had a nosebleed and seemed light-headed, so I was helping her."

Bay's eyes narrowed. "Diana? I didn't know she was in today after…" she left her thought unfinished.

"After what?" Cass leaned in like a hawk ready to pounce.

Bay flushed. "We should eat lunch, Cass. I'm famished."

Before Cass could pin down Bay, there was a short knock on the door, and Diana walked in with Bay's food order. Seeing Cass startled her, and she almost lost her footing.

Bay greeted her kindly. "Hi Diana. I'm glad you're here today. Are you feeling better?"

Diana's puzzled expression traveled from Bay to Cass and back again. "I'm not feeling all that well actually, but I know how busy it is this week, so I thought I should come in. I hope you two enjoy your lunch." With that, she backed out the door.

Bay avoided her sister's piercing eyes and chose to fuss with the food order from All Thái'd Up. The pad Thai was the best in the area, and its generous portion made it perfect for sharing. Bay opened the brown bag and frowned, then looked at the slip attached to the outside of the bag. Sure enough, her name was printed on the bag.

"Is there a problem?" Cass blinked.

"Grr. I've had this happen once before. Someone in the office decided my order looked better than theirs and switched the tags."

Bay pulled out packages of crackers and a large Styrofoam container of soup from Stu's Soups. It looked like plain Jane chicken noodle.

"Oh well, soup and sandwich it is, I guess. It's okay, Professor." At this point, Cass just wanted to get lunch over with.

Bay pulled two coffee cups from her back shelf and lifted the plastic lid to divide the soup. Steam rose from the soup, and it smelled nice, but what in the world…Bay shrieked and stood up, pushing her chair away.

"What is that?" Cass bent her head over the container and using a spoon, inelegantly retrieved a plastic male figure floating face down in the soup.

Bay laid out a napkin, and Cass set the doll face up on it. Both women stared at the doll, then each other. The plastic doll had been carefully dressed as an artist. He wore a painter's cap and held a paint brush in one hand and a pallet of paints in the other. His hair was dark, and he had a beard and mustache.

Both women felt their skin crawl, but for different reasons. Bay vaulted around the desk and out the door to question Diana and Trevor, who were both eating in the break room.

"You two. Were you out there when the food arrived?"

Trevor nodded while Diana looked blank.

Bay looked around the break room for other deliveries, but they'd likely been taken directly to their offices. "I ordered from the Thai place. Did anyone else?'

Trevor and Diana shrugged. "We didn't really look at the orders, just the names on the slips."

Bay realized that probably didn't matter anyway. "Did you

see the delivery person?"

It was common for the Fast Foodie delivery driver to congregate orders from the area and make one delivery for the sake of time and to make more money.

"It was one of the regular delivery people, Jordy. You'd probably recognize him." Trevor was patiently waiting for an explanation. "Is something wrong with your order?" He couldn't imagine Bay being this upset about a mistake in food.

"Well, I, it's just that I didn't get Thai food. I ended up with a soup order from Stu's. I thought maybe someone decided to swap." She was aware she sounded petty, and that's exactly what she didn't want. "Never mind. It must have been a mix-up on their end." Bay's brain was racing to fill in a face for Jordy the delivery driver, but she failed. She knew that everyone on their floor was supposed to be on the lookout for the motorbike man, though.

Bay retreated to her office where Cass was giving the plastic artist a thorough going over, using two plastic sporks like a pair of tongs.

"What are you doing, Cass?"

"I wanted to examine the evidence before you called the detective. I'm guessing that's the plan, right?" Cass took photos of the figure from every angle with her phone. "Something you want to tell me?"

Bay collapsed into her chair, wondering how much to say. Finally, she came clean about her morning walk in the subdivision and experience with the guy on the motorbike who must have been the same guy who paid the dry cleaner to swap her coat with a murder victim's.

"And you think this guy put the doll into your soup? You

think this guy is the Medusa?" Cass couldn't make sense of the threads.

Bay shook her head. "No, I think the motorbike guy is an errand boy and doesn't know he's helping out a killer. But the doll in the soup is an artist, and that connects back to Virginia Lowe and the notes about the Cesari or Vasari paintings. Maybe another note is waiting for me somewhere." At the thought, Bay scrutinized the paper bag inside and out. Other than her name and the register receipt for the soup, there was nothing.

Cass was lost in her own thoughts and paid little attention to Bay. She found herself teetering on the edge of a precipice, staring into a void. She seldom if ever found herself unable to see the outcome of an event, and she marveled at the realization of something unexpected. At the same time, she shuddered, encountering the darkness. ◾

CHAPTER 21
ALL THE FEELS

Bay waited for Cass to leave before reporting the floating figure to Downing.

"What?" Downing stood up at his desk and slammed his hand against it, then cursed. "Was there a note with it? A phone call? Anything in your mailbox?"

"No to all of the above." Bay felt surprisingly calm, maybe because one raving person was enough for now. "Do you want the doll?"

"Of course. You didn't get fingerprints on it, did you?"

"No. My sister fished it out with a plastic spoon onto a napkin. It's still laying on my desk, face up." Bay laughed in spite of the situation.

"You and your sister are a lot of trouble, Professor. Leave it there and I'll come fetch it."

Bay barely refocused her attention to her reading material when a quiet rap on the door interrupted her. Not enough time had passed for Downing to arrive.

"Come in," she said a little testily.

Jen Yoo peeked warily around the edge of the door. "Am I interrupting? Sorry. I just wanted to check in to see how you're doing." Jen abruptly changed courses. "What in the world is that?" She pointed to the plastic artist.

"That," Bay poked her finger toward the doll, "was in my lunch order, floating in my soup. Soup I didn't even order, mind you."

Jen squinted and bent her face over the tiny figure. "What does it mean? Did it come with a message?"

"That was the message, I guess. I can't be sure what it means, but it's an artist, so either it's connected to the murdered art dealer, or an artist is going to be the next victim." No sooner did she say the words than she clasped her hand over her mouth.

Jen gasped. "An artist! You don't suppose the killer is coming after me? Maybe I know too much."

Bay inwardly chided herself for speaking out of turn. "No, I don't think you're in any danger, Jen. I'm sorry I said that."

Jen stood up to leave. "Just the same, when I'm done here today, I'm going to the gym for a kickboxing refresher." She spun around to face Bay, jabbing her pointer finger in the air. "And if I were you, Bay, I'd get to the gym, too." Jen crossed her arms over her chest in a hug sign and left.

A while later, Downing paraded through the door without knocking, causing Bay to jump out of her seat.

"You toad! Haven't you heard of knocking on a closed door?" Bay yelped.

Downing looked offended, then laughed heartily. "Toad? Is that the best you could come up with?"

Bay frowned. "Look, Downing, as an English professor, I

express myself in an array of vocabulary choices. Any oaf can swear. I like to borrow from Shakespeare or elsewhere." She lifted her chin in false haughtiness.

Downing shook his head, donned a pair of latex gloves, and sat across the desk. "So, this is the soup du jour, huh?" He smiled as he turned the plastic figure to examine it. "I don't see anything cryptic on it, but it's going into evidence, and we'll print it. I doubt we'll get any prints though."

"Is there any other news on the case?" Was it wrong to be hopeful, she wondered?

Downing removed the gloves and sat back. "There's no break, if that's what you're asking."

Bay could see she'd have to bait the hook today if she was going to catch anything. "What's your theory about the drowned psychologist? How do you think he got into the tank wearing cement shoes?"

Downing flashed an expression indicating he knew what she was up to but answered anyway. "Well, if you're buying what Fabulous Fiona is selling, the killer hypnotized the shrink and got him to go willingly."

Bay smirked. "But I'm guessing you know better."

"We found plaster residue on the boom's platform and the shrink's fingerprints on the platform rails. How Medusa dumped him overboard, I don't know. He'd be heavy with plaster shoes and diving apparatus."

"How big was Paul Johnson?"

"Not that big. We estimate his premortem weight at around 140 pounds. He was a short man, too, so if Medusa is taller and larger, he or she could have pushed him over the platform."

Bay remembered the prismatic medallion in her bag and

considered its mesmerizing properties. "I wouldn't rule out Fiona's methods, Detective. None of Medusa's victims appeared to fight back, so she either had their cooperation or she had an accomplice."

Downing scrunched his face. "Let's just say we're considering all the angles. I honestly don't know why Medusa bothered to use the diving tank. It seemed like a lot of fuss for only ten minutes of oxygen."

"What do you mean?"

"The aquarium's oxygen tanks are logged for minutes used when they're checked out and back in again. This tank only had 10 minutes of air, while the others had thirty minutes. If Medusa wanted to give the shrink a chance, she would have used a thirty-minute tank. I'm thinking she used ten minutes because that's the longest she needed to get away while all the attention was on the shrink."

Bay recalled Medusa's note. "'Three must drown if Time wills it.' But Paul Johnson never had a chance." Bay shuddered.

Downing handed Bay a slip of paper. "I've got to get this back to the station, and I have a couple more leads to chase down today." He nodded toward the slip of paper. "I hope you don't have plans for tomorrow."

Bay read the paper: Meet Mandy, noon, at the Pig Squeal. "What's this about?"

"Mandy's offered to teach you self-defense moves. It's a good idea, don't you think, Bay?"

Bay had mixed emotions. Taking lessons from Mandy was an excellent idea. A woman would know exactly how and where to hit. She was put off, however, by Downing's sneaky methods, setting up lessons behind her back, then calling her by her given name to get his way.

"I'll go but hold up a minute." Bay opened her closet and presented a foil bag to Downing. He took it gingerly as if it might bite him.

"This is a special tea blend made by my aunt. It's good for digestion and heartburn." Bay smiled.

Downing's lopsided grin conveyed uncertainty. "I guess no good deed goes unpunished, huh?" He swung the bag of tea in the air and left.

Sunday morning dawned a glorious array of gold and pink sky accompanied by temperatures that made Bay itching to be outside walking away her troubles. She was dressed in layers and about to make her escape after filling her portable water bottle when Cass emerged from her room, dressed in jogging pants and an old pair of Bay's hiking shoes.

"You're not going out the door without me, I hope," Cass announced. "Do you have another water bottle I can use?"

Bay scowled. "Walking time is my thinking time. I like the quiet."

Cass was beside her searching through cupboards for a water bottle. "So, I can be quiet. You won't even know I'm there." She located a trove of various travel bottles and selected one with a carabiner to attach to her travel pack.

Bay pointed to the nylon pack fastened around Cass's waist and laughed. "What in the world is that geeky thing for? We're not going on a ten-mile walk through the barren wasteland."

Cass wasn't offended. "I don't go anywhere without tools. We might need Band-Aids, tissues, wet wipes, a mini flashlight, pepper spray—who knows? Unlike you, I was a Girl Scout."

Bay didn't feel like arguing. "Let's get going then. We're

wasting the best part of the day. Blissful peace, lovely birds, and a glorious sunrise." She skipped out the door without looking for Cass to follow.

The empty subdivision conjured raw reminders of yesterday, so Bay crossed the street to Elfenham Park to walk along its numerous trails. She walked briskly, in part to elevate her heart rate, but also to discourage lengthy conversation with Cass.

Cass was shorter than Bay by a few inches, and she worked hard to keep pace with her. After they finished a one-mile loop, Bay stopped for water.

"Do you want to walk the yellow trail now? It's the same length, but winds uphill to a pretty view of Breezy Prairie and Token Creek to the east. It should be bathed in sunshine about now."

Cass nodded, gulped more water, and trotted beside Bay. The upward descent was gradual but uneven, and the two used tree limbs for leverage to scramble over rocks sticking through the snow cover. Halfway up the trail, their reward was worth the climb as the new sun pulsated along the surface of the prairie, making the snow cover sparkle, while the skeletal trees resembled black ebony.

"You know I haven't quite acclimated to Wisconsin winter yet. But I do see why you enjoy walking in the morning. There's something peaceful out here and the cold air makes a person feel more alive somehow." Cass was seldom philosophical when it came to nature, and Bay smiled.

"It's not Florida—that's for sure." Bay took a photo with her phone and grabbed a long drink. "Here, stand facing me, and I'll take your picture with the prairie behind you. You know, in case you ever need proof that you spend time outdoors." Bay laughed, but the irony that her sister, an indoor gal, worked for Outfitters wasn't lost on her.

"Very funny." Cass posed with a cheesy smile and peace sign fingers. "What's on your agenda today—more crime consulting?"

Bay groaned. "You had to remind me. Up here, it's easy to forget there's trouble in the world."

The other half of the yellow trail began its descent after a quarter mile of level ground.

"Actually, I'm going to take self-defense lessons from a police recruit. That and some leisure reading was what I had in mind."

Cass's eyes widened in surprise. "Good for you. You should learn some self-defense moves. Maybe I wouldn't have to worry about you so much. I'm glad you're not going into the office today." Cass said it so casually, she didn't think Bay would notice.

"Why are you glad about that?" Bay inquired suspiciously, and Cass wondered if it would always be like this between them.

"Because you've been there every day this week and could use a break. It's good for your head, you know. And, because I don't imagine there's anyone around on a Sunday." She let the comment dangle.

Bay grinned. "Well, thanks for your concern. It's a good thing I'm learning self-defense so I can take care of myself."

To shut down the conversation, Bay picked up the pace. The trail narrowed to accommodate single file walking through the packed snow. Bay's foot caught on an exposed tree root from a towering oak, which propelled her forward, tumbling down the trail. As she skidded faster, she grabbed a sapling on the trail's edge, slowing her descent enough for her to dig in her boot heels and stop.

Cass wasn't far behind, but she stayed on her feet by grabbing branches and watching the trail below her. She sat down next to Bay on a large boulder just off the path.

"Are you hurt?"

"Just my dignity." Bay rubbed her left ankle and removed the glove from her right hand where the sharp end of a stick speared her palm, leaving a small bloody hole and broken blood vessels that were already purpling.

Cass opened her pack, located a bandage and ointment, and took her sister's hand. She was surprised not to sense anything from Bay in the contact, and wondered if her perceptions were out of whack.

"This is your fault you know, Cass. If you hadn't bothered to pack all that stuff, I wouldn't have needed it, so I definitely blame you." Bay punched her sister playfully and smiled.

Cass grinned, finished her work, and they regained the trail at a slower pace all the way to level ground again. A few cars were parked at the entrance now that the community was waking up, and the pair saw a family of four carrying snowshoes toward the prairie trail leading to a large open field that skirted Token Creek.

"Have you ever been snowshoeing, Professor? I think we should try that next." Cass laughed.

Bay decided having company on her walk wasn't half bad, but she had no plans to let Cass know it. Outside the park, the graffiti painted wall stood waiting to remind Bay a killer was at large, and she was a target. The wall had been covered in a black hurricane tarp to preserve the artwork as evidence and to keep gawkers away. The tarp flapped menacingly against the bricks like a stalking vulture. Bay saw the graffiti in her mind's eye every time she looked out the window. The glaring eyes of Anubis, the mirror, the prying eye of Ra, the message of vengeance. Would she ever be able to look at the park again?

Bay packed a gym bag with everyday clothes after donning lightweight camping slacks, a T-shirt, and nonskid socks for her meeting at The Pig Squeal. She didn't own shin, arm, or wrist guards and wondered if they would be worth the investment. Right now, Bay thought any advantage that kept her alive was worth the price.

It wasn't quite noon, and the Pig Squeal appeared to be closed, but there were three vehicles in the parking lot, and Bay hoped one of them belonged to Mandy.

She walked sheepishly up to the front entrance and knocked. Nothing. She skirted to the next entrance where a large outdoor roaster was smoking what must be pork. The tantalizing smell tried to make Bay forget why she was there.

She knocked on the back door. "It's open," a raspy voice came through the window, which was open an inch or so.

Bay reluctantly walked into the kitchen area where the bouncer stood shredding pork onto a giant stone slab, then liberally dousing it with barbecue sauce. He looked up at Bay in recognition.

"Hey. Mandy's waiting for you out there. You can go that way." The bouncer indicated the door to the dining room.

"Thank you. That looks delicious, by the way."

The bouncer grunted. "Won't last long. Sunday's our busiest day. Family time, ya know."

Bay chuckled, thinking about family day at The Pig Squeal, and wondering what that must entail. She saw Mandy sitting at one of the tables, strapping on shin guards. Mandy waved.

"I'm so glad you decided to take me up on my offer,

Dr. Browning."

"It's Bay, please, no Dr. stuff, Mandy." Bay looked at the shin guards then at the table where a pair of arm guards lay waiting.

"I'm sorry, I don't have any guards to wear," Bay apologized.

"No worries. I'm the one getting beat up today, not you." Mandy winked. "Come on. Follow me to the dungeon."

At the back end of the dining hall, beyond the restrooms, a door emerged which revealed a staircase to a basement, otherwise known as the dungeon. Mandy hit the lights at the top of the stairs and a huge gym was illuminated below.

"This is one of the bonuses to having our own place. The police held fundraisers to remodel and equip this for specialized training and privacy during workouts. The floor was padded, and weights, bikes, tread mills, steppers and more took up the perimeter. There was even a small boxing ring and a variety of punching bags—one resembled a human body.

"This is amazing," Bay blew out a whoosh of air. "The force must have very successful fundraisers."

Mandy spun around to face Bay. "We do, but you should know that half of all the money we raise goes back to the community for something Prairie Ridge needs. The money helps families, schools, parks, the hospital and more. This place, though, is our haven and we keep it going without any help from the city."

Bay understood Mandy's sober speech. The police didn't want an outsider to get any negative ideas about them. There was enough of that in the public already. The Prairie Ridge force went above and beyond to give back to the community.

"Okay. Let's get to work. You need to be a badass, Bay, and I'm going to show you the most common ways women are attacked and the most effective ways to fight back. You won't need a gun or knife. Your body will be your best defense." Suddenly Mandy transformed from sweet server to savage warrior.

She instructed Bay how to focus on the most vulnerable areas on an attacker's body: eyes, nose, throat and yes, between the legs. "The groin is easily injured no matter the attacker's gender," Mandy explained, "it's a series of small muscles between the lower abdomen and thigh. You don't have to aim for the pubic bone or scrotum to disable someone."

Bay tried her best to hide her amusement at Mandy's statement. She closed her eyes and channeled the inner warrior she summoned during yoga practice, and warmed up her muscles with squats, punches, and kicks in the air before Mandy deemed she was ready to land some real punches.

Mandy demonstrated how to use car keys in your fist and make hammer strikes on an attacker. "Aim for the face, especially the eyes, nose, and throat for the most impact. Here, you try it on the dummy, holding your keys outward through your fist."

Bay felt immediate satisfaction as she thrust her right fist into the dummy's face. Already, the tension she'd been carrying was finding release.

"Good job, but try to thrust downward for the most force. You're tall enough, luckily, so you can match up with many assailants."

Bay practiced again and again, feeling more powerful with each focused thrust.

"Another way you can use your keys is to hang them from a lanyard and swing them overhand like you're throwing a stick or a dart at a target. You have plenty of keys, so you could always divide yours into two weapons. Or go buy some more." Mandy went to her gym bag and produced a set of 20 or more keys hanging from a rawhide lanyard.

"Impressive, Mandy."

Mandy smiled deviously. "And, once you're good at kicking ass, you can use the rawhide to do even more damage."

After several rounds of swinging Mandy's heavy lanyard at her substitute attacker, Bay stopped for a water break. Sweat was dripping from every pore.

Mandy nodded, satisfied at her student's progress. "After you take a breather, let's work on groin kicks. I'll demonstrate and then you can try it."

Bay watched Mandy's slick movements as she centered her body, drove her knee forward, then extended her leg thrusting full throttle into the dummy's groin. She repeated the move a few more times, then gestured for Bay to try.

Bay was a little off balance the first three tries, but then found her footing to deliver a solid blow to the dummy's vulnerable area.

Mandy smiled. "Good for your first practice. Remember that you have to face your attacker to make this work, and that can be intimidating. If the assailant is too close to you, just drive your knee upward as hard as you can. It's going to take some self-talk to find your courage. Just keep telling yourself that you're in charge, that you're not the victim."

Bay practiced a few more well-placed kicks before Mandy stopped her.

"I want you to perform some kicks on me now. I'm going to gear up."

Bay hesitated, shaking her head in doubt, but Mandy insisted she could take anything Bay dished out. Bay landed two perfect kicks out of eight.

"That's enough for today. You're in shape, but you'll be sore tomorrow. Let's meet again; how about the day after tomorrow? Practice is the name of the game."

Bay high-fived Mandy. "Thank you so much for this. You're an amazing mentor. I can't wait to see you on the force."

While Bay was occupied at The Pig Squeal's underbelly, Cassandra conducted a mission of her own. She took a bus to Flourish College and dusted off her breaking and entering skills at Gale Hall, the humanities building.

Cass thought she might have to skirt around people since classes would be starting in a week, but it appeared everyone was willing to take Sunday off to regroup, and the campus was empty. She avoided the only security station in operation by trekking through the wooded area that led to the large dumpsters behind Humanities.

Dressed in camo pants and jacket she'd purchased with her discount from Outfitters, Cass pulled her climbing gear from her backpack. The climbing gear was another work purchase and now her secret stash of gate money was nearly gone.

After attaching the harness, Cass chalked her hands and began the ascent straight up the building. She moved two floors initially, then one floor at a time, gripping the back window ledges as she climbed. Her aim was the rooftop which should provide the easiest break-in access. Rooftop doors typically had one or two locks to break through, and they were often outdated.

She paused on the roof to survey her surroundings. She didn't see anyone or any vehicles either, so she proceeded to the first of two doors providing roof access.

Cass produced a foxy smile of pleasure. She loved the view from the top, but more importantly, she loved the freedom and control she experienced from sneaking into places. The door was padlocked, too simple to present any challenge. Cass carried a set of dental tools she'd found in Bay's bathroom, finding success with her first choice in springing the lock pin.

She scampered back to the side of the roof, pulled up her climbing gear, and dumped everything in a heap. The door opened with a groan and Cass squatted on her haunches to avoid being on camera. She duckwalked down the first flight of stairs to the sixth-floor door where no cameras were mounted. She pushed on the door and proceeded to the elevator.

Cass held her breath, listening for any alarms, as the elevator descended to the fifth floor. The door opened onto a dark reception area and two main hallways, illuminated by red exit signs. Staying close to the wall, she crept past reception to the far hallway where Bay's office was located.

"Office doors are a cinch to open," Cass scolded the lock for giving way in one small turn of the pick. "Guess I'll leave the light off. Better safe than sorry."

Cass pulled the blinds open on the wide window that overlooked one of the campus green spaces. Of course, that space was nothing but white mixed with dirty mounds of old snow, and bare trees.

She closed her eyes and turned away from the window. She took a deep breath which heightened her senses. First, she smelled leather and wood polish. A quarter turn and there was the slightly stagnant smell of industrial carpeting. After another quarter turn, her nose picked up a mixture of earth, whiskey, dry leaves, and honey which belonged to Bay's favorite candle.

A whiff of coffee brushed her senses, probably a used mug or cardboard cup in the trash. One final spin put a painting in view. It sent her nostrils flaring with the assault of paint. She could see the brushstrokes teeming with emotions and the scent of thick acrylics as if they'd been stroked on canvas just yesterday. It was enough.

Cass opened her eyes and sat in Bay's chair to reclaim her calm. She gingerly crept to the wall where the unforgettable painting hung. Bay had insisted it was her treasure, a remnant of the perfect Penelope, their mother. *Poor Bay, my poor sister,* Cass thought.

Before she dared to touch the painting, she snapped a photo of it with her phone, then stood on tiptoe to remove the canvas from the wall and laid it on Bay's desk. Standing over it with her eyes closed, Cass touched the painted images which were braille under her fingers.

Cass recited aloud what she saw under her fingers. "There are two children standing on the shore. The one on the left is a dark-haired beauty wearing a crown of laurel leaves. I can smell the herbal bay leaves, even though they are a lie. The girl on the right is golden haired, crowned by the moon in all its phases. I smell the cold deception of the moon." Her fingers went numb.

"Both girls are bathed in radiant light coming from the top of the painting, and now I can feel their tears, hard frozen drops on their faces, as the beauties gaze at the swan sailing away from them. The pure white swan wears Penelope's golden eyes, eyes that can only look ahead at the river's path." Cass could feel the downy feathers under her fingers but pulled them away quickly in the searing heat. The swan sailed into a current of inescapable flames. Indeed, Cass smelled the char of feathers that had already blackened at the tips.

In the bottom corner, she felt the signature of the artist, pulled her hand away, and wept in despair. She emptied her eyes and heart and repeated the journey through the painting. Painful as it was, she did it for Bay. She did it because they must find the Medusa and she believed the canvas was a map to the killer.

Cass made one new discovery on her second trip around the canvas. Something reminded her of her encounter with Diana. "I think it's time to look at Diana's personnel file," Cass whispered.

She played a child's game of "icka bicka soda cracker" wondering which office housed the files. She doubts they're in the main reception area because of their confidential nature. That leaves the three deans' offices.

She decided on Stasia Andino's, which was just as easily unlocked as Bay's. Cass's senses were muddled by the trinkets adorning every nook and cranny, like a strange Turkish bazaar. She plugged her nose and headed to the file cabinet, also locked.

Cass laughed when she opened the top desk drawer, her fingers clutching the key to the cabinet. "People always leave the cabinet keys close by." The top drawer contained administrative files associated with finances. The second drawer was a winner, loaded with personnel records in alphabetical order, except Cass can't remember Diana's last name.

There was only one Diana. Diana Poulin. Cass pulled out the slim folder. Diana Poulin was born in Montreal on May 12, 1998. Cass paused to consider Diana's age, a bit old for a college sophomore. Diana's college transcript indicates she's been at Flourish for a year on a student visa, having transferred from an online college in Montreal. Her major is listed as criminal justice.

Cass grasped Diana's application for office assistant in both hands and closed her eyes. She was immediately barraged by unbearable emotions that she could not sort out. She dropped the paper as if it were coated in acid. Enough for one day. ∎

CHAPTER 22
PLAYING HOOKY

Bay returned to her office Monday and settled into a familiar routine that made her believe everything was normal. She had a delightful conversation with the new hire, Meg Wegman, a semi-retired transplant from Indianapolis, who shared the same teaching values as Bay. It appeared they would mesh well together. Stasia was tied up in meetings all day with the two head deans and the provost, so Bay felt free to wade through her books and projects at her leisure.

Before noon, her phone jangled the Darth Vader theme that she'd assigned to Detective Downing.

"I knew it was too good to be true that I'd have a whole day to myself." Bay hoped she sounded annoyed enough.

"Good morning to you, too, princess." Without skipping a beat, Downing added, "there's been a break in the case."

The line went silent. "Wait, don't hang up on me. What's going on?"

Downing let out a quick laugh. "We found the guy we've

been calling Chance. He works for Eats and Runs, one of the food delivery services."

Bay began to sputter with a series of half-asked questions.

"Simmer down, Professor. Before you get too excited, Chance doesn't know much. He admitted to being an errand boy for a female he met at The Gizmo, that gaming café on Madison's east side. He said they always met at the café to exchange the errand for money, and she always wore a dark hoodie that hid her face. He thinks she has dark hair and might be around twenty."

Bay groaned. "You called it a break in the case, Downing."

"Well, we got one of the players out of the game. Chance is going to cop a plea, so he doesn't go away for a long time as an accessory to murder. He's cooperating and might even go undercover if the female wants another favor. It's half a loaf, Professor."

Bay conceded his point. "I had a wonderful self-defense lesson with Mandy yesterday. So, thank you for suggesting it. I'm going back tomorrow night for another round."

"Glad to hear it. It's never a bad idea for women to know how to protect themselves, especially in the world we live in." He sighed heavily.

"What is it? There's something more, isn't there?" Bay felt the fluttery return of nausea. Had there been another victim?

"I hesitate to tell you, because it hasn't produced any fruit yet, but the psychiatrist who viewed the tape of Virginia Lowe's stepson agrees with me and you. She's certain he was abused by the uncle, maybe even by Virginia. Anyway, she's flying out to California to meet with him, and he's agreed to speak with a police liaison at the same time."

"What do you hope to find out?" Bay remembered the

stepson had a solid alibi for Virginia's murder.

"It's a long shot, but maybe he can tell us the names of the two stepchildren we can't locate. We're trying to see if the New York husband might know, too. But everything gets filtered through his attorney. And then there're the authorities in Canada—another slower than molasses operation." All of the red tape made Downing disagreeable.

He changed the subject. "How about grabbing a bite at The Pig Squeal after your self-defense session? Gotta eat, right?"

Bay couldn't argue with that logic. "My session's at five, so let's make it six-thirty?"

Downing's call came at a good time. Bay needed a break and considered ordering lunch. Then thoughts of a doll swimming in her soup loomed large in her mind. What she needed was a brisk walk across campus to the coffee shop.

She donned her coat and collided with Jen Yoo as soon as she opened the office door.

Jen grabbed her hand, tugging hard.

"Come with me, Bay. I have to show you something."

Jen wore her winter coat, too, and she pulled Bay toward the elevator, entered, and pushed the ground floor button.

"Are you going to tell me where we're going, Jen?" Bay slid her cell phone into her purse after pulling away from Jen's grip.

"We're going to the Luxe Art Museum. The new exhibit is being unveiled next week, but faculty are allowed to take a sneak peek." Jen's pitch was higher than normal, and she grabbed Bay's arm when the elevator door opened.

"Why do I get the feeling you've already seen the exhibit?"

Jen didn't answer and Bay had to trot at a fast pace to keep up with her. It only took a few minutes, and they were entering the ornate double doors of the Luxe. The Atrium stood regally at one end of the entrance hall where it was already being set up for the faculty spring semester potluck on Saturday.

The special exhibit hall was located on the second floor, overlooking the Atrium. Exhibits changed each semester and Bay wondered if Jen had collaborated on this one.

As if reading her mind, Jen filled in the blanks. "I worked on the last special exhibition of Asian art from the pre-classical through the neo-classical periods, so I wasn't involved in this one."

Bay and Jen created a duet of sharp staccato footfalls up the marble staircase to the exhibit hall. Bay paused to read the entrance sign: Special Mannerist Exhibit sponsored by Victor and Deirdre Vogel with the assistance of Dean Pamela Foyt and Art Department Co-Chair Danita Smits. Bay gasped sharply as her brain processed the word *Mannerist*.

Jen grabbed her hand again and pulled her swiftly past many pieces of artwork and around a corner where a wall emerged with three stunning paintings on display.

Jen pointed to the first painting, *Diana and Actaeon*, by Giuseppe Cesari, circa 1602–1603, Arpino. Before Bay could move in for a closer look, Jen held her back.

"Wait, look at the center painting. It's Giorgio Vasari's *Allegory of Justice and Truth*."

Bay immediately recalled the painting of Justice crowning Truth with a laurel wreath. Truth held two doves of innocence and she leaned on an ostrich. The painting was a reminder of the graffiti mural, Anubis holding the ostrich feather, the note with Virginia Lowe's body saying the truth cannot be hidden, and the riddle Bay had received in her office. The same riddle found pinned on the comic creator. She began to feel dizzy, but Jen pulled on her sleeve and brought her back to the present.

"Look at the third painting. It's called *An Allegory of Truth and Time* by Annibale Carracci." Jen pointed out the main figures. "See, there is Truth holding a mirror, with Father Time having just helped her from the depths of the well out of which he climbs. Truth radiates light while this figure, two-faced Deceit, is trampled under her feet."

Bay stared at the painting. Could this piece of art be another clue to the murders? "Jen, do you think Virginia Lowe was meeting with the Vogels to coordinate part of this exhibit? And, who else knew that Virginia would be in Madison?"

Jen shrugged. "I can ask Danita since she worked on the project. But paintings like these are requested for exhibit months or more in advance. Anything the Vogels held in their private collection might be easily offered for display, but these paintings came from all over the world."

Bay mechanically snapped photos of the paintings with her cell phone, lost in a haze of shock and fear. The contents of the notes mingled with the mural and paintings into a mosh pit of turmoil and confusion. Her pulse raced at a thunderous beat, blocking out all other sounds. Jen caught her as she began to crumple to the floor.

Jen held onto Bay as she dug into her purse, happy when her fingers found the small bottle of an essential blend she kept on hand for clarity. The oil was Jen's go-to revival after hours staring at a computer screen or paperwork. She sat on the cool tile floor with Bay lying at her feet, opened the bottle, and gently waved it under Bay's nose, then applied a drop to her forehead. Bay began to stir, then slowly sat up with Jen's help.

"For a minute I thought you were my Aunt Venus. The scent reminds me of her. What happened to me?" Bay didn't remember fainting, in fact, she couldn't recall ever fainting in her life.

Jen helped Bay to her feet. "One minute you were staring at the paintings, then you became dizzy and pale as a ghost before crumpling to the floor. Well, I did catch you before you landed."

"Thanks, Jen." Bay applied a couple more drops of the oil blend to her temples and one under her nostrils as Jen instructed.

"It's my mother's recommended cure-all. A blend of rosemary, peppermint, and frankincense. I admit, it's helped me out any time I'm fatigued from the kind of work we do. It was all I could think of to do." Jen raised concerned eyes toward Bay. "Are you sure you're going to be up for teaching the first week of classes? Maybe you should take some time away, Bay."

Bay was shocked at the suggestion and adamant as well. "I can't take time off now, Jen. I'm the department chair. How would that look?" She softened. "But thank you for helping me. You're a good friend." Bay patted Jen's hand.

Jen grabbed Bay's hand and searched her face. "I'm truly worried about you, about your safety." She swallowed a hard lump of emotion. "I'm sorry to say this, but I'd be terrified if I were in your shoes. What are you going to do? Are the police giving you protection?" Jen stopped her rant, thinking she sounded more like her mother than ever.

Bay smiled weakly, happy to have someone she could consider a true friend. "What I'm going to do, I guess, is keep on keepin' on. I can't let this control my life, which it sort of is." She tilted her chin defiantly. "I am taking self-defense lessons, though."

Jen's smile was thin at best. "Good for you. You may need them. Come on, let's get back to our offices. You need to call the detective with your latest report. But first, we're stopping at the campus coffee shop. When's the last time you ate something?"

The egg salad cucumber sandwich on sprouted grain bread hit the spot. Bay resisted adding another caffeinated drink to her already struggling body and opted for an iced herbal tea. Jen insisted they sit at a table to eat instead of racing back to the office where they would gobble their food in a hot minute.

"Are you going to the faculty potluck Saturday night?" Jen tried to normalize the conversation.

"Yes, I plan to. Are you going?" Bay picked a honeydew melon chunk from the fruit bowl Jen set in the middle of the table to share.

"I wouldn't miss it." Jen's face said otherwise. "I'm expected to be there. Dean Pamela said all the department heads should be there to set a good example for the lower-level faculty. I just hate those social hoo-has."

Bay laughed at Jen's word choice. "When did the dean say that?" Bay couldn't remember and she wondered if she'd been missing other vital information since a crazy killer had taken over her life.

"At the faculty meeting last week. You were there." Jen's concern was back on display.

"Oh right. Well, there was a lot said at that meeting." Bay remembered her mind was wandering while the deans droned on. "Let's plan to meet there and make fun of the faculty members we don't like."

Jen's stern expression quickly melted into a chuckle. "Deal. But you know we have to mingle with our department people, too."

Lunch revived Bay's spirits, so she wasn't looking forward to calling Downing with her latest report. The last thing she needed was another reminder about the danger she might be in from the Medusa, but she knew she had to call him. Any detail might lead to an arrest, ending the nightmare.

"Doctor Browning, I presume. Do you miss me already?" Downing seemed less somber than normal.

Bay relayed the information about the Mannerist exhibit at the Luxe, including the name of the painting that comprised the trio. "It could be a coincidence." Bay was weary of it all.

"Professor, neither one of us believes in coincidences at this point. I'll drive down to look at the paintings myself and compare them to my notes. And you—well you be careful."

Bay nodded absently on her end. "You should know, Detective, that our department is hosting a potluck party Saturday night as a kickoff to the spring semester. It's going to be in the Atrium at the Luxe, right below the special exhibit wing."

There was that signature Downing sigh of exasperation. "And I suppose you're going to this party?"

"I have to. The deans require department chairs to be there. We're expected to mingle with our faculty members."

"Hmmm. Can you bring a date?"

"Sorry, but I'm taken. I'm going with Jen Yoo, the art history chair." Bay disconnected.

The afternoon passed all too slowly. Bay's mind often wandered off the pages of the book she was reading, and at one point, she face-planted into its fragrant depths. Instead of jolting back to reality, the heady scent of vanilla and the woods in autumn gifted her a temporary daydream of playing in the old library with Cass. Aunt Venus, Barrett, and Penelope regularly took the sisters to used-book shops and libraries, which all carried the same addictive smell.

Bay was only halfway out of her reverie when a devious idea sprang to life. She looked at the time. "Bodkins," she mumbled the Shakespearian oath. It was three o'clock, and Cass had probably punched in at work. She was on second shift this week. Still, she sent her a text.

Do you have a dinner break?

Cass answered immediately. *Yes at 7. ?*

Are you up for a mission?

Yes.

In their childhood, Bay and Cass excelled at making up secret missions, calling themselves the "Sly Spies." Bay was Harriet the Spy from her favorite book, but naturally Cass had to be someone more sophisticated, calling herself Jane Bond. With all the unsupervised time around their father, the girls listened in on adult conversations not meant for children and wandered around the streets of many foreign cities looking for mysteries to solve.

Bay hoped she could recreate the devil-may-care approach tonight at The Gizmo. She was tired of waiting for Medusa to find her. Tonight, she would be the hunter. ∎

CHAPTER 23
A MOMENT OF TRUTH

Bay dressed in Morticia Adams black, complete with the knee length lululemon and a black knitted cap. She brought a matching black cap, a long black coat, and black boots for Cass, all purchased at the local thrift store on her way home.

Cass waited by the back entrance of Outfitters for Bay. "What are you wearing, may I ask?"

Bay smiled slyly. "Come on. You only have an hour, right? Put these on." Bay tossed a plastic bag at Cass, then pointed at the floor. "Black boots, too. We're going hunting."

Cass smiled like the Cheshire cat with a belly full of cream. "You are going to fill me in, right?"

"We're going to a gaming café called The Gizmo. The Medusa hangs out there. Maybe tonight we'll be able to find her." Bay provided a quick update that Chance, the errand boy, had been nabbed, and that he received his orders from a hooded female who hangs out at The Gizmo.

"Wait a minute, Sister. You think that I might get a vibe from someone there? Is that the plan?"

Bay couldn't tell if Cass relished the risk or was provoked by Bay's audacity.

"Well," she said, faltering. "It was an impulsive plan, but yes. I thought we could keep our eyes and ears open. And, well you could keep a channel open?"

Cass laughed. "I can tell you're rusty at the spy game, but sure, why not. Do you know anything about gaming?"

Bay didn't. "I haven't played anything but the Sims. Is that still a happening thing?"

Cass laughed. "It is, but not at this café. You're going to have to follow my lead." Cass tucked her hair underneath the knit cap, and Bay followed suit.

Bay was relieved that Cass agreed to play along, and she hoped the adrenaline pumping through her system would hold out for the next hour.

The Gizmo was a dimly lit space with rows of tables and computer screens, each positioned with a futuristic designed office chair in brilliant orange. A large digital screen separated competing teams at two of the six-player set ups. Red vinyl couches lined one wall with slim individual stands holding screens and slots for controllers.

Bay saw four people using VR headsets, standing on an electronic game platform. A few more people sat playing games in individual booths. All of them wore dark hoodies. A couple of them even wore blue hospital face masks.

"What is this, a hoodie con?" Bay whispered lightly, trying to make a sad joke.

"Lots of gamers relish their privacy. Stick with me and let me do the talking." Cass wore the expression of a coyote on the prowl.

Two teens manned the front counter, checking people in, taking money, and handing out gaming equipment. Bay noticed neither of them wore hoodies, but both looked to be all of twelve years old.

"What can I do for you two?" the acne-coated teen with bright yellow bristly hair asked.

"What's the group game tonight, and can we get in on it?" Cass used an exaggerated questioning teen voice.

"*Epic Clash* starts in five. Do you both want in?" The teen couldn't meet Cassandra's intimidating stare down.

Bay telegraphed a firm no to her sister. She didn't want in. She wanted to watch and wander around.

"Just me. My friend likes to watch." Cass snickered, making the teen blush. He handed Cass a headset, charged her ten bucks, and directed her to seat number three.

"Hey, you have to buy something if you want to hang out in here," the teen squawked at Bay, his voice cascading from a deep baritone to soprano.

Poor Mason, thought Bay, reading his nametag. *I remember those awkward days.* "I'll have a large Coke, Mason," Bay tried to mimic the vocals of an irritated teenage girl.

Bay did an initial walk-through using the slinky casual stroll of a teen on the lookout for a potential hookup. At least she hoped that's what she looked like. At first, she tried to appear invisible so she could study the patrons, but that tack didn't work. Most of them stared outward from the depth of their hoods, sizing her up.

She turned toward the front window, pulled her cap down further to conceal more of her features, and donned a pair of sunglasses from her bag. Maybe now nobody would know where she was looking at least. *But how will I recognize Medusa if she's here? What does a serial killer look like, anyway?*

Minutes later Cass cleared her throat loudly, her head raised in Bay's direction. Once Cass got her attention, she strolled over to their game table. It turned out observing a dim room filled with darkly clad people wasn't the best plan when one wore sunglasses, so Bay removed them and slid them into her coat pocket.

The *Epic Clash* opening graphics lit up the screen, and each player logged in with one of six assigned roles: alpha, beta, gamma, delta, kappa, or omega. In the third player seat, Cass was automatically the gamma player. Her gaming name was Oracle500, and Bay wondered if her sister played games before or during prison.

Bay guessed the alpha player was team leader on either side of the competition, and it appeared the omega player held special powers in the game. A private chat was open on the side of the screen for communicating between players, and Bay could already see that Cass was trying to feel out the others.

Bay felt like she was lurking and that it might draw attention, so she pulled a stool away from another game console and placed it behind Cass, far enough away from her personal space, but close enough to scrutinize the game play.

Players noticed Cass was making newbie errors on her turns and called her out. *Oracle, you gotta talk to that NPC you just walked past.* That message came from Bucksnort BB, the alpha.

Cass thanked Bucksnort signed with a smiley emoji before taking her player back to the NPC or nonplayer character, a stocked character in every game. On Cass's next turn, she picked up a sword and started on a dead run after a sorcerer into a cave where a cache of goodies likely awaited.

The chat lit up with a combination of corrective measures and annoyance. *Gamma, you play like my gramma,* Nightshade2, the omega player quipped. *This your first rodeo, Oracle?* chatted Cowgirl Boots, the beta player. Bucksnort BB was back with a gentle reminder to *take the longer path, gamma.*

Cass knew gaming etiquette but hoped she could draw out the Medusa, so she had to look like a noob who didn't know better. She chatted an apology to the team and retraced her steps from the cave back through a murky marsh where danger lurked at every turn. Every time Cass was able to earn a new weapon or learn a skill, Bucksnort BB high-fived her game play.

Bay sucked the last of her Coke and checked the time. Thirty minutes had passed like a flash of lightning, and Bay feared Cass wasn't going to make it back to Outfitters before her break ended. She lifted Cass's headset and whispered. "How long does this game go on? What about your job?"

Cass shoved Bay's head away and snapped her headset back in place. Hands on hips, Bay glared at her sister. "Okay then. Guess I'll be figuring this part out myself."

Bay trotted to the restroom, but there were three other hoods in there, so she walked out to the front of the café to place a call to Outfitters.

"Security. Did you mean to call retail? I can transfer you."

"Wait, don't hang up. It's Cassandra. I have a pounding headache, so I'm done for tonight, er ah," Bay, fake-coughed, hoping the voice on the other end would identify himself.

"It's Jason. Cass, you sound like you're losing your voice. Just get some sleep and I'll catch you tomorrow. And don't worry. I'm going to keep you clocked in until the shift is over."

Bay balked at Jason's carefree attitude toward time theft, and she was about to protest but clamped her mouth shut. Wasn't she being dishonest by pretending to be her sister, who wasn't even sick? "'Kay, thanks, Jason." She disconnected.

Bay was met with an accusatory stare from Mason when she walked back into the café, prompting her to the counter to order another drink. "Thanks, Mason. I'm trying to learn by watching, you know."

He smiled shyly, then leaned across the counter, gesturing for Bay to do the same. He spoke quietly.

"Your friend in seat three. She's being watched." Mason stared toward the game table. "Don't turn around now. The player in seat six, Nightshade Two. She's got a rep for being vicious."

"Thank you," Bay meant it. But how was she supposed to warn Cass? She smiled deviously. "You don't know my friend. She can hold her own."

Mason nodded, but his eyes held concern just the same.

Back at the gaming arena, the quest was in full swing, and Bay noticed she'd missed a lot of back-and-forth banter between both sides of the table. Cass appeared to have hit her stride and, con artist or not, Bay got the impression her sister enjoyed the thrill of the quest.

Oracle500 slashed through a briar thicket, chased down a flesh-eating Lepus, and slayed it with one stroke of an ice blade. Her teammates cheered, and her opponents knelt in mock worship. *Looks like someone's been faking on us*, came a message from Sandwich Delivery, the opposing alpha. Most players chimed in with either surprise or laughing emojis, but Nightshade2 delivered an angry emoji surrounded by flames.

Cass sat back a moment, stretched, and began typing in the

chat. *Just getting back into the arena after a long break. Anybody have any cheat codes to trade in Titans?*

The popular *Titan World* was a classic game loaded with mythological stories and figures. Cass hoped to bait the Medusa out of hiding if she was there.

Nightshade2 replied first. *Wha'dya have in mind?*

Bay bet if Medusa was there, that Nightshade2 character was pick of the litter. She worried about Cass going too far.

Oracle500 was deep in thought, too far away for Bay to reach her with any kind of sisterly vibe. Cass's hands clicked away rapidly on the keyboard. *Something to help me defeat Medusa. I lose every time in the battle royale. How do you defeat that MF?*

The chat thread lit up once again with emojis varying from shrugs to zippered lips to an exploding clown head. Nightshade2 was silent. Sandwich Delivery left their chair for a break after responding with a rage emoji and an hourglass.

Sandwich Delivery's departure was met with two more players rising to use the restroom or buy something at the café counter. Cass rose to take advantage of the break and chat with Bay. She motioned toward the front door.

"What's going on? I think I'm following most of the chat, but I don't speak gamer or whatever generation's language is driving the chat." Bay looked around as she spoke, careful to keep her voice down.

"Nightshade Two is giving me a negative vibe, Sister, but so is Sandwich Delivery. I know I've gotten under their skin, but I need to make body contact to see just how bad it is." Cass grinned slyly.

Bay sucked in her breath. "Don't do it, Cass. It's too dangerous."

Cass's nostrils flared and her eyes became slits. "Then why did we come here, LuLu?"

Bay looked at her feet. "I called you in sick for the rest of the night."

Cass laughed and punched her shoulder. "Okay, let's finish this game."

Mason and the other server were busy filling orders at the counter when Cass got into the queue to get a drink for the second half of the game. Bay headed to the restroom, her two drinks screaming for release, but was met with a line vying for the two stalls.

The tiny room was a cramped space and Bay considered waiting in the hallway, but it was blocked by two other gamers with the same purpose. Nightshade2 glared when she bumped into Bay, who was partially blocking the hand dryer. Bay answered the glare with a shrug, while her annoyed inner voice muttered a curse from Macbeth directed at the scrappy looking gamer.

After doing her business, Bay stood at the sink to splash some cool water on her face. The knit hat was hot and itchy, and she couldn't wait to get out of the café and the undercover garb she wore. *What's with these gaming types anyway? They don't even talk unless they're in the chat box.* Maybe that's why they looked so sullen; they could use some real social interaction.

Bay wiped her face and peered at herself in the mirror again. She jumped, unable to disguise her fright, when she saw the figure of Sandwich Delivery standing at the next sink. She was too close for comfort, and Bay saw it as a sign of intimidation. Bay stared back, however, unwilling to drop her eyes in deference. She could make out pale skin and large eyes caked with dark makeup, along with lips that protruded either naturally or by emotional design.

Sandwich Delivery made a guttural sound and moved to the hand dryer, her shapeless body blocking Bay's way out the door. Bay waited, then did something she would never have imagined. She pushed past the gamer, wiped her hands on the back of her hoodie, and charged out of the restroom.

Cass was standing by her console, stretching like she was warming up for a boxing match. The look on Bay's face stopped her cold.

"You look like you've seen a ghost. What's the matter?"

Bay stared somewhere into space. "I honestly don't know. Good luck, Cass. Finish strong."

Cass took a long swig of Dr. Pepper and gave Bay a thumbs-up sign, just before the fire alarm blared through the café. The exit lights illuminated more brightly than before while Mason and the other clerk stood in the center of the café directing people out the front entrance.

Bay and Cass noticed a few players left out the back door and they followed them, suspicious of their decision to slip away. Certainly, one of them must have pulled the fire alarm unless there was a real fire. Either way, the sisters didn't plan to hang around to find out. Unfortunately, the gamers had slipped away quickly, either into the shadows or, in a couple of cases, into two cars screeching out of the back lot.

The sisters trotted down the alley to the street in front of the café, hurrying to flee the scene before the fire trucks showed up. Bay slammed the car into drive as sirens whined in the distance.

Cass fired up the tea kettle in the apartment while Bay peeled off the sweat-soaked clothing and ducked into the shower. She emerged in plaid pajama pants and a solid red top and wandered into the kitchen where Cass was pouring hot water into mugs.

"Thanks. This is just what I need after drinking two Cokes. I might not come down from the moon until tomorrow with all that caffeine and sugar." Bay spotted Aunt Venus's calming tea mixture on the counter.

Cass covered the two mugs with coasters. She still had the whole black getup on except for the knitted hat, which she'd flung on the floor and Minerva had adopted as a bed. The black cat melded with the black hat, and it was difficult to determine where one began and the other one ended.

Cass was lost in thought and began to giggle, not unlike the giggle of a carefree child. She looked at her sister. "I don't know about you, but that's the most fun I've had since I got out of prison."

Bay decided to be honest, wondering if she should encourage her sister. "There was something wild about tonight, but skipping work isn't a good habit to get into, Cass. You just started that job."

Cass pouted on purpose. "I know, I know. You don't have to lecture me. But you have to admit, taking risks is like riding a giant wave across the ocean. Exhilarating." She elongated the last word.

Bay agreed. She saw Cass in a new light for the first time in their adult lives. Cass glowed and some of her youth returned to her face, especially her eyes, which were alive with light. "Thanks for coming with me."

"I wouldn't have missed it for the world. Now, I'm going to slither out of this and take a shower while the tea steeps."

Bay picked up her lululemon from the back of the chair where she'd deposited it to hang it up in her closet. The pocket bulged and she remembered stowing her sunglasses there. Her tidy nature kicked into gear, so she pulled the glasses out to return them to their case. Something fell out of the pocket with the glasses. A piece of folded paper was stuck to one of the bows.

Bay's heart thumped loudly in her chest as she unfolded the paper, expecting a note from Medusa. Ugh, she was tired of being right. She laid it on her night table and turned on the bedside lamp. The note was simple and direct: "The answer is in the mirror. Your mirror."

Instinctively, Bay opened her closet door where a full-length mirror waited. She turned on every light in the room. What was she supposed to see? She looked at herself. That was no help at all.

She swung the door around for the mirror to reveal all the pieces of the room it could. Her bed. Her dresser. The walls. The window? Wait a minute. Bay opened the blinds to look at the view. Her bedroom overlooked the landscaped walkway around the apartment complex. There was a fountain, not running since it was January, benches for sitting, and a trail that ran through a green space and exited at a strip mall. She would have to look again in daylight.

She closed the closet door, hoping to shut out the invasion she felt. How dare this Medusa killer taunt and torment her. What had she done to deserve it? She grabbed the note, began to crumple it with the notion of ripping it apart. Instead, she cried.

By now, the shower had stopped, and Cass could hear Bay sobbing on the other side of the wall.

"LuLu, what is it?" Cass barged into the room wrapped in a

towel and found her sister sitting on the floor next to the night table.

Bay pointed to the note and wiped her eyes on her sleeves. "I found it in my coat pocket with my sunglasses." Cass read the note and handed her a tissue at the same time.

Cass muttered the phrase "your mirror" repeatedly, deep in thought.

"I'm sorry, LuLu. I could sense Medusa was at the café, but I couldn't get a precise read on any one person. I think I made contact with her in the throng of people rushing from the café when the alarm went off, but I can't be sure which body was hers. Can you remember running into someone who had access to your pocket?"

Bay shrugged. "The restroom, maybe. I waited in line a few minutes and two people bumped into me by the sink. Wait a minute!" She stood up and walked around the room. "There was someone staring at me in the restroom mirror at the next sink. It was unnerving, that cold penetrating stare."

Cass pondered the detail. "Are you thinking Medusa was the person in the mirror at the café? If that's true, she had to be certain the two of you would end up standing at the mirror at the same time. I'm not sure about that."

Bay resumed pacing. "I looked in my closet mirror, but you're welcome to try it. Maybe you'll see something I don't. Meanwhile, I'm going to look in both bathroom mirrors." Bay needed to be proactive; besides she knew a call to Detective Downing was imminent and she wanted to investigate first.

Cass stayed out of Bay's space until she left each room, and the two reconvened in the kitchen where their tea was fully steeped, but cold.

Cass lifted the mugs and placed them into the microwave to reheat. "I wrote down everything that could be seen from the mirrors in all three rooms. I saw you doing that, too. Let's compare notes and drink some strong tea."

After reviewing their notes, the women added a couple of details gleaned from the other's. Bay sighed. "It's going to take time to think this over because there's nothing obvious staring at us. And, sorry to say, I need to call Downing."

"I'll keep studying the notes," Cass decided, "and I'm going to walk around the apartment again to make sure we didn't miss a mirror anywhere." Suddenly, Cass's skin crawled with the realization that Medusa must have been in the apartment. How else could she know where the mirrors were and what would be revealed? She kept that thought to herself for the moment.

Bay sat on her favorite reading chair and swiped Downing's number. She looked at the time. It was almost ten p.m.

"Professor? What's wrong?" Downing's voice held sincere concern.

"Another note for me from Medusa, Detective. I'm home if you want to come over. I doubt I'm going to sleep tonight."

"Read it to me."

Bay read the short note. Downing swore on the other end. "I don't like this. I'm coming over to get more details and the note."

Minutes later, Downing rapped quietly on the door and identified himself. Bay greeted him with a mug of calming digestive tea.

"What the hell is this stuff?" Downing barely swallowed down what he planned to spit out.

Bay laughed despite the situation. "It's a tea to help with stress and digestion. It's the same tea I gave you yesterday. Guess you haven't tried it yet."

Downing sneered. "I hate to ask, but do you have anything you can add to this to make it better?"

Cass heard the exchange from the kitchen and brought a squeeze bottle of agave nectar to the dining table. "This will help until you get used to the flavor of herbal teas." She squeezed a teaspoon full into the detective's mug.

"Better. But I doubt anyone can get used to this." He snorted.

Bay gestured for Cass to sit, then handed Downing the note, which was typed.

"Let's start at the beginning. When and where did you find this? Where have you been today, and do you remember leaving your coat unattended?" He flipped open his notebook to a fresh page and held his pen ready.

Bay hesitated, knowing the onslaught of Downing's wrath was about to be unleashed. She explained the trip to The Gizmo right down to a description of their undercover garb.

Downing turned beet red, and his face puffed up like a Macy's parade balloon about to explode. He stood up and began a stream of incoherent speech mixed with swear words Bay could pick out of the rant. He walked between the dining and living rooms, whirled around like a dervish when he met a dead end and repeated the activity. Finally, he gathered his thoughts enough to deliver a lecture.

"First of all, you completely blew my investigation. Chance, remember him? He was supposed to go there tomorrow to meet with Medusa. He agreed to wear a wire and a little camera so he could ID her at the café. What the F were you thinking? You're playing with fire, Professor." He turned and shook his finger at Cass. "And you, too. Who do you think you are—Batman and Robin?"

Cass and Bay exchanged smug expressions they hoped Downing didn't see. "I was thinking more like two Amazon warriors, Detective." Cass smiled sweetly. Bay made a cut the crap gesture at her.

"We're sorry. I'm sorry, Downing. It's sort of your fault, though. You did tell me where Medusa hangs out. I thought I could help or…" Bay trailed off. The truth was, Bay needed some kind of control over the situation, and inaction was not part of her personality.

Downing's face had cooled from flaming red to rosy. He sat back down, glared from one woman to the next, then took a couple of deep breaths.

"Let's see what we have to work with here. I want every detail of every encounter you had with anyone. I want descriptions of each person you had contact with. Any kind of contact—verbal or physical. Got it?"

Cass and Bay both mentioned the two gamers who made insulting or angry comments in the chat, Nightshade2 and Sandwich Delivery. The two, coincidentally or not, were the same people who jostled against Bay in the restroom.

The sisters fell short, however, when describing them. People in dark hoodies and baggy clothes often look alike. "The only reason I'll say both are female is because they were in the women's restroom. But you never know." Bay offered the most helpful information she could.

Downing closed his eyes and raised his empty mug to his lips, then held it out to Cass. "Got any more of this potion? My stomach suddenly seems less grumpy."

Cass took the mug and went to the kitchen, and Downing

used the opportunity to level with Bay.

"I get why you thought this was a good plan, Bay, but you don't know what you're dealing with, and you're not trained." He shushed her before she could retort. "Promise me you're not going to pull any more stunts without running them past me first."

Bay swallowed a defiant response. "I promise, but don't ever shush me again. I'm not a little kid, and I don't appreciate it." She relaxed a bit after getting that off her chest. "I am sorry if I messed up the investigation. We didn't really give you anything to go on."

Downing raised a finger and spoke gently. "Ah, but you did, Professor. If Nightshade and Sandwich are regulars at The Gizmo, the manager and clerks might know their real names. They might have purchased something on a card. They might have registered for tournaments. Other gamers there might be helpful, too."

Cass brought Downing another mug of tea laced with agave nectar. She handed him the squeeze bottle of agave. "Take this with you until you get used to drinking the tea."

Downing gave Cass a half-grin. "Just so you know, I have no reason to report any of this to your parole officer, Cassandra. That is, unless you pulled the fire alarm?"

Bay smiled in appreciation. "I think Medusa pulled the alarm to get rid of us. Maybe we were too close for comfort. And thank you for not ratting on Cass. This was all my fault. I even called her in sick for the second half of her shift."

Downing cocked one eyebrow and directed his comment to Cass. "You know Ms. Browning, I'm beginning to think your sister here is the real troublemaker." He told Bay he'd see her tomorrow night at The Pig Squeal and left.

Bay smiled slyly. "You're softening toward the detective. Offering him sweets. I saw the way you looked at him when he said I was the troublemaker. You like him." Bay's sarcasm was coated in angelic sweetness.

Cass huffed and said good night. ∎

CHAPTER 24
CONNECTIONS

An overload of adrenaline must have been the catalyst for sleep because Bay and Cass awoke refreshed the next morning. Bay managed to convince Cass to join her in yoga practice, which proved auspicious because promptly at seven o'clock, a heavy knock issued upon the door.

Bay unfolded from her lotus position, leaving Cass lying in repose on the mat. The face of Kelly Weber appeared in the peephole. Bay opened the door at once.

"Good morning, Professor Browning. Doing a little yoga, I see?" The parole officer was all business, dressed in a black skirt, white blouse, and black jacket that sported her badge. She held a clipboard in one hand and pen in the other.

"I came to check on Cassandra." Kelly Weber padded into the living room and stared down at Cass as if she were a lab specimen. "Are you alive down there, Cassandra?"

Cass opened one eye gingerly, trying to concoct a good story quickly. Kelly nudged Cass's foot with one toe of her leather pumps and pushed the pen behind one ear. She offered a hand to Cass to get up.

"If you could just sit down at the table, please. I'll get busy with my inspection. It shouldn't take long. You keep a tidy home here, Professor."

Bay and Cass obediently sat at the dining table. "Can I get you any tea or coffee, Officer Weber?" Bay figured hospitality was in order.

The officer called out a no from Cass's bedroom.

"She knows I called in sick last night. That's why she's here. I'm sure of it." Cass spoke calmly, unflappable as usual.

Bay's eyes flew open, alarmed, like a cornered squirrel.

In a matter of minutes, Kelly joined them at the table. "I didn't find any weapons other than the posh chef's knives in your kitchen. Don't worry. They don't count. Besides, they're all accounted for, still sitting pretty in their holders. No illegal substances. Everything appears to be in order." Kelly pointed to the bottom of page two of the report. "If you could sign here, Professor. Your signature agrees with my findings."

The officer gestured toward Cass's bedroom. "I see you're taking up painting, Cassandra. Very therapeutic, whatever that's supposed to be in there."

Kelly Weber's reference to the wall mural made Bay smile and Cass frown at the apparent critique. Bay breathed a sigh of relief, signed her name on the document, and sat back in her seat, but Kelly wasn't finished.

"Now then. About last night." Her eyes bore holes through Cassandra's skull, yet Cass didn't even fidget.

"I called in sick after my dinner break. I don't know if it was something I ate, but I had a raging headache." Cass was a proficient liar.

The officer's eyes didn't waver. "Yes, I am aware. You do know that the night manager has to report an absence of any kind and any length, Cassandra."

Cass nodded. Bay jumped in. "I can attest that she was with me all night, Officer Weber. I even picked her up from work." Bay's wide-eyed innocence and nervous tick registered with the parole officer.

"I'm happy to see that you're taking an interest in your sister's well-being, Professor. I'll note that in my file." She turned back to face Cass. "And you, you're feeling better today?"

Cass nodded. "Fit as a fiddle after a good night's sleep and therapeutic yoga." Bay wanted to slap her sister for her smug response, which she knew was on display for Officer Weber.

Kelly Weber didn't even blink or alter her expression. It seemed Cass may have met her match. "A word of advice, Cassandra." Her tone was that of the spider in striking mode. "Your co-worker Jason is a fool, a nice guy, but a fool. Don't participate in any cheating on your timecard, no matter whose idea it is. Got it?"

Cass nodded. She'd already pegged Jason for a fool on the first night of work.

Bay took advantage of the haul of books and files she'd brought home with her from Flourish and curled up in her reading chair with another book from the American literature course she'd be teaching, *Their Eyes Were Watching God* by Zora Neale Hurston. Although she'd read it a few times, there was always something new to discover. Bay admired Janie's spirit and feminist qualities, which she utilized in her journey to self-discovery. Janie always seemed to whisper in Bay's ear to figure out her own history and come to terms with her mother's loss.

Today, however, the demons Janie wrestled conjured Bay's own demons, or one, that is. She wouldn't be able to escape the Medusa until she was caught, until Bay had answers. *What does this monster want from me, from my family?*

Bay forced herself to concentrate on the novel and craft thoughtful discussion questions for small groups to grapple over. Once she finished this novel, she only had one more to tackle for the semester.

Blessedly, Cass left Bay alone to work by visiting their father for the morning. She took Barrett a third of the scrumptious Dutch Baby she'd concocted for breakfast, using leeks, bacon, and French herbs, along with a couple of oranges and bananas. She knew her father wasn't good at keeping fresh produce around.

Barrett always took the path of least resistance when life got messy, so Cass wasn't surprised when he didn't ask about the Medusa case, or even inquire about Bay's state of mind. No, she wasn't surprised, but that didn't stop her from being annoyed.

"So, you and your sister seem to be getting along. I told you things would all work out." Barrett was pleased with himself for making the proclamation, as if he could snap his fingers and make it so.

"It's a work in progress, Dad," Cass conveyed her aggravation. "You know she's in danger, right? That this killer, for whatever reason, is stalking her."

"Now, now, Cassie. We don't know that for certain. Why are you mad at me? I can't do anything about it." Barrett wore that charming but helpless expression that always worked on women.

Cass stomped her foot. "Stop it, Dad. You know what I'm

talking about. It always comes back to this terrible secret we're keeping from Bay. She's an adult. We're all adults. Don't you think it's time to get it out in the open and deal with it?"

Barrett's face reddened and his bottom lip quivered. "You know we can't. A promise is a promise. I don't want to talk about this." Barrett turned away in his chair to finish his breakfast in silence.

Cass stewed on the inside, silently fuming. How was she supposed to keep her promise and be honest with her sister? It was an impossible conundrum. One thing she knew for sure, she and Bay could never be the sisters they were as children if she didn't tell her the truth. Maybe not even then.

"Come on Cassie. Please don't stay mad at me. Let's play some chess. I need to get into practice for the local tournament at the community center in three weeks." Barret's tack was predictable. He couldn't handle sensitive issues or conflict. He'd always been that kind of father—sweep it all under the rug and paste on a smile. Cass knew she was the worthiest opponent her father would have to contend with, and she acquiesced.

In the middle of their third game, Barrett's landline rang, and Cass rose to answer it. The caller ID displayed Aunt Venus. Cass picked up the portable phone and made a beeline for the bathroom, locking the door behind her and turning on the overhead fan.

"Hi Aunt Venus, it's Cass. I'm glad you called." Cass closed the lid on the toilet and took a seat.

"Cassandra? You must be at your father's. Oh-oh. Did LuLu give you the boot?" Venus sounded more playful than concerned.

"No. Nothing like that. She's trying to work at home today,

so I'm giving her some space. Dad and I are perfecting his chess game for an upcoming tournament, and of course, avoiding any serious conversation."

"Which is why I called. I'm sensing there's something wrong up there. What is it, Cassandra?" The philosophical prophetic Venus was back.

Cass gave her aunt an outline of the Medusa story and its trail of victims as she knew it. "You'd be proud of LuLu. She's taking self-defense classes and helping the police with the investigation."

Aunt Venus didn't know what to make of the situation. "No wonder Barrett called me," she mumbled aloud. "Well, I'm happy to hear that you and your sister are finding a way to trust each other again, even it is under the most unusual circumstances."

"Yes, I suppose so." Cass sounded less enthused than her aunt. After all, the trust they were building now was nothing more than dandelion fluff. It could quickly blow away in the wind when the case was solved.

Venus was lost in her thoughts on the other end of the call. "Do you need me to come to Wisconsin?" It was a tenuous query, lacking sincerity.

Cass picked up on her aunt's anemic tone. "How are things in Hawaii?" Cass couldn't imagine leaving the tropical paradise for icy Wisconsin in January, but she suspected Aunt Venus had another reason for her hesitation. She was probably entangled in a new romance.

"Hawaii is bliss, Cassandra. I'm living in a small village in Kauai where I'm using my gifts to teach meditation. The beach is my classroom. It's where I first saw Marty, playing music. He taught me to play the ukelele in a week. I'm a natural, he said."

Venus was bubbling over in joy. Cass had seen this movie time and time again. Aunt Venus gravitated toward men she could control, usually younger than her. She put her charms on full display, and they flocked to her like kids at a candy shop. They almost always had money to spare, and if they did, they would buy her an expensive bauble, which Venus collected like shells on the beach. It was only a matter of time when Marty, like the others, would be discarded.

"You'd like Marty. Perhaps I can coax him to accompany me to Wisconsin for a visit. He's a native, you know, so his soul belongs to the island. Ah, this island life is utopia. The breezes carry new affirmations to me every day. I truly feel kinship here." Cass sensed she'd drifted away from their conversation. Venus seemed to be talking to an otherworldly spirit.

"Of course, you don't have to leave your life behind and come here. You'd hate it, Auntie Vee. Everything is stark and gray, and the only breezes blowing here have a negative windchill." Cass laughed to lighten the tension she felt in placating her aunt.

Venus audibly sighed in relief. "You know I'll come on a moment's notice if you need me, Cassandra. I love you and LuLu; you're my earth children."

Whatever that meant, Cass couldn't be sure, but she knew now was her chance to confront Aunt Venus with her conundrum. "Aunt Vee, before you go, I need to tell you something. It's about the promise you and Dad asked me to keep. You remember?"

Kauai had a strong grip on Venus, and she was reluctant to step backward into the past. "Hmm. Are you talking about the secret, Dear?"

Cass sprung like a snake through the phone line. "Yes, exactly that. I can't keep my promise, Aunt Venus. It's not fair, and it no longer serves any purpose. I'm telling LuLu the truth."

Venus sucked in foul air and her tone dripped with acid. "If that's the case, what do you want me to say, Cassandra? You've always been too headstrong. Barrett never controlled you, and despite my best efforts, the Universe didn't help me where you're concerned."

Cass teetered under an emotional weight. How unfair of Aunt Venus to accuse her this way. She was a child when she made the promise, under duress. She felt used by the two adults in her life she was supposed to count on. "I don't want your permission or favor, Aunt Venus. I just want you to know and prepare for the backlash. Enjoy your moment in the sun, while it lasts." Cass punched the button that ended the call.

Thanks to the change of scenery and the quiet atmosphere at home, Bay felt the success of a day well spent in reading and crafting discussion questions that would broaden her students' outlook on the world; at least that was the goal.

She was grateful Cass had vacated the apartment to spend time with their father, although she'd returned unusually quiet and sullen. She'd dressed for work, said her goodbyes, and quickly left.

The day was already darkening with the threat of snow, and Bay felt the need for a nap or movement from sitting too long. She rose to get ready for self-defense lesson number two and did fifteen minutes of stretches to refresh her stiff joints.

At least she'd had the sense to fuel her body for the workout ahead, again, thanks to Cass. Since her sister's arrival, Bay's kitchen was stocked with healthy foods and fresh produce, so she'd made some whole grain toast with smashed avocado for lunch, apple slices on the side.

The snow had kept its promise, falling gently from leaden clouds, as Bay left the parking garage. Commuter traffic lined Grand Avenue in a trail of red taillights broken up by an aerial show of spitting snowflakes. Her car's thermometer read twenty-nine degrees, and the dampness permeated Bay's body, making her feel lethargic. This was the optimum time for a zesty workout.

The Pig Squeal was alive with activity. Fully lit in the darkness, it emitted an inviting glow like an old-time tavern in a storm. She parked near the back entrance and knocked on the kitchen door, the same way she'd entered on Sunday.

The same raspy voice said to come in. The bouncer/chef was pulling apart a slab of brisket the size of a small horse, pushing it into large stainless-steel pans, and dousing it with barbecue sauce. He acknowledged Bay with a grunt and pointed to the swinging door that led to the dining room.

"Mandy's out there. I think she's ready for you."

Bay thanked him and Sunday's scene repeated itself with Mandy tying on shin guards. But this time, a second pair sat next to her on the floor near a plastic tub with the name "Harris" printed in marker.

"Hey, Bay. Glad you're here because this weather makes me want to kick down some walls. You know what I'm saying? Here. These guards are for you. Strap on." Mandy offered the padded guards to Bay, giving her a sinister side-eye.

Bay laughed and adjusted the Velcro straps on the first shin guard. "Do these belong to Officer Harris?" She pointed to the plastic bin.

Mandy tilted her head back in an eruption of laughter. "No,

no, no. You mean Nolan Harris? That's my big brother, and probably the reason I'm going to be a cop."

Bay's face lit up in surprise and she scrutinized Mandy with fresh eyes. "I see some resemblance. You have the same kind smile."

Mandy smiled. "Yep, but Nolan's got a lot more bulk than I do, if you know what I mean. The truth is, I was heading for trouble in high school, and Nolan saved my ass more than once. He encouraged me to get my head on straight."

"Sounds like a good brother to me. I'm curious. He works with Downing, but he's an officer, not a detective. How does that work?"

Mandy sat up straighter. "My brother has been in training for the past few months. He'll be officially promoted to detective on the thirtieth." Bay could tell Mandy was proud of him.

"This Medusa case must be like baptism by fire for someone new in the field. I can't imagine cutting my teeth on a case like this." Bay blew out a sympathetic breath.

Mandy just grinned. "It's what he signed up for. Now, his wife Yvonne, I don't think she's thrilled about it. They have two little ones at home, and she's a worrier."

"I guess that's why Downing's not married, huh? It would be difficult to have a family and be a detective."

Mandy protested. "It's like many other jobs out there. You have to find balance. Downing has his own battles to fight. That's why he isn't married. That man has a sad past, so he buries his sadness in work. And he's damn good at his job, but it comes with a price."

Bay knitted her brows and prodded Mandy for more details. "A sad past? What happened to him?"

There was that devious smile. Mandy was good at concealing. "It's not my story, Bay. Come on, let's go kick and punch stuff."

After more than an hour of beating on bags and each other, the two sweat-soaked women laid on the gym mat, panting and laughing.

"That was the best I've felt in a good while, Mandy. Thank you." Bay stared upward at the ceiling tiles.

"You're welcome. I should be thanking you, though. It's so much better to spar with someone than just punching a sandbag. There's the shower room if you like. That's where I'm headed." Mandy pointed to a small side hallway leading to four shower stalls.

Bay felt more than refreshed under the lukewarm spray. Rivulets of tension released from her body, and she watched them gurgle down the drain. But now she was hungry, and the promise of delicious food awaited upstairs.

She found Mandy in the gym sanitizing the punching bags they'd been beating on.

"Hey, I'm meeting Downing upstairs for dinner. Do you want to join us?"

"I'd like that, but I'm working. I'll probably be serving you two. My shift starts in ten minutes."

Bay was about to apologize but her ringing cell, playing the Darth Vader Imperial March, cut off her comment. Downing must be running behind.

"Sorry, Professor, but I'm not going to make it for dinner. There's been a break in the case, and Harris and I are seeing it through." Downing sounded edgy and excited at once.

"Great. Tell me about it?" Bay wanted a share in the thrill of the hunt.

Downing snorted and exhaled loudly. "I guess I should have guessed that was coming. Are you somewhere private?"

"I'm downstairs in the gym at The Pig Squeal. There's nobody here but Mandy and, oh she's waving goodbye right now. Her shift is starting." Bay looked around for a place to sit. She scurried to a nearby weight bench, took paper and pen from her bag, and sat down.

"Harris found a connection between the comic creator and Virginia Lowe." Bay registered how pleased Downing sounded.

"You're kidding! That's marvelous. What's the connection?" Bay wanted answers.

"All of this is off the book Ms. Enquiring Minds want to know." Still, Downing sounded good-natured, almost like a big brother.

"Yes, of course. Go on." Bay had pen in position.

"Harris found a receipt among the comic creator's files. They paid Virginia Lowe for an acquisition of sketches. All of them were mythological figures. The comic creator paid for the rights to use them for his series." Downing paused to let the information sink in.

Bay wrote hastily to keep up. "So, you think Medusa saw both of the victims as betrayers?" Bay couldn't sync this development to the rest of the case. How did this connect to her family?

"No. I think the artist who drew the sketches is the key. His name is Lucien Nadeau, and he was Virginia's third spouse. We're about to deep dive on Nadeau and figure out how the Medusa is connected to him."

"So, maybe Nadeau has family out for revenge. Family who wanted those sketches, who definitely didn't want them to be used for erotica." Bay could see a motive forming, even as questions skittered around her mind. *How is the psychiatrist involved? How am I connected?*

"One more thing, Professor. Harris found a contract between the comic creator and a movie studio to produce three feature films based on the *Vengeful Venuses* series. If Medusa knew this, it may provide further motivation to kill. Got to run." Downing clicked off.

Bay made a split-second decision to order some Pig Squeal food to go for the two detectives hard at work on the Medusa case. ■

CHAPTER 25
SOME ASSEMBLY REQUIRED

Bay was disappointed to find another person sitting at the reception desk when she got off the elevator at the Prairie Ridge police station. This individual, unlike Carol, was not a ray of sunshine, more like a dark cloud that matched the weather outside.

"Is there something I can help you with, Madam?" Officer Steele said, a frown etched on his face, accented by deep lines suggesting this was a permanent fixture. His hair was iron gray as was the bushy mustache in need of a trim. Upon closer inspection, Bay noticed his eyes were watery gray, a clear indication his features matched his name.

"I'm here to see Detective Downing and Officer Harris. My name is L.L. Browning." Bay smiled confidently, hoping to convey she belonged there.

"And what's in that bag, Madam?" Officer Steele stood, bent over the top of the desk like a question mark. "We have to inspect everything that comes into the building."

Bay's smile was more like a sneer. She'd already passed through the metal detectors at the station entrance, and the officer there had no qualms about the shopping bag. "But I've already been through inspection at the front entrance."

Officer Steele stood up straight and hiked up his pants, puffing out his chest as he did so. "Well, the night officer is a rookie, so I better take a look myself."

Bay could see a small line of drool had developed on his lips as his mouth watered. He could smell the food, and he clearly wanted a cut. She reluctantly set the bag down on his desk with a loud plunk.

Steele opened the bag and began rifling, even lifting the covers off the Styrofoam containers. He inhaled deeply, then eyed her suspiciously. "Suppose you tell me how you got food at The Pig Squeal? You're no cop."

Bay faltered but regained her tenacity. "I met a friend there. Look, Officer Steele, you're holding me up, and the food's getting cold. Would you kindly let the officers know I'm here?"

Steele folded his arms across his chest and sat down.

Bay made a bold decision. "Never mind. I know my way." She picked up the bag and walked toward Downing's office, Steele yelling after her.

By the time Bay opened Downing's door, the reception officer was right behind her, out of breath.

"Lady, you can't just barge in." He looked helplessly at Downing and Harris, whose faces remained expressionless.

"It's all right. We ordered dinner. We knew she was coming. Thank you, Steele." Downing played along.

Bay set the food out on the worktable next to Harris. "I figured you two would just keep working and probably grab something disgusting from the vending machine, so I brought rescue sustenance."

Harris inhaled deeply and grinned. "Thank you, Dr. Browning. I for one work better on a full stomach. Can't just run on caffeine." Harris jerked his thumb toward Downing.

Downing snorted. "Don't play into her hand, Harris. She just came to snoop. Bringing dinner was a good excuse."

Bay didn't know if she should be insulted or amused; Downing could be such a pain to read. "Now, now, Detective. I brought food for myself, too, although I thought I was going to have to sacrifice it to Officer Steele. He seems like a pompous jerk."

Downing and Harris dove into the brisket, scooped it onto buns, added slaw, and took generous bites. Both smiled appreciatively.

Harris swallowed and commented on Steele. "You need to understand where Steele's coming from. He's about ready to retire, so they pulled him off the street and stuck him behind a desk where he can't get into trouble."

"Oh, so it's like caging a bear then?" Bay offered.

Both men nodded.

"Okay. If I see him again, I'll be nicer. If I can." Bay figured the two could see right through her sincerity act, but they didn't say anything.

In less than ten minutes, Downing and Harris had traversed the entire take-out bag and were back at their desks, digging through files, browsing their computers. Bay was invisible.

She cleared her throat once, twice, then an exaggerated third time.

Downing didn't attend to her in the slightest, but Harris

looked up. "What is it?"

"Okay, you two. Aren't you going to tell me anything? Give me something to do? Assign something for me to study?" Bay begged to be included.

Downing cut Harris off, slicing the air with his hand. He spoke to Bay over a pair of reading glasses that sat stoutly on his nose. "No, no, and no. You need to go home, get a good night's sleep, and go to work tomorrow at the college. Get ready for your new semester and let us do our job." He punctuated nearly every word as if it were a stand-alone sentence.

Bay pouted but knew better than to push it. She quietly left. On her way out she told Officer Steele to have a nice night.

By morning, several inches of snow hid the gray and black patches of old snow mounds, wrapped itself around tree trunks, and clung to the pine boughs at Elfenham Park. Bay looked out the living room window like a child waiting for Santa Claus, entertained by the squirrels jumping from pine bough to pine bough, creating new snow falls each time. She barely noticed the tarp that covered the graffiti mural, instead smiling at a pair of cardinals, colorful against the pure white snow.

Cass stood next to Bay in a robe she'd borrowed from Bay's closet. "What's your plan today? Will you go into the office?"

Bay nodded. "I will but not for an hour or so. I'll wait for the snowplows and salt trucks to do their thing first. How was work last night? Everything okay between you and your co-workers?" The last thing Bay wanted was for Cass to get fired.

Cass yawned. "Fine. Jason didn't know any better. He still thinks he pulled one over on management and that they have no idea he fudged my time sheet."

"And what about your manager?"

Cass smirked. "The manager is just happy to have a warm body that shows up for work and has a modicum of common sense. Do you know how hard it is to find reliable employees?"

Bay laughed at the irritation in Cass's voice, as if she were the human resources manager herself. "Well, I've heard there are way more jobs than people in the work force these days."

Cass smiled brightly. "That's what I call job security, Sister. And how was your self-defense lesson last night?"

Bay's eyes brightened with pride and energy. "Fantastic. Once I have a few more lessons, I'll bring you along if you like. Maybe we can spar each other."

"Wouldn't that be something?" Cass was impressed by Bay's zeal for the art of combat, but Bay was clueless about Cass's skills.

"And what's your plan today before work?" Bay asked without an agenda, making her wonder if she was beginning to trust her sister.

"I'm going to the library. I have some research to do, and I hope to find some books. I'm getting bored around here. I mean, look outside. Winter's an awfully long season, and without a bank to break into or a con to run, what's a girl to do?" Cass raised her arms in a helpless gesture and batted her eyelashes innocently. And Bay responded by slugging her on the shoulder.

Bay greeted Jen Yoo on the elevator of Gale Hall with a cheery good morning. Jen stared back in surprise, double-checking to see if she was standing next to Bay or someone else.

"You seem quite perky today, Bay. Is the case solved?"

"No, it's not. But the new snow has made everything beautiful and the air smells clean. Maybe it's a sign, Jen."

Bay's optimism didn't rub off on Jen. The art history

professor kicked snow off the tote bag she'd set on the elevator floor, yanked off her hat, and tried to smooth away the static in her long hair.

"I hate winter," she pronounced. "My mother keeps telling me I should have stayed in California. Maybe she's right."

Bay used her scarf to wipe excess snow off Jen's tote bag. "You don't like California. Too close to family. That's what you told me. Besides, it's only three more months till spring," Bay chirped.

"Ugh. It took three tries to start my car and the heater never kicked in during the drive."

"I keep telling you to take it in. Maybe it's time for a new car. Didn't you drive that one in high school?" Bay poked fun at Jen's ancient Fiat, a car no dealership in the area sold.

"Very funny, Bay. My car's not that old. Anyway, it's been so reliable." She shrugged. "I guess I better take it somewhere."

The elevator doors opened. Bay took Jen by the arm.

"Come with me. I have some spray that will take the static out of your hair." The two walked to Bay's office where she retrieved the spray from her closet shelf.

"What do you know? This stuff actually works." Jen was impressed. "It's hump day of the last week of our vacation." Jen made air quotes around the word vacation. Most educators didn't take much time off between semesters, yet the public continued to describe it as a vacation, nonetheless.

"I'm going to start the last book for my new American lit class, so I think I'm ready to wrap things up and start teaching next week. How about you?"

Jen nodded. "I'm teaching a newish class. I've taught it before, but it's been a few years, so I've been getting up to speed on modern art again. I have to say, it's not my favorite subject." Jen was a classical gal all the way.

"Speaking of modern art, have you heard of an artist named Lucien Nadeau?" Bay figured she might as well probe the only art expert she knew.

Jen thought for a minute. "The name doesn't ring a bell. What kind of art does he do? Where's he from? What's his time period?"

Bay gave her friend credit. She knew the right questions to ask. "Those are all good questions, but I don't know the answer to any of them. I looked him up yesterday on the web, and nothing. Not even a hit."

Jen scoffed. "And you expect me to know the guy? Tell you what, when I have a chance, I'll look him up in my supersecret specialized database of unknown artists, okay?" Jen picked up her bag and waved to Bay.

Bay wondered: sarcasm or not? Is there a supersecret database? Maybe she'd find out later. For now, Arthur Miller's timeless tale of the Salem witch hunts beckoned. Bay loved the layers of intrigue waiting to be peeled back in *The Crucible*. She had solid plans in mind for discussion, in which her students would find a companion piece to read on their own and present to the class in lieu of another essay exam. Lillian Hellman's *Scoundrel Time* came to mind, the writer's firsthand account of life during the Red Scare, and there were numerous others.

The Crucible, a play in four acts, read quickly. Bay finished with lunch on the horizon and weighed her options. She opened her desk drawer and pulled out her collection of take-out menus from area restaurants. Maybe she should call Jen to see if a shared lunch was possible.

The comfort of soup beckoned from the Stu's Soups menu. A clanging alarm echoed in Bay's head, making her dizzy. She held her head between her hands and leaned on her desk begging for the clanging to cease.

When it did, she was left with a stunning revelation. The last time she'd had a soup delivery from Stu's, it came with a floating artist. Not only could it be a depiction of Lucien Nadeau, but she might know the delivery person.

She swiped on her contact list and pressed Downing's number.

"Professor Browning, I presume."

Downing seemed to be in good spirits. Maybe he would elaborate.

"Detective. I have a hunch. Maybe it's crazy. I don't know." Bay started pacing in front of her office window.

"Just stop fuming and start talking." Downing didn't enjoy hemming and hawing.

"Okay. Remember when I had the plastic artist floating in my soup?"

"Yep. Go on."

"The gamer. Her username is Sandwich Delivery. And she used Chance to run errands. Chance also works for a delivery service. What if Sandwich Delivery is Medusa? I mean, she'd easily get into places without having to break in or sneak in. Delivery people come and go. They're practically invisible."

Downing slapped his desk. "She's been hiding in plain sight. I'll get in touch with people at The Gizmo as my next priority, and we'll set up a stakeout. Did you figure anything out with the mirror note?"

Bay frowned, unhappy once more. There was always another

puzzle to solve. "No, afraid not. I've been taking your advice and working, Detective."

"If that's the truth, what made you come up with the gamer theory?"

"Well, it was time to order lunch. I've got a drawer full of food delivery options." Bay laughed and disconnected.

After a quiet lunch by herself at Fresh and Green Canteen, Flourish's main cafeteria, Bay spent an extra fifteen minutes walking briskly around the college grounds, now decorated in white. She wondered if she should bug Jen Yoo about the artist, Lucien Nadeau, but didn't want to be a pest.

She also softened her perspective on Detective Downing. As she thought about all the clues and details associated with the case, she adopted deep respect for the work being done by the police department. She also wondered how many other behind-the-scenes professionals were being kept busy every day staring at computer screens, looking at the victims' receipts and other belongings. Realizing that Harris made a connection between victims with one sales receipt, she could see how a small detail could bust a case wide open.

Circling back to her building, she passed by the library and brushed shoulders with McNelly. Bay scowled. She hadn't seen the man in a few days, and truth be told, that's how she liked it. McNelly carried a large cardboard box along with a heavy backpack slung over one shoulder and walked with his head down, a man on a mission.

"Hello McNelly. Where are you off to in such a rush?" Bay's pleasantry held a salty undertone.

"Oh, L.L. It's you," McNelly stopped to shift the box around. "Just finished at the library and bookstore. I'm leaving some things with the Criminal Justice department over at Ham Hall." Ham Hall was the nickname of the Social Sciences Building, named for Supreme Court Justice Shirley Abrahamson, Wisconsin's first female justice.

McNelly was out of breath and decided to set down his burden. The irony of McNelly running course materials between Ham and Gale Halls wasn't lost on Bay. She couldn't resist a little poke. "You know, if you'd stayed at Ham Hall, your office would be in the same building as your classes. By the way, you should wear your backpack over both shoulders, so you don't hurt your back."

McNelly grimaced and bent down to pick up the box. Bay summoned her better angels, trying to figure out a way she could be helpful. "Here, put the box back down. Let's see if we can divide and conquer."

McNelly's quizzical expression met Bay's next move. She lifted the lid off the overfilled box just as a breeze kicked up the top papers, scattering them across the sidewalk. She slammed the cover back over the box and ran around collecting stray papers in the snow, like a squirrel looking for buried acorns.

At first, McNelly said a few words unbecoming of a man of the cloth, even a former one, then he burst into action, gathering papers, too. When the two bent over the box at the same time, they knocked heads and stood up rubbing their foreheads, perfectly synchronized. There was nothing to do but laugh, and after making snarly faces at one another, that's exactly what they did.

"No good deed goes unpunished," Bay finally spit out after a few rounds of raucous laughter.

McNelly's expression shifted from giddy to stern. "You don't really mean that, L.L. Has life been treating you that poorly?"

Bay's wide-eyed glare at McNelly conveyed how clueless he was. "Yes, as a matter of fact, things haven't been too great lately, McNelly." She stood up straight and jutted out her chin, remembering the Browning motto of stiff upper lip, like many British families. "There are others who have it much worse."

McNelly nodded. "I'm sorry. I wasn't aware. Would you care to talk about it? I've been known to be a good listener."

Bay smirked. "Pardon me, but no thank you. Now, can I help you get these over to Ham Hall before you break your back?"

McNelly smiled warmly, opened the box gingerly and pulled out a second box nestled under the top papers. It was smaller, covered, and probably weighed around ten pounds. "If you really don't mind, I think you can manage this, and it will take off some weight."

Bay took the box and the two walked the next few minutes in silence to Ham Hall, where Bay left McNelly at the ground floor elevator. McNelly thanked her with a tip of his hat.

Bay returned to Gale Hall with a light step. It felt good to do something kind for someone, especially someone she didn't care for. The small act made her wonder how long it had been since she last helped someone without an agenda. A small warm glow kindled inside of her. A little remorse was good for her soul.

Jen Yoo was waiting outside Bay's office when she returned.

"Where have you been? Did you already have lunch?" Jen trotted in behind Bay and closed the door.

"Yes, I'm sorry. I didn't want to bother you in case you were in the middle of something. Besides, I needed the fresh air to clear my head—again." Bay lost count of how many times she used a walk outside as a remedy for her muddled brain.

"No, it's fine. I have a dinner date tonight, so I'm skipping lunch anyway."

"Date? Who with?" Bay leaned across the desk.

"Hmm, great grammar, Ms. English Professor. I don't think you know him. He's one of the new adjunct hires in the history department. Andrew Peng." Jen looked toward the window instead of at Bay's prying eyes.

"Don't say anything, Bay. The Asian population around here isn't that big, and my parents really want me to give an Asian guy a chance. I'm forty for Pete's sake. You'd think it wouldn't matter to me what they think." Jen covered her face with both hands.

"You're never too old to care what your parents think, Jen. It's all good. Maybe Andrew Peng will turn out to be your Prince Charming," Bay snickered.

"I'm not getting ahead of myself. But, anyway, I'm here because I looked up your artist, the mysterious Lucien Nadeau. He was indeed married to Virginia Lowe, but he wasn't an artist of any consequence." She paused and took a folded paper from her pocket for reference.

"He preferred sketching mythology subjects and sometimes painted in acrylics. In fact, he was a painting instructor for several years from the 1990s to early 2000s. He died in 2009. Nothing is mentioned about any pieces attributed to him."

Bay nodded, taking in the lackluster information. Somehow, she'd hoped for more. "Who else was Nadeau married to? Did he have any children?"

Jen reviewed her notes once more. "There's nothing in here indicating he was married to anyone else. And this database is only going to discuss children if they became consequential. Sorry this wasn't more helpful."

"At least you found him. That's something. I don't suppose there was a picture of him?"

Jen shook her head. "Sorry, Bay. I need to bail. I want to go home and obsess about what to wear tonight to dinner." Jen tossed her hair back like a drama queen, a sultry expression on her face.

"That reminds me, could I borrow your magic antistatic spray for my hair? It's one of my best attributes."

"Sure. Just let me check my windblown do, first. I forgot to look after my lunch walk." Bay opened her closet door and looked in the mirror, retrieved the can of spray, and gave the top of her dark head a few spritzes, shook her head, and picked up the comb from the closet shelf. That's when she noticed the painting behind her in the mirror, Penelope's treasured artwork that Bay had claimed for herself.

Bay's face drained of color, and Jen touched her back, then caught her as she momentarily lost her balance. She regained her composure after Jen pushed her into a chair.

"Hey friend, we've got to stop meeting like this," Jen was glib, but concerned.

"The painting." Bay pointed to the wall opposite the closet where the acrylic piece hung, depicting two girls watching a swan swim toward fire.

Jen rose to inspect the piece. "What is it? I guess we never talked about it, even though it's been on your wall since you started here."

"My mother painted this. The dark-haired girl with the laurel crown is me. My middle name is Laurel. The blond girl crowned with the phases of the moon is Cassandra. Her middle name is Selene, the moon goddess. She always called us her little goddesses. My mother is the swan, sailing away from us into the fire. You see, she was ill and died when we were young."

Jen's eyes widened as she tried to examine the painting's details and her breathing became shallow, so as not to damage the surface. "May I take this with me to the lab? I want a closer look, Bay."

"Sure. Why, though? Do you see something?" Bay stammered, frustrated. "If this is the truth I'm supposed to see in the mirror, I don't understand it. How does this help me find Medusa?"

Jen gestured for Bay to follow her. "I'm going to take it to the lab right now. Want to come with me?"

Bay nodded and stood up. "Wait. What about Andrew Peng?"

Jen's eyes were lit with tiny flames. "I'll call him and change our dinner time. It will be a good first test, don't you think?" She winked at Bay.

The art history lab was in the building's basement and was a cramped cold cubby with two workspaces where various tools of the trade sat on cheesecloth. Jen unlocked the lab, donned her lab coat, and handed a second coat to Bay. She pulled two pairs of gloves from the pop-up box by the door and handed one pair to Bay. Both women tucked their hair into large gauze coverings.

Now Jen felt better about handling the painting, which she set upright on an easel. She sprayed the table with an antimicrobial cleaner and let the surface air dry. She set the painting on the exam table and mentally divided it into quadrants to study with a lighted magnifying glass. She didn't' speak and Bay held her breath during the process.

Jen's brows were two question marks of anticipation when

she turned toward Bay. "Okay, I'm interested in something, so I'm going to put the painting on the light table. The light shines from the bottom of the painting to illuminate things that are hidden or difficult to see clearly because of thick paint, overlaid images, or age."

After a few minutes, Jen raised her head from the light table in triumph. "Come here, Bay. You need to see this."

Jen pointed to the signature in the bottom right-hand corner of the piece. The paint was dark and thick there, textured to resemble the flowing river the swan sailed upon. Jen held the magnifier, revealing the letters "cuL" and below them, "daN."

Bay shrugged. "I'm a failure at art history. Cul Dan? What's that supposed to mean?"

Jen's voice warmed with enthusiasm. "Some artists will disguise their signature as a trick or a secret by writing their name backwards. That's why the capital letter L and N are at the end of the signature."

Bay was baffled and still in the dark.

Jen moved the magnifier from right to left across the first letters. "Do you see? There are more letters, just fainter. Right here. The same on the bottom. Right here."

Comprehension arrived like a freight train. "Lucien Nadeau. He's the artist. Not my mother." Bay's lips began to tremble. Was this the truth she was supposed to see? But what did it mean?

Jen took Bay's hand and forced her to sit down. "Look at me. You trust me, right?"

Jen nodded which made Bay nod along with her.

"Good. I'm going to give you my opinion about this piece. You know this is what I do right?"

Bay nodded again, reluctantly.

"This piece is full of sadness. If the swan is supposed to be your mother and the artist is Lucien Nadeau, then your mother is sailing away from him, from all of you. Do you see this light radiating on the two girls? The name Lucien means light. He is the light, but the swan is swimming into darkness and flames. You can see that her feathers are already turning black in the water. The two girls are crying. It looks like their tears formed the river she's sailing on."

Bay swallowed a hard lump. "Do you think he loved my mother? That he loved me and Cass? I don't know him, Jen. There are gaps in my childhood that are just black holes." Bay felt haunted by the past, and the chill in the lab seeped through her whole body.

"I can't answer your questions, Bay. But I think your father can. You need to talk to him. You probably should call the detective, too."

Keeping the gloves on, Bay carried the painting back to her office, thanked Jen, and prepared to go home and face the past. "I hope Andrew Peng is as kind as you are, Jen Yoo. Thanks for being honest with me." The two hugged each other tightly.

Bay wrapped the painting in a large plastic bag she had in the closet and carried it to her car, called Downing, then abruptly hung up before he answered. *What am I doing? As soon as he knows about the painting, he's going to take it away. Worse, he'll interrogate Dad, Cass, and me about what it means. I don't need an invasion of my family privacy until I have a chance to hear it first.* ◼

CHAPTER 27
FAMILY AFFAIRS

Bay mixed herself a brandy old-fashioned and sat in her reading chair, staring at the painting from her office that leaned against the nearby wall. She took small sips between ping-pong matches playing in her head and found herself whispering to the painting.

"All this time. I thought my mother painted you as a tribute to her daughters. All this time."

She raised her glass in a toast. "Well done. What a grand deception. What will my father say?"

Bay's emotions bubbled up inside her, threatening to break free in angry tears. She rehearsed questions in her mind before calling her father. Should she wait for Cass, she wondered? At least her sister was working second shift and would be home around ten. It was decided. All of the family should hear the story at the same time. She owed Cass that much. Penelope was her mother, too.

Bay drained the cocktail and made a second one, a rarity.

Halfway through, she regretted it or at least regretted drinking on an empty stomach. She rose and teetered several woozy steps to the kitchen where she opened the fridge to examine its contents. She frowned. No leftovers to be had. In the old days, she'd make a bowl of oatmeal with some fruit, a reliable standby.

She opened the cupboard, pulled out a package of instant multigrain oats, added water, dribbling some with her unsteady hand, and microwaved it. She found an apple, cut it in half without peeling it, chopped up some of it, and left the rest on the counter. She added the apple pieces to the oats and poured some oat milk over the top. Her stomach lurched, displeased with the smell of food. *More likely displeased with my choice of appetizer.*

"Zounds, what a pittikins you are!" She cursed herself for being a lightweight.

Leaning on the counter, she took a small spoonful of oatmeal and swallowed quickly. It went down like a wad of bubble gum. She picked out an apple and chewed it about 50 times before attempting to swallow it. She feared her stomach planned a rebellion.

Bay left the kitchen, making a direct line for the bathroom. She was dizzy and stumbled against the cool porcelain toilet where she collapsed in a wilted heap. Heat rose from her stomach to her face, while her legs and feet were ice. She couldn't remember how much brandy she'd used in her drinks. Obviously, too much.

When Cass arrived home two hours later, she found Bay curled up on the bathroom floor covered in a bath towel, passed out. Cass helped her to her bed which she tumbled into with little resistance. Cass covered her up and retraced her sister's steps that evening. Even as she discovered the partially empty cocktail and barely touched oatmeal, Cass was certain of one thing. The painting standing against the wall was her accuser, and the moment of truth was at hand.

When Bay woke up just after five the next morning, she felt surprisingly refreshed. Apparently, a brandy-induced sleep dulled her senses and her memory. She'd slept like the proverbial log. When she crawled out of bed, she realized she was still in yesterday's clothes, and vaguely remembered someone had helped her into bed the night before.

She didn't want to wake Cass, so she tiptoed into the bathroom to brush her teeth, then threw on jeans and a sweatshirt. She intended to skip yoga and head straight for coffee, followed by a visit to her father. Her head was clear this morning, another benefit of a sound sleep, and there would be no more procrastination about the painting and its secrets.

Bay jumped when she saw Cass sitting on the sofa sipping a cup of tea, an expectant look on her face. Cass was dressed, or maybe she'd never gotten undressed last night either, Bay supposed.

"How are you feeling this morning, Professor?" Cass spoke softly and hesitantly, making Bay wonder why.

"I slept like a babe in the arms of Morpheus," Bay released a small giggle. "I suspect you helped me to bed, so thank you, Cassandra."

"Why are you up so early? Change in your work schedule messing with you?" Bay asked.

"I've been awake most of the night, fixated on that." Cass pointed to the painting.

Bay snorted. "That painting has a story to tell, and I'm going to get Dad up here ASAP to fill us both in."

Cass frowned and her eyes swept downward away from her sister's sight. The change in Cassandra's demeanor suddenly made sense to Bay.

"Look at me, Cass. You know something about this painting, don't you?"

"And you said you didn't possess any of the Charming qualities. You read people very well, Sister." Cass turned a sad serious face upward, and invited Bay to sit down next to her on the sofa.

"Maybe I should hear what you have to say, standing up. Hmm?" But Bay sat down keeping space between the two of them. "Okay, just tell me. Rip off the Band-Aid."

Cass looked down at her hands and tried to keep them from fluttering. "I suspect you already know something, but I don't want to play games anymore, LuLu. I've kept this secret far too long."

Bay's silence hung between them like an invisible barrier, just when both sisters dared to hope their relationship was on the mend.

"I know you always thought this painting was done by our mother, but it was done by her art instructor, Lucien Nadeau."

"So, Nadeau gave mom art lessons? I remember she was taking art lessons. She wanted to do more than look at art. She wanted to paint, to create. I can hear her telling me that." Bay tried to pull on the memory thread and conjure Penelope's face and voice.

Cass nodded. "Yes, that's true. She'd always wanted to learn to paint. Dad found Lucien Nadeau during one of his anthropology workshops. They hit it off immediately, and it turned out that Lucien was going to be spending a semester as a guest art instructor in Chicago, our home at the time."

Bay acknowledged the information but couldn't bring up visuals of a Chicago home other than Aunt Venus's.

"Was he in love with our mother?" The words stuck in Bay's throat like molasses.

Cass nodded. "Yes. They were in love. It wasn't one-sided, LuLu." A small tear slid down Cass's cheek, and she paused to gather her thoughts or wait for Bay's reaction.

Bay's query was a scratchy whisper. "How do you know that? We were so young."

"You were young, LuLu. I was old enough to know, old enough to figure it out. Besides, I saw them. I caught them." Cass spit out the word "I" like a flying dart tipped in venom.

"What are you talking about?" Bay's incredulity matched her sister's bitterness.

"Mom lost track of time during her art lesson, or she didn't remember she was taking me to the dentist that day. I came home early from school and found them…together." Finally, Cass felt the release of a long-kept secret. Yet, there was more to be said.

"Did you tell Dad?" Bay's voice edged on accusatory.

Cass's eyes flew open as she stood up, hands on her hips, glaring at Bay. "Of course, I didn't tell him. Mom did. She had no choice, really. She couldn't ask her nine-year-old daughter to keep quiet."

Bay sat very still and tried to fit this new information into her memory gap between age five and seven. She closed her eyes and raised her hand to stop Cass from saying anything.

"I guess I understand better why there are strange gaps in my memory. Mom and Dad split up for a while, didn't they?"

"Yes. During those two years, we lived all over the place. Sometimes with Dad at one of his work sites. Sometimes with Auntie Vee in Chicago. Mom came to visit on and off."

Bay nodded. Her fuzzy memories began to make sense. "That's why I remember Mom at Auntie Vee's but also remember her coming to see us in Italy. She seemed happy and sad at the same time. I didn't understand it."

"Do you remember Dad telling us she was studying art in Canada on a sabbatical?" Cass sneered. "I knew she wasn't on sabbatical. She was living with Lucien Nadeau."

"Did you ask Dad if that was true?" Bay wondered.

"No. I knew he wouldn't tell me the truth, so I told Auntie Vee what I knew to trick her into telling me the truth." Cass folded her arms stubbornly across her chest, probably the same way she did years ago when confronting Auntie Vee.

"Did it work?"

"Yes. My first con job, I suppose. That's when she made me promise not to tell you. Ever. Years later, after Mom came back to us to stay, she made me promise to keep it a secret from you. Dad, too. Even when Mom got sick, she reminded me of my promise. I was supposed to keep it a secret. Forever." Cass lost it on the last word and broke into quaking sobs.

Finally, Bay understood why Cass had rebelled. Keeping a secret from a beloved sister had morphed into a monster Cass couldn't tame. Being a con artist, living in aliases and disguises, allowed the secret to be kept under wraps. Bay pulled Cass into a tight hug and stroked her hair.

After Cass calmed down, Bay stepped back and sat again. "I wish you'd told me this sooner. I could have handled it once I got older. And Dad is not off the hook. We need to confront him, painful or not."

Cass agreed. "You know how Dad is. He doesn't like conflict, and he wants to remember Mom his way. Just like you, Bay. The perfect Penelope."

"But that's not fair to you, Cass. You can't carry the truth alone. And, I have to deal with it. I wish I could understand what made her fall for Lucien Nadeau. I always thought our parents were happy." Bay's voice warbled and tears threatened, but something inside her stopped the flow. She didn't want to cry. She wanted to process her family history.

In typical Bay fashion, she checked the time and concocted an outline for the day ahead. It was only six a.m. Barrett would be up by seven or so, and she didn't want to wake him early. She needed coffee and breakfast. She was ahead of schedule at the college, a blessing for sure. She could take the morning off, or even the whole day. She must call Detective Downing.

"Where's your head, LuLu?" Cass interrupted her brainstorm.

Bay smiled weakly. "Just deciding a plan of action. Feel like going out for breakfast? I'm famished. I didn't eat supper last night. My stomach revolted once I started drinking."

"I know. First, I found you on the bathroom floor. Then I found your attempt at a meal in the kitchen. How much did you drink anyway?" The look on Cass's face brought back memories of their Grandma Charming, whom Cass favored.

"I had one old-fashioned and half of a second one."

"You're kidding. You either need to drink more often or just stop already," Cass laughed.

The sisters enjoyed a quiet breakfast in the nearly empty Sunrise Café. Bay placed her emotions on hold until she could come to terms with what Cass told her. She didn't know whether she was angry with Cass or her father, but she was angry, and that anger needed a place of resolution.

They sat in the café, talking about everyday life and work routines, until Cass looked at her phone and proclaimed it was time to go home and talk to Barrett.

Bay called their dad and asked him to meet them at her apartment in twenty minutes.

Cass prepared a pot of Auntie Vee's special blend of tea she aptly named "tragedy blend." The tea was reserved for the worst of occasions and its ingredients included cardamom, cacao, cinnamon, rose hips, and even a pinch of ground coffee. Three mugs perched at the ready on the coffee table when Barrett knocked on the door.

"What's going on? Has the killer been caught?" Barrett looked expectantly from Bay to Cass and back again.

"Why don't we sit down where we can talk? Cass made tea." Bay took her father's arm and gently pulled him to the overstuffed chair that she'd scooted closer to the coffee table and sofa. She sat down next to Cass, and Cass covered her hand over Bay's to steady their resolve.

"Dad," Bay began. "It's about that painting." She pointed at the piece that stood against the wall closest to Barrett.

Barrett looked over with a jolt, noting the painting as if for the first time. "I didn't know you still had that thing, LuLu." A pained look crept over his face.

Cass squeezed Bay's hand lest she abandon their plan. "Dad, I always thought Mom painted this. But she didn't. Lucien Nadeau painted it. My art history friend, Jen Yoo, told me that yesterday. That's why I brought it home. I need to ask you about the artist."

Barrett's face drained of color, replaced by the ashen appearance of the dead. "Cass," he whispered, as if Bay couldn't hear him.

"Dad," Bay redirected his attention with a firm command. "I want to hear the truth from you. Who was Lucien Nadeau?" After several minutes of stammering, Barrett tearfully rolled out the same story Bay had heard from Cass. "I loved your mother. That's why we made an agreement for her to come back to me. To us."

"Did the agreement include never talking about her relationship with Lucien Nadeau? To keep it a secret? And what about this painting? Why do we even have it, Dad?" The questions poured out of Bay like rainfall.

Barrett sat up straighter in face of the onslaught. "Please, LuLu. I am your father, after all. We had to make some rules. I insisted we never speak of her absence. We were wiping the slate clean and starting over. She insisted she keep the painting. It was important to her. It marked the end of her time with him and her return to us."

Cass scoffed. "I'd say she kept is as memento of their love. He painted his feelings all over that canvas, and it was her keepsake." Cass didn't care to be cautious with Barrett's own feelings, having harbored their secret for far too long.

Bay shot her sister a warning look to tone down a little. "This painting is related to these murders, Dad. The last note from Medusa told me to find the truth in the mirror. My closet mirror in my office showed the painting. Lucien Nadeau was married to Virginia, the art curator who was murdered. Did you know that?"

Barrett took a long drink of tea, but it didn't change his

gray pallor. "Oh, dear God. No, I didn't keep track of Nadeau after your mother and I reunited. I wanted to forget the man. I brought them together in the first place. How do you think that made me feel?"

Despite the fact her father looked lost and helpless, Bay pressed on. "The police are looking for Nadeau's children. Do you know anything about them?"

Something inside Barrett boiled up hot and prickly. Bay and Cass both noticed it at once.

"You do know something. Tell us," Cass insisted.

"Maybe he and Virginia had a child. I don't know. Why does it matter?"

Bay shook her head, reached over, and grabbed her father's hand. "The children are Virginia's stepchildren. I know this is difficult for you but tell us the truth."

Barrett looked toward the fireplace. "Your mother left me because she was pregnant with his child. I sent her away. I didn't want you two to see her pregnant and ask questions." He pulled his hand away from Bay and covered his face.

Bay and Cass exchanged looks of shock, sorrow, and horror. What had their father done?

"That's why you said she was on sabbatical. You didn't know how long she'd be away, but you kept her away from us until after the baby was born." Cass's anger bubbled over.

"What happened to the child?" Bay couldn't imagine the choice Penelope faced. She had to leave her children behind to have a new child but had to abandon that child to return to her family. Suddenly, Bay felt empty inside.

Barrett shrugged and withdrew inward, crouched over toward the corner like a tiny gnome.

"I don't know. I told her I wouldn't hear anything about the child. I don't even know if it was a boy or girl. If she'd had a boy, I couldn't bear it."

So many lives were damaged by the affair and made worse by keeping it all a secret. Bay's heart sunk heavily in her chest, but Cass had been calculating time in her head and had a revelation of her own.

"I think I know what happened to her. The child." Cass recalled her encounter with Diana Poulin at Bay's office and remembered the strong connection set off between them. "I think Diana Poulin is their child, our half sister, LuLu."

"How can that be?" Bay thought about her knowledge of Diana. Her age seemed off. She was too young, but she was from Canada and did have a stepmother. Then there was McNelly, insisting she be hired and insisting Bay take her under her wing. Did McNelly know the truth? Was that part of the confession she'd made? If so, then Diana must know Bay is her half sister. Bay didn't think her brain could accommodate any more truth now.

Cass covered her hand back over Bay's. "You know I have that weird perception of the truth that happens when I touch people. The day I bumped into Diana, the two of us were like a conduit of electricity. Both of us saw images. I'm certain of it. That's when she suffered that bloody nose. Her body couldn't handle the shock. She's one of us. I'm sure of it, LuLu."

Bay stood up abruptly. "I need to call Downing. Right now." ■

CHAPTER 28
POTLUCK SURPRISE

After Bay's lengthy phone call with Downing, she returned to the tableau she'd vacated in her living room. Cass and Barrett were silently sitting apart, the only sound coming from the sipping of tea. At least there was silence, Bay thought. Maybe the tragedy blend had some sort of magical effects.

"Dad, I think you should go home. Detective Downing wants the three of us to lay low for a bit. He didn't tell me his plans, but insists I stay away from the college today." The call to Downing brought back some normalcy to Bay's world.

"Am I under house arrest or what?" Barrett demanded. "It's Thursday. I have a card tournament at one, and I'm playing chess at four." He jutted out his bottom lip like a defiant toddler.

"The detective said you can go about your regular routine as long as the police know where to expect you to be. I already told him about your plans, Dad." Bay kept her voice even and absent of emotion. The truth was, she didn't know how she felt.

Barrett stood up and smoothed out his slacks. "Well, I'm sure

I'll get a warmer welcome at the club than I'm getting here with my own children anyway."

He began walking toward the door while Cass fumed to herself, trying to decide whether or not to speak her mind. Bay warded off her oncoming tirade with one hand. Barrett left in silence.

"Cass, I understand how mad you are at Dad right now." Bay held up her hand again as Cass was ready to defend her feelings. "You have every right to be angry. They were adults, and they screwed up. But he is our father. Just hold that thought for now."

"What do you think is going on with Downing? He's going to pull in Diana and question her, maybe even arrest her, isn't he?" Cassandra's prophetic nature was highly acute at present.

"Why shouldn't he? Maybe Diana is Medusa."

"You don't believe that LuLu, any more than I do. It cannot be." Cass stopped, closed her eyes, and tuned into another frequency. "But she knows something. She can help them."

Bay stared at Cass, looking for a reason to suspect her of a con. Finding none, Bay held her hand lightly. "I believe you, Sister."

Cass exhaled. It was the first time she could remember her words being accepted at face value, without proof. She smiled.

For two days, Bay heard nothing from Downing; in fact, he didn't return her calls. Tempted as she was, she didn't venture into the police station, fearing she'd be thrown out. The fifth floor of Gale Hall and beyond was abuzz with talk about Diana Poulin being in police custody. Bay avoided all conversations with the excuse she had to prepare for next semester.

She only bumped into McNelly once, and he sidestepped her, pretending to be on his cell phone. He wouldn't look her in the eye, a certainty he knew more about Diana, and what he knew must be connected to Bay.

Bay narrowed her eyes in a death stare and muttered, "You rapscallion," under her breath.

She spent most of Friday in her office, pretending she wasn't there. She didn't respond to door knocks or Jen Yoo's inquiries on the other side.

That afternoon, under a winter weather alert, the campus planned to empty out by one o'clock. Bay gathered a syllabus from each of her courses, stuffed them in her paisley-printed tote bag, and prepared for a quiet weekend without schoolwork.

Stasia had made last-minute rounds to check that her charges were ready for Monday and reminded everyone she'd be seeing them at the Luxe tomorrow night for the potluck party. "I can't wait to celebrate the beginning of spring semester with you all," she gushed as only Stasia could, sounding more like a croak than a croon.

When Bay opened her office door to leave, Jen Yoo was standing against the wall next to it.

"Aha, you've been avoiding me, Bay. What's going on? Is it true? Is our office assistant a serial killer?" Jen was on a roll. "She did have the opportunity to leave you those notes. But I have to say, she seems way too mousey to be a cold-blooded killer."

"Stop Jen. I don't want to talk about this. It's been a rough couple of days, and I just can't right now. I need to focus on my job." Bay paused when she saw Jen's offended expression.

"I'm sorry. You've been such a good friend to me. I really don't know anything, though. The police have stopped talking to me."

They walked to the elevator side-by-side.

"Are you still going to the Luxe tomorrow?" Jen asked.

"Yes. I've been told to keep my plans and routines." She pressed the down button and lowered her voice. "I agree with you, Jen. I can't see Diana being Medusa. It doesn't fit."

Life at the apartment wasn't much better than the college office. Bay managed to avoid her father, which wasn't difficult since Barrett had retreated from his daughters' lives as well. Cass was unusually quiet and, along with Bay, constantly on high alert for intruders or mysterious notes. Everything, however, was eerily quiet in their lives.

Cass worked second shift all week with the potential to make it her permanent schedule. Bay spent two hours practicing self-defense moves with Mandy at The Pig Squeal Thursday evening, hoping the exhaustive workout would produce sleep. It almost worked for a couple of hours, until Minerva stirred during the night, made mournful meows, and jumped at spirits. After an hour of that, both Bay and Cass were up for the remainder of the night and watched old TV shows.

On Saturday morning, Bay suggested Cass accompany her to The Pig Squeal for a morning session with Mandy Harris.

"You don't have to twist my arm. I'm there." Cass welcomed a physical distraction to alleviate the heavy atmosphere surrounding her family.

Mandy and Bay were impressed by Cassandra's power and flexibility. No wonder she made such a good cat burglar on occasion, Bay thought, but didn't share her viewpoint in front of Mandy. The less Mandy knew about Bay's family history, the better.

After more than an hour, Mandy mopped sweat off her neck and forehead with a towel and called a time-out.

"Bay, you're making excellent progress. I'm especially impressed on your reaction time and how automatic your moves are becoming." Mandy patted Bay on the back.

Bay brightened. "Well, I'm appropriately motivated, I guess you could say." The three women laughed despite the dangerous situation.

"I sure wish I knew how the case was going. I haven't heard from Downing or your brother since they took Diana into custody. It's awful not knowing what's happening."

Mandy nodded in empathy. "I understand how you must feel. But I'm going to give you the cop response to that. Let them do their job. If you're not hearing from them, you shouldn't worry. Have a little faith. Downing's as good as any big city detective, Bay and Cass."

Bay and Cass exchanged a lackluster look and sighed heavily in unison. Mandy said she'd see Bay again Tuesday after work. Monday, the start of the new semester, would be a loaded day for Bay, and she couldn't promise to keep an appointment. Her lightest days of the week would be Thursday and Friday, but she didn't want to have a big gap in her self-defense training, so Tuesday would have to do.

Bay and Cass stopped for groceries on the way home, so Bay could prepare her baked ziti dish for the potluck. But plans change, and Cass convinced Bay to bring something less predictable and more modern.

"I'm home all day, so I'll help you prepare the dish," Cass promised.

They gathered fresh brussels sprouts, thyme, parsley, Parmigiano cheese, and anchovies for a brussels sprouts Caesar salad. Cass was certain they had grapeseed oil and red wine vinegar already, but they stopped at the bakery department and found a delicious looking focaccia bread for the croutons.

Bay smiled at the prospect of bringing a dish with pizzazz to the party that night, then frowned remembering she'd signed up to bring a main dish.

"No worries, Sister. We can pick up a rotisserie chicken and whip up a main dish with it."

Bay envied Cassandra's cooking confidence and wondered if she could still learn her way around the kitchen with comfort. She was so skilled at ordering out, that she'd made it an organized art form.

Cass's eyes lit up with an idea. "I know something easy. We'll make white chicken chili. We can double it and have leftovers of our own."

White chili was simple and heartwarming, the perfect cold weather dish. Cass sent Bay to the deli to grab two cooked chickens while she raced up the aisles for chicken stock, canned tomatoes, and cannellini beans. A trip to the produce section yielded fresh cilantro, garlic, and green chiles.

All afternoon, Bay's kitchen was filled with the aroma of simmering chicken chili and shaved Parmigiano, a combination made in heaven.

While Bay dressed for the party in her traditional first-day-of-classes garb, Cass packed a box with the pot of chili wrapped in a large towel and a second box with the salad and dressing, which would be poured on right before serving. She'd had the forethought to pick up sour cream, sliced green onions, and tortilla chips to garnish the chili and placed them in one of Bay's tote bags.

Bay and Cass each carried a box to the parking garage and set them on the floor of Bay's back seat. The sisters smiled warmly at what they'd accomplished, and Bay gave Cass a spontaneous squeeze.

"Have a good time tonight and try to relax. Promise?"

"Promise."

Bay was early enough to score a front row parking space at the Luxe, handy since she had to make two trips to get the boxes to the Atrium. One of the bartenders pointed out a table just for hot foods where Bay could plug in the chicken chili. Another table showed a lineup of stainless-steel chiller trays where Bay set the salad and dressing.

While she waited for one of the kitchen staff to bring her serving spoons for her dishes, she spied Jen Yoo coming through the Atrium archway, carrying a large bamboo steamer basket. Bay waved to get her attention by the hot foods.

The spring and fall potluck semester kickoffs were casual parties, but the professors were encouraged to wear their first-day-of-school outfits as a tradition. Jen Yoo always dressed like a piece of abstract art, and Bay admired her friend's choice for this event.

The swing dress, primary colors on a beige background, looked like a Kandinsky spatter painting. The red, blue, and yellow swashes, dots, dribbles, and swirls resembled textured paint. An oversized yellow plastic belt complimented the dress, made more noticeable with its giant black eyelets that looked like eyes with lashes. Jen wore her hair down, wrapped in a silk scarf with zigzag stripes of red, blue, and yellow.

Jen set down the bamboo basket of steamed dumplings and a sauce dish on the hot table next to Bay's chili, and sidled up to Bay, as she stirred her dish and placed the serving spoon on a paper towel next to it.

"Let me guess. You brought your mother's famous steamed dumplings and sauce?" Bay made a yummy noise to show her approval when Jen nodded.

Jen lifted the lid from the chili and smiled, puzzled. "What, no baked ziti?"

"Cass convinced me to modernize my potluck choices. I made two dishes, with her help."

"Wow. I guess you and your sister are getting along better these days?"

Bay nodded. "That's a fantastic outfit, by the way. You've outdone yourself from last year."

Jen gave a little twirl to show off the fullness of the skirt. "I see you're wearing your typical 'I'm in mourning' ensemble." Jen's mouth puckered as she surveyed Bay's drapey black pants, silk black blouse, and textured black jacket.

Bay smiled proudly. "I have to dress dark and more mature for my students, or they won't respect me. I want to convey mystery and make them feel a little apprehension." Bay held up one foot to show Jen the short leather black boots trimmed in pewter buckles.

Jen laughed. "Someday, you'll be confident enough to wear whatever makes you happy. You'll see. Come on. Let's go scout out the bartender and get this party started." She glanced around and spied Stasia Andino working the room.

"Quick," Jen grabbed Bay's wrist. "Before Stasia finds us." She giggled.

"What is Stasia wearing? Her dress looks like a comic book collage or maybe railcar graffiti?" Stasia wore a loose-fitting shift of many colors. The block print dress sported a prominent curvy eye, a bubble-style flower, and large red lips puckered for a kiss.

Jen laughed. "I have a theory. I think she gets her clothes from Giorgio's left-behinds at the dry cleaner's."

When Stasia approached Jen and Bay, the two women held glasses of wine and small plates of nibbles. Stasia was empty-handed and gazed longingly at the full wine glasses.

"Good evening, Jen and Bay. I see you both dressed for the occasion."

The professors exchanged meaningful looks. Was Stasia fishing for a compliment? They capitalized on the moment to take sips of their wine.

"Bay, I'm glad I had a chance to catch you early enough. I wanted to let you know that Diana will be coming tonight. She was released from police custody yesterday. I didn't want it to be a shock to you." Stasia leaned in and stood on tiptoe to reach Bay's ear.

A flutter of panic threatened to overtake Bay, but she inhaled deeply to push it away. "Thank you for letting me know. I guess that means she's not in any legal trouble then?" It was a question she expected Stasia to answer.

Stasia puffed out her ample chest and large lips simultaneously. "The police assured me they have no evidence to hold her. We need to treat her kindly." Stasia waggled a finger under Bay's and Jen's noses. "Innocent until proven guilty." Stasia's proclamation might have been delivered by the Wicked Witch of the West.

Even so, Bay knew the assistant dean was right, but she wasn't sure she could be that gracious, given the circumstances. If Diana was her half sister that would be difficult enough to handle, but if she was in cahoots with Medusa, that was unforgiveable.

"Stasia, you're not drinking anything, and this red blend is delightful. You should get a glass before they run out of it." There was Jen Yoo to the rescue, pointing toward the portable bar where she and Bay found the wine.

Bay was on the lookout for Diana, and by the time she arrived, the party was well underway, and most people had filled their plates from the food tables. Bay selected a quiet corner table next to a lush parlor palm where she could observe Diana as she passed through the food line.

The candy pink cardigan she wore made her look innocent and angelic, but was it a ruse? Bay noticed her face was splotchy, from nerves, stress, or crying, Bay couldn't be certain, but Diana seemed to have aged in the past few days. Or maybe that's because Bay now knew she probably wasn't twenty, more like twenty-five, if she was indeed her half sister.

The office assistant looked around doubtfully for a place to sit, then Bay noticed she smiled weakly at someone on the other side of the room. McNelly. Bay sipped to the bottom of the wine glass. Jen had gone fishing for dessert and a second drink. Bay had to give McNelly credit. At least he wasn't judgmental.

"Here, I brought us a plate full of dessert options to share. And here's another glass of red blend."

Bay wondered if she could manage two glasses and a tower of desserts, too, now that she'd been training her body for dexterity and balance. She waved away the second wine.

"I think one glass is my limit." The memory of the cocktail and a half was too recent for Bay to risk a repeat performance of sleeping on the bathroom floor.

"Suit yourself. I won't let it go to waste." Jen smiled. "I see you've been keeping an eye on Diana. Are you worried?"

"No. Not really." Bay faltered. She wasn't sure how she felt.

The women shared desserts and compared their semester workloads and student rosters.

"Well, time to mingle with our fellow colleagues, Bay. I saw a few profs from your department hanging out near the chamber musicians. Several of mine are stuck in a corner with Dean Pamela. I guess I'll go rescue them." She waved and encouraged Bay to put on a brave face.

The chamber musicians were setting up under the glass domed atrium circle, the prettiest spot in the room. Flowering plants and tall palms outlined the circle, illuminated by hanging crackled globe lights. A crystal chandelier was the star of the circle, a dazzling cascade of prismatic stars and teardrops.

Bay greeted the five department professors and adjuncts who were chatting with two of the violinists. They made small talk about hope for an early spring, their travel plans for spring break in two months, as well as what their partners, children, or pets were up to these days. Bay shared her acquisition of Minerva the cat, her attempt at being personal. She wasn't ready to talk about sharing the apartment with her fresh-out-of-prison sister.

Out of the corner of one eye, she glimpsed Diana moving up the center stairs toward the special exhibit on the next floor. She excused herself from the group, asking them to save her a seat for the performance.

Just steps away from the Atrium, the exhibit hall was unusually quiet. Its vastness and dark hall gave Bay the chills. The central trio of paintings in the large exhibit room were lit from below, casting eerie reflections off the faces of the artwork.

Diana stood against the semi-circular railing, surveying the painting, *Allegory of Justice and Truth*. Bay wished she could read people so she might know what Diana was thinking as she studied the painting.

"Hello, Diana. I see the police let you go." Bay spoke impulsively having no clear idea of an appropriate conversation starter with the woman.

"Good evening, Professor Browning. It's nice to see you." Diana's voice was coated in sincerity, leaving Bay to wonder if Diana knew the danger Bay was in.

Diana gazed from the marble floor to the vaulted ceiling, imploring any available divine assistance. "I need to speak with you."

Bay steeled herself for the impending conversation, which was cut short when a figure dressed in black sailed past Bay and jumped on Diana, knocking her to the floor.

The figure in black wore a jacket, its logo read "Fast Foodie" in red, its letters tilted with speed streaks emanating from them as if they could run away. She didn't appear to be holding a weapon, but a nylon insulated food delivery bag was slung over her shoulder.

The figure expertly pinned Diana to the floor and held her there, at the same time she unzipped the bag and yanked out a plaster gun. She spun the gun into one hand, pulled Diana off the floor and held her in front of her body like a shield. The move caused the figure's hood to fall away, revealing a female face with dark raccoon-like eyes. Bay recognized her from The Gizmo.

Time stood still and rushed forward at once for Bay as she attempted to register the spectacle in front of her.

Below the exhibit hall, the chamber music started, drowning Diana's attempted scream. The figure, who could only be Medusa, covered Diana's mouth.

It was clear to Bay that Medusa wanted to show something to her, but the killer was at a distinct disadvantage. She only had two hands and one was busy covering Diana's mouth while the other held a weapon.

Adrenaline began to find its way through Bay's body, but she instinctively paused, waiting for the opportune time.

Medusa dropped her hold on Diana, and Diana took her chance and dashed out of sight. Bay hoped she was going for help, but who knew?

This was the face-off Bay feared and anticipated. Medusa approached Bay, training the plaster gun from her face to her feet, a sinister smile planted on her face. Medusa was dark-haired and would have been pretty if not for the monstrous grin and menacing eyes.

Bay snarled at the woman, startling her momentarily. An unknown force propelled Bay forward. She lunged, and with one well-placed kick, knocked the plaster gun from her hand. Medusa stared at her throbbing hand in surprise while the gun skittered loudly across the marble floor into darkness.

Bay was ready, but not for what happened next. Medusa laughed, a maniacal peal that echoed around the exhibit hall. She pulled something out from underneath her shirt that hung around her neck. A medallion.

Bay slowly walked backwards out of the hall toward the center stairs, Medusa creeping steadily toward her swinging the medallion side to side. The shiny coin must have come from Fabulous Fiona's class.

Bay kept her movements slow and deliberate, but the railing separating the second floor from the Atrium stopped her abruptly. She'd run out of back-up space. Medusa kept coming and Bay was caught in her orbit, held immobile by a strange force she didn't understand.

She heard Fiona's voice telling her to close her eyes. Bay obeyed. At the same time, she reached into her jacket pocket. Medusa began a slow stream of commands for Bay to open her eyes and face her accuser.

Bay's eyes forced themselves open despite her unwilling mind. Medusa was almost chanting, her voice a steady cadence, a stream of practiced verses emitted forth.

"You are number four. Your sister is number five. You are no longer needed. You cannot protect her. I am the protector." Repeatedly, Medusa droned the phrases.

Bay was ready. Fiona's medallion cradled in Bay's hand, and she swung it out freely, inches from Medusa's face. She had phrases of her own. All the time she spent in theater productions and presentations might pay off in a new way.

"Medusa. You are a monster, not a protector. You can't hurt me. Your time is over." Bay repeated the phrases, competing with Medusa's own incantation.

For a moment, Bay believed she had the upper hand when Medusa stopped chanting and stared into space. But she'd underestimated the frenzy of a sick person.

Medusa's face suddenly transformed into a mask of rage and determination. She thrust forward intending to push Bay over the railing. Bay read the move and instantly reacted by thrusting her fist, the medallion wrapped around it, into Medusa's throat, throwing the killer off-balance.

Bay began to run sideways toward the stairs but not close enough to end up being pushed down them. As she kept her sights on Medusa's movement, two unexpected things happened.

Diana emerged from the dark hallway, wielding Medusa's plaster gun and yelling like a warrior. Cassandra darted in from the opposite hallway, carrying one of Bay's tote bags. Energized, Bay charged head-on toward Medusa, shining the medallion in her eyes, hoping to confuse her.

Cass was steps away and when she swung the tote bag at Medusa's head, the killer crumpled to the floor instantly. Bay planted a thick boot heel on Medusa's chest, while Cass pinned her arms over her head. Diana joined the two, pointing the plaster gun directly in Medusa's face, an otherworldly look in her eyes.

"No, Diana. Don't do anything. It's over. One of us needs to call the police." Bay didn't recognize the calmness in her voice.

Diana grinned. "I called them right after I ran away. They should be here any minute."

As if on cue, officers appeared from every direction; one bounded up the stairs and the others came from parts unknown. They instructed Diana to drop the plaster gun and told Bay and Cass to move aside.

Downing and Harris were on the heels of the arresting officers, standing on the sidelines as protocol dictated.

After Medusa was hauled away, Downing embraced all three women, beginning with Bay, who then walked over to thank Harris and hug him, too.

Downing winked at Bay. "Nice going, Professor. Bet you didn't know those self-defense lessons would come in handy so soon. I'll catch up with you later. You three have some things to discuss."

The detectives briefed the horrified partygoers and instructed them to remain downstairs or to feel free to leave, indicating the danger was over.

Upstairs, under the watchful eyes of a police officer, Bay and Cass hooked arms, and sat on a bench. The two looked at Diana and spoke at the same time. "I think you should go first."

Diana sat on an adjacent bench. "Daphne is my sister. My twin." She broke into a cascade of tears.

Bay and Cass didn't know what to say. "Did you know she was a killer?"

Diana shook her head. "Not at first. After our father died, Daphne and I were raised by my grandmother until she died. We were seventeen and tried to keep her death a secret from the authorities so they wouldn't place us in custody with Virginia. She was our legal guardian after my grandmother's death. Daphne ran away, and I enrolled in college classes with the help of my counselor. I managed to stay under the radar until I turned eighteen, then I moved to Montreal."

"What about Daphne?" Bay asked, trying to fit the pieces together.

"Daphne showed up in my life again two years ago. I could tell there was something wrong with her. I knew she was damaged from our childhood, and I asked her to see a therapist with me. She refused and demanded I stop seeing one, too. She said she would always be my protector, just like when we were kids. She also said she had a plan to stop the people who hurt us." Diana sobbed harder.

Cass and Bay left the bench and placed their arms around

her. She clung to them briefly, then sat straighter.

"I need to finish what I have to say…for now anyway."

"I had to get away from Daphne and my therapist agreed, so I took the first chance I got, which was to apply for a student visa and come to the U.S. to continue my education. I lied about my age on my financial aid application because I already had an associate degree, and I didn't think I'd be eligible for aid here."

Bay nodded, understanding how the system might work against Diana, even though the rules in America differed from Canada.

"The first time I suspected Daphne was when the police asked questions around the department after Virginia's death. I didn't know it was my stepmother until I looked up the story. That's when I thought it might be Daphne."

"Why didn't you contact the police?" Bay asked.

"I hadn't heard from Daphne and didn't know where she was. I convinced myself it must be someone else, thinking my sister couldn't be in the U.S." Diana looked at her hands in her lap. "But after my therapist was found at the aquarium, I knew it had to be Daphne. She still didn't contact me, and I didn't have a way to contact her. I didn't' know where she was."

"And you must have been afraid." Cass offered.

Diana nodded. "But I should have been braver. Daphne was always the brave one. She protected me from Virginia's brother. He tried to molest me, and Daphne hit him over the head with a skillet. But he tried again. I think he may have molested her."

Bay nodded and tears filled her eyes. She knew Virginia's brother, the pedophile, had molested at least one of Virginia's stepchildren, probably Daphne, too. No wonder she was so screwed up.

"This isn't your fault, Diana. I'm guessing you helped the police after they took you into custody."

Diana nodded. "I told them everything I knew that might help, but I still had no contact with Daphne. The police kept me in protective custody once they cleared me of wrongdoing, but they asked me to come to the party tonight to draw out Daphne. They were certain she was ready to strike again." Diana's voice broke. "And they were right."

"So, the police must have been nearby when you called them tonight?" Bay wondered how the police were on the scene so quickly. Diana nodded.

Cass was curious about Daphne's Medusa persona. "Do you know why your sister became Medusa?"

Diana shrugged. "I'm not sure, but Daphne was always interested in my father's art. She was quite artistic herself. My father favored mythology subjects in his works. Medusa protected her sisters, and Daphne was fierce about protecting me."

Cass steered the subject away from the murders to something more personal. "You and Daphne. You're Lucien Nadeau's daughters?"

Diana nodded. "We took my grandmother's last name. My father promised his mother that if he had daughters, they would carry on the old tradition of taking the last name of the woman who was head of the family. His mother, Anne-Marie Poulin, was my grandmother."

Cass forced the next words to come. "And who was your mother? Did you know her?"

Diana's lips quivered nervously. "You both know who our mother is. Penelope Browning. We are half sisters."

Hearing it from Diana felt like a tidal wave to both Bay and Cass. Bay held up her hand as if it could push away the truth.

"That's enough for now. We've all been through a lot, and we still need to give the police our statements. We'll talk again soon."

It was nearly eleven p.m. when Bay and Cass returned to the apartment. They were talked out and exhausted from the ordeal.

Before retiring, Bay padded out to her patio balcony in her pajamas and slippers and inhaled the cold air in long drinks. This was the beginning of a changed life. She stared upward at the black sky and its magic carpet of twinkling stars. The sky was moonless, and Bay recalled Medusa's manifesto, the note that stated she would kill number four and five in the new moon. She shivered, thinking if just one detail had changed, she or Cass or Diana might be dead now.

Cass called through the patio door for Bay to come back inside. "You'll freeze to death out there."

Bay reluctantly padded back inside where Cass handed her a mug of relaxation blend tea.

"Thank you. What made you show up at the Luxe, anyway? Premonition?" Bay and Cass had been separated to give individual statements to the police, leaving gaps in their stories.

Cass presented a one-sided smile. "Not a premonition that I know of, but you'd forgotten the bag of garnishes for your dishes, so I borrowed Dad's car to bring them. My timing was perfect because I saw the woman in her food delivery uniform and knew it was Medusa. I followed her up the back stairs."

Bay exhaled in relief. "And thank goodness you did. I'm still confused. Did you hit her in the head with the bag of garnishes?"

Cass laughed loudly. "No. Your tote bag of books was next to the bag of garnishes, and I grabbed the wrong bag. Turned out that books pack a punch, which just proves that knowledge is power. Isn't that what you always say?"

Bay applauded her sister's wit. "That was certainly a happy accident, Cass."

Cass screwed her face into a smirk. "Oh, I don't think so. I don't believe in coincidences." ■

CHAPTER 29
FAMILY MATTERS

On Tuesday, Detective Downing called Bay to set up a lunch date at The Pig Squeal and invited Cass to join them. He called it a debriefing, and after three days that felt like a whirlwind, Bay was ready for more information.

Downing arrived in advance and the sisters found him seated in a corner away from anyone. The table was already loaded with food.

Downing stood and motioned them to sit. "I ordered in advance, so we wouldn't be disturbed."

He picked up a pitcher of iced tea and filled three glasses, then served up pulled pork piled on buttery buns, German potato salad, and slaw.

Downing began with what he considered the highlights of the case.

"Your tip on the gamer named Sandwich Delivery was golden. It allowed us to whittle down suspects to just a few women. Diana helped us narrow that down with a description of her twin. Then we contacted the aquarium to see which food delivery service they typically used there." He paused and spooned in a bite of potato salad and took a drink.

"That's why it was so easy for Daphne to get into places unnoticed." Bay added.

"Yeah, and by the time the victims realized they were in danger, it was too late. She had control. I'll admit, she was good with that hypnotism nonsense." Downing was ever the skeptic.

Bay smiled. "Well, I don't know much about hypnotism, but I used Fabulous Fiona's medallion to confuse Daphne. I just repeated the same phrases to question her motive and authority, and it worked. Well, in part."

Cass interjected. "What made you bring the medallion to the potluck anyway?"

Bay snorted a laugh. "I've been carrying it with me like some kind of talisman ever since Fiona gave it to me."

A bemused Downing continued his narrative. "Medusa had a backup plan in case her medallion failed to work. She stole some hypodermic needles of sedatives from the local hospital on at least one delivery. That's how she was able to get scuba gear on Dr. Johnson. Then she let gravity take over when she dumped him into the tank."

Cass took a jab at that theory. "A sedated man would be dead weight. How did she get him onto the boom platform?"

"She used the medallion first, we think. Whatever she said to him, lured him onto the boom. Once it was raised, he might have tried to fight her off. Besides, she had to abandon the medallion to get him in the scuba gear."

"Was anyone else drugged? Virginia? The comic creator?"

Downing shook his head. "We think the comic creator was

taken off guard, probably by the delivery of the ordered food. There were no signs of needle marks or drugs on the tox screen. We know that Daphne confronted Virginia. She wanted her stepmother to know why she was there and what was about to happen to her."

Downing shook his head from side to side as if dislodging a moth from his ear, while inside his stomach, his lunch staged a minor mutiny. "Daphne was excited to narrate the tale of killing Virginia."

Cass, who had heard plenty of stories from bragging prisoners, pursed her lips and frowned. But she had one burning question: "Did Daphne's chronicle of self-glorification explain why she used a plaster gun on her victims?"

Downing's face was strained and weary. "She was Medusa, right? She believed Medusa was invincible, immortal. Daphne knew she couldn't turn anyone to stone, but a plaster gun could. She carefully chose which pieces of her victims to cement."

Bay had heard all she cared to in one sitting. "What's next for you, Detective?"

Downing grinned. "My sister keeps insisting I come down for a visit. She lives in Florida."

"I imagine you have months of vacation stacked up," Bay grinned.

"I do. You're very intuitive, Professor."

Cass cleared her throat, feeling invisible as a small spark passed between Bay and Downing. "Why did you involve my sister in this case? As she pointed out to me, she's not an expert investigator, nor art historian. I'm not sure how much her knowledge of mythology helped either."

Downing chuckled at the scathing look Bay gave Cass before

he answered.

"It wasn't my idea. That decision was made by the chief. I admit, keeping the professor busy allowed us to do a better job."

Bay kicked Downing under the table, but she couldn't comprehend the chief's decision either, and wondered if an outside influencer was involved.

Bay rose and shook Downing's hand warmly. "Thank you again, for everything. Enjoy your vacation. It'll do you a world of good, Bryce."

Downing bowed in deference. "Have a successful and stress-free semester, Bay."

The parting comments between the two seemed anticlimactic after the ordeal of the past weeks.

Cass snorted, waved to Downing, and walked briskly out the door to wait in the car.

The following weekend, Bay vacuumed the apartment for the third time. Cass had arranged for Diana and Barrett to come for lunch and get acquainted as a family. Bay's nervous energy couldn't be contained. It was hard to fathom that her sister would initiate a family gathering. Maybe Bay underestimated Cassandra's desire to be a real family again. Maybe Bay was too stubborn for her own good. She'd always considered Cass her protector, which proved true after Cass had kept the secret about their mother to preserve Bay's untarnished memory of Penelope. Now Bay felt she needed to protect her family. Maybe allowing an outsider into their fold wasn't a good idea. Did the Brownings owe Diana Poulin anything?

The humming vacuum stopped abruptly. Bay turned around to see Cass holding the cord with a smirk on her face.

"You're going to wear the carpet out. Diana will be here any minute."

Bay gave her father some credit. He was as wary of Diana as Bay was, the stepdaughter who was a painful reminder of his wife's infidelity. To her credit, Diana was sweet and gentle, and seemed genuine, Bay had to admit.

When Diana saw the painting leaning against the apartment wall, her face drained of color, then a deep pink spread from her neck upward. She excused herself to the bathroom, and Barrett took her exit as an opportunity to escape.

"I'm very tired, girls. This has all been too much for me. The murders. Diana showing up. Twins? For God's sake!" Barrett tossed his napkin on the floor and stomped toward the door. "Excuse me. I need some time alone."

Bay and Cass said solemn goodbyes and let him be, but they were unwilling to let him off the hook. Confrontation and discussion would ensue another time.

Diana noticed Barrett's absence. "I hope I didn't upset him too much. Please apologize for me if I did."

"None of this is your fault, Diana. You didn't make this happen. But, once you get to know our father, you'll see he wears his heart on his sleeve." Cass gently patted Diana's hand.

Diana gazed from one sister to the other, hesitating to proceed. "May I show you something?" She opened the photos on her phone and scrolled until she found the photo she wanted. It was a picture of a young Penelope holding the twin daughters next to the painting. Bay's painting.

Bay gasped to see her mother as she remembered her, beautiful and motherly. Except she was giving her mother love to someone else. Tears filled Bay's eyes and she had to look away and blink them back.

Cass took the phone to examine the photo. "What do you know about this painting?" She pointed to the real specimen in the room.

Diana swallowed. "My father told us about it during our childhood. He had a large, framed picture of mother holding us next to the painting as a keepsake. He said he painted it as a goodbye gift to her. He said she left us because she had to. She is the swan sailing away, leaving suffering and destruction behind. My father's light shines on us, trying to be enough for us in her absence. I'm the blonde with the crown of moons, Diana, the moon goddess. Daphne wears the laurel crown. Mother named her from the myth of Daphne being turned into a laurel tree to escape Apollo's pursuit."

Bay gasped; a flood of emotions assaulted her all at once. All this time, she and Cass believed they were the daughters in the painting. All this time, Bay thought her mother was the artist. All this time, she thought Penelope painted it because she knew she was dying. All this time. "All this time, I've been wrong. The painting is a lie."

Weeks later, Bay had settled into the new semester as a matter of routine. Her encounters with Diana at Gale Hall were cordial, and Bay still suspected McNelly knew about their relationship. She didn't have the heart to ask him, though. Her emotions were still being sorted out.

Spring was trying to influence the curmudgeonly winter, and occasionally the sun promised it would win the day.

Bay felt at odds with the universe. She always had a plan and most often executed it victoriously. Now, she faltered every time she thought about the future. She and Cass were gaining ground on their way back to sisterhood. But their goals differed. Cass wanted Diana to be part of the family, and Bay wasn't ready.

A walk through the subdivision conjured the emotions that tugged inside Bay, threatening to break her apart. Like the subdivision, Bay's life was under construction. Houses were being built there now. Bay imagined homes with flower gardens and kids riding bikes, giggling in their freedom as she and Cass had once done.

Her steps halted at the main entrance where an almost-completed office stood. Three crows held a meeting on the welcome sign, bobbing their heads hypnotically and cawing in chorus. They shifted their perches on the sign when Bay approached, but they didn't fly away. She looked below the crows to find an enclosure filled with brochures. She raised her eyes to query the crows. Her hand mechanically lifted the glass door to clasp a Morningside Grove Community brochure. She stared upward at one of the glossy creatures and shrugged. "Life's a mystery, isn't it?"

About the Author

Joy Ann Ribar is an RV author, writing on the road wherever her husband and their Winnebago View wanders. Joy's cocktail of careers includes news reporter, paralegal, English educator, and aquaponics greenhouse technician, all of which prove useful in penning mysteries. She loves to bake, read, do wine research, and explore nature. Joy's writing is inspired by Wisconsin's four distinct seasons, natural beauty, and kind-hearted, but sometimes quirky, people.

Joy holds a BA in Journalism from UW-Madison and an MS in Education from UW–Oshkosh. She is a member of Mystery Writers of America, Sisters in Crime, Blackbird Writers, and Wisconsin Writers Association.

You may contact the author at *joyribar.com*
Go to *https://joyribar.com/signup to* sign up for newsletters

 Joy Ann Ribar Wisconsin Author

---

Also by Joy Ann Ribar

If you like bakery without the calories, wine without the hangover, and drama without the backlash, try my Deep Lakes Cozy Mystery Series. Make friends with Frankie Champagne—full time baker, vintner and Bubble & Bake shop owner with her business partner/best friend, Carmen Martinez.

Frankie's sideline is a sleuthing regional reporter for Point Press, giving her the opportunity to stick her nose into crimes in the small tourist town of Deep Lakes, Wisconsin. Of course, her investigations curl the toes of her life-long pal Sheriff Alonzo Goodman, especially since she enlists the help of her romantic partner, Coroner Garrett Iverson. The laugh-out-loud humor and strong female relationships make a winning recipe for this mystery series. Recipes are included in each book.

Deep Lakes
Cozy Mystery Series · Book 5

Deep Wedded Blues

Frankie's plans for her daughter Sophie's wedding are anything but spring breezes and blossoms. An unexpected hot spell ushers in a wave of mysterious deaths, at a time when Whitman County is missing its coroner. Garrett, who is also Frankie's beau, is called away to Duluth to assist his former partner with a string of homicides. When Sophie becomes an AWOL bride, Frankie jumps into action to find her and lands in the middle of a spreading health crisis. In Frankie's struggle to overcome the blues, she questions the future of romance—both Sophie's and her own.

You're invited to save the date for *Deep Wedded Blues.*

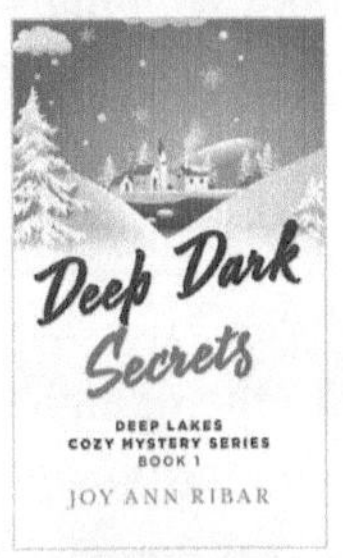

Other books in the Deep Lakes Cozy Mystery Series

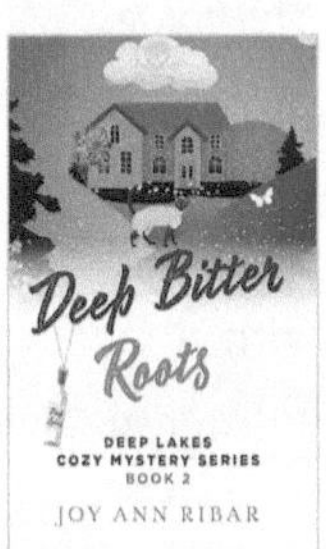

Deep Dark Secrets
Book 1

Deep Bitter Roots
Book 2

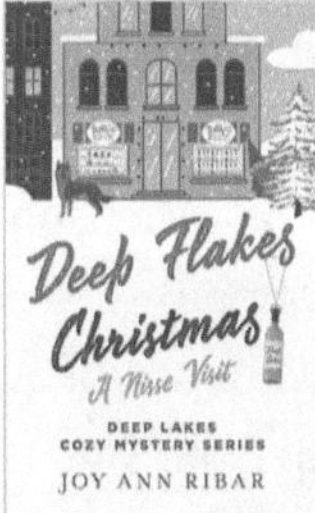

Deep Green Envy
Book 3

Deep Dire Harvest
Book 4

Deep Flakes Christmas
A Nisse Visit · Prequel

Acknowledgments

Thank you to my creative team: editor Kay Rettenmund, designer Terry Rydberg at Fine Print Design, and my husband, LJ Ribar. You are all indispensable and therefore, under contract indefinitely. Where would an author be without her street team? Thank you to my ARC readers: Valerie Biel, Laurie Buchanan, Christine DeSmet, Debra Goldstein, Sharon Lynn, Amanda Marbais, Sharon Michalov, Tracey S. Phillips, Judy Rinehimer, T.K. Sheffield, and Kelly Young. I value your reading chops and writing expertise beyond measure, and I appreciate your careful reading and generous offering of your time.

The use of Edith Hamilton's *Timeless Tales of Gods and Heroes,* Ovid's Metamorphoses, and Geraldine Pinch's *Egyptian Mythology: A Guide to the Gods, Goddesses, and Traditions of Ancient Egypt,* harken to the wonderful days of teaching mythology to my high school students, who devoured it. The compiled information in these handbooks provide students with a general understanding of the stories, history, and rich culture of ancient empires and gives us insight into the thought processes and values of their peoples. For those who ask: why study ancient myths? I say the more we learn about the past, the better we understand ourselves. Culture to culture, we share universal truths and questions, and we express them in the stories we tell.

I studied art history via textbook in a few courses at UW–Madison and in person at the Elvehjem Art Center on campus before it was expanded and renamed The Chazen Museum of Art. Nothing compares to seeing works of art in person, but the wonder of modern technology invites us to explore art housed around the world with the click of a mouse. The pieces written about in this novel are real pieces, which you can and should look at. Any description I've provided is inadequate when a visual paints what a million words cannot convey.

Diana and Actaeon, painted with oil on copper, by Giuseppe Cesari, ca. 1602–1603, can be seen online by searching for the Museum of Fine Arts, Budapest, where the piece is cataloged. Johann König's *The Death of Niobe's Children*, ca. 1600–1642 may be viewed online on various sites. The oil on canvas painting was sold at a Christie's auction in May 2023 for over $88,000. Finally, Giorgio Vasari's *Allegory of Justice and Truth,* 1543, can be seen in all its complexity and grandeur at the National Museum of Capodimonte in Naples, Italy if you're fortunate to be in the neighborhood. If not, view the large oil on panel via the Google Arts and Culture search engine or Wikimedia, as well as other websites. Once you gaze upon these art pieces online, I hope you're inspired to visit an art museum near you. Maybe, like me, you'll marvel at the wonders captured by artists around the world.

www.ingramcontent.com/pod-product-compliance
Lightning Source LLC
Chambersburg PA
CBHW061558190726
48288CB00007B/2075